Jack McCauley is at a dead end. He's run out of money, luck, and love. There'd be no one to mourn him if he died tomorrow. Out of the blue, he's given the chance to begin anew—another identity, another life, another chance at love. Should he take it? Should he start over?

Jack is young, good-looking, and desperate for his next acting gig. His boyfriend is history, his rent is unpaid, and his agent isn't returning his calls. He's offered one chance at redemption—a small part in a western being shot in Arizona—if only he can make his way there from LA by noon the following day.

Hitching a ride with Martin Brenner seems just the ticket. Martin is on his way to a new life in Phoenix and seems pleased to pick up an extra passenger.

Little does Jack know that a simple pickup will lead to the acting job he least expected—the role of a lifetime. But nothing in Phoenix is what it seems on the surface. Can Jack act his way out of an intricate jigsaw of lies, blackmail, and murder?

PHOENIX

BARRY CREYTON

A NineStar Press Publication

www.ninestarpress.com

Phoenix

© 2023 Barry Creyton
Cover Art © 2023 Jaycee DeLorenzo
Edited by Elizabetta McKay

First Edition, May 2023

ISBN: 978-1-64890-651-0

Also available in eBook, ISBN: 978-1-64890-650-3

CONTENT WARNING:
This book contains sexual content, which may only be suitable for mature readers. Depictions of racist and homophobic slurs, fat othering and misogynist language, graphic violence in a murder scene, plotting to commit violence, use of guns, and arson.

De las cenizas nos levantaremos

Anonymous 1910

Mexican Revolution

Chapter One

LOS ANGELES
WEDNESDAY, JULY 13
2:59 P.M.

"YOUR NAME?"

The voice came from somewhere beyond the glare of the lights. It was deep, resonant, and weary.

A pinpoint of light reflected from the camera lens; Jack smiled at this tiny beacon—a warm, open smile with a hint of vulnerability, as he'd learned in drama class. He held up the slate bearing his name and said, "Jackson McCauley."

There followed a weighty silence broken by a gurgle

as Jack's stomach protested a skipped breakfast. He hoped the mic hadn't picked it up. Not that breakfast was beyond what he had in his wallet, but when it came to auditions and screen tests, the void in his gut admitted a butterfly or two.

He sneaked a glance into the gloom and saw a tight closeup of his face on a floor monitor. He was shiny from the heat of the lamps, but it was an evenly proportioned face with strong bones, piercing blue eyes, and a shock of carefully casual sandy-blond hair—a handsome face, a face, he'd been told, that would take him far.

It had taken him as far as this ancient, rundown sound stage in the back blocks of Hollywood.

"Jackson McCauley?" The weary man intoned the name as if trying to place it.

Jack turned his gaze back to the camera lens. "Most people just call me Jack—Jack McCauley. But, professionally…"

There was a terse rustle of paper. "How old are you?"

"It's on my résumé."

The man sighed and said as if to a kindergarten dropout, "We'd rather like to hear your voice."

"Twenty-three."

Silence. Jack grabbed another look at his image in the monitor. He'd worn what he thought was appropriate to test for a western—a neat, sky-blue, long-sleeved denim shirt with tabbed pockets, faded 501s, and cowboy boots that were only slightly down at heel, a souvenir from a gig as an extra on a TV series; they added an inch or so to his lean six feet.

"Profile." A female voice—the voice of the casting director who'd called him out of the blue that afternoon—Michelle? Nicole? Something French sounding. That was about thirty minutes before the phone company ended their bumpy relationship with him and killed his cell account.

He turned to his left, offering what he considered to be his best side to the camera. Across the dark stage in the yellow glow of a work light, he saw a bored grip gazing at the floor. Even from this distance, Jack could tell the only thought on the guy's mind was getting the hell out of there for a cigarette.

"Other side."

Jack did a one-eighty. His view from this angle was even more depressing: Another actor around Jack's age stood in the dust-defined beam of a grid, rigid with nerves. His glance shifted back and forth from Jack to a page of script.

"Jack—Jackson—whatever…" Her voice had a husky, tough edge but sounded young; he could see nothing of her except the glint of a bracelet as she moved her hand in a casual, dismissive wave. "Tell us something about yourself."

Jack turned back to the lens. "Okay. Um, I was born right here in LA. I always wanted to act, I guess. Always."

"How about your folks?"

He shifted his weight from one leg to the other, unaware he'd done so, but this subtle movement, coupled with a second's hesitation, was enough to suggest to anyone with the most elementary knowledge of psychology that this was a painful subject.

"I never knew my mom." He let this sit for a moment, then added, "She, um, she left when I was just a month old. And—my dad died when I was twelve. My grandmother took care of me until—"

"Any other family?"

"No, no one." What had his drama coach advised? *Use it! Use the emotion!* He lowered his eyes, subtly suggesting loss. This was good. He was getting to give them a range of expression without having read a word of the script.

"What've you done?" the baritone asked.

"Uh, let's see…I did a spot in *Girl About the House* for Disney. That was a while back. I did an ep of *Sands of Time*—"

"The soap?"

"Yeah."

"That was canceled a year ago." Now the baritone sounded impatient; his precious time was being wasted by the nonevent of Jack's career.

But the woman sounded interested. "How about recently?"

"I was in *True West*. HBO."

"Oh?" This elicited a hint of interest from the man. "Which character?"

"Um, day player."

The interest evaporated. "An extra."

"Yeah, but I'm good with horses, so they wrote up the part a bit."

"But no lines."

Jack shook his head.

"Anything else?"

"You want to know about the theater I've done?"

"God no," the man said. "Just give him the copy."

A disembodied hand darted into Jack's pool of light and thrust a page at him.

"Can I have a minute…?"

"From sight," the man said. "I'll cue you." He read in a monotone: "'You wouldn't mind living in the nicest house in town. Buying your wife a lot of fine clothes, going to New York on a business trip a couple of times a year. Maybe to Europe once in a while?'"

Jack's eyes darted over the page trying to find the place. He realized he was squinting and eased the tension from his face.

Keep it simple.

"'I know what I'm going to do tomorrow and the next day and next.'" The words were familiar. They triggered a faint memory of something rare and bright in a shadow-filled childhood. He couldn't pin it down without losing concentration, but the emotion it generated was a gift to an actor. "'And I'm going to build things! I'm going to build airfields! I'm going to build skyscrapers a hundred stories high! I'm going to build a bridge a mile long!'"

"Okay, that'll do," the man said.

Jack turned the page over and back, then peered into the void beyond the camera with a puzzled frown. "Isn't this from *It's a Wonderful Life*?"

"We just want to see how you handle dialogue," the man said.

Jack smiled his easy, all-American smile. "Can I take it again?"

The request was ignored. There was a whispered exchange in the dark. He strained to catch the voices.

First the baritone: "…strictly an under five…"

Then the woman: "…exactly what I want…"

A little more muttering and then a firm "I *know* what I

want!" from the woman.

"You're a good-looking guy," the man said. It sounded more like an accusation than a compliment. Jack lowered his head modestly anyway. "Can you be in Flagstaff by noon tomorrow?"

"Flagstaff, Arizona?"

The baritone sighed. "It's the only Flagstaff I know. It's not a big part. You'll have to get there on your own."

Realization hit—he'd got the part!

A chair scraped as the woman rose, and Jack heard the sound of her high heels as she crossed the concrete floor to an exit. A stagehand opened the door, and Jack saw her trim silhouette as she left the stage.

"Be there twelve noon on the dot, or we'll have to cast a local," she said as she vanished into the light.

*

3:21 P.M.

THE OFFICE THAT fronted the dilapidated sound stage was a sterile recent addition. No boastful movie posters adorned the walls, but the extravagantly tattooed girl at the desk more than compensated for the absence of decoration. Having ascertained Jack was "between agents", she shoved a basic agreement across the desk. The money wasn't great, but given his circumstances, food stamps would've been a plus.

Jack winced a little as he noted the girl's pierced tongue and wondered if it got in the way when she kissed or ate. It certainly made a mush of the rote information she imparted.

"Twelve noon for makeup and wardrobe."

Jack was relieved he was not expected to provide his own costume.

"Sign here, initial here, and here."

He wanted to tell someone about his good fortune but realized, with no rancor, there was no one. Everyone to whom he'd been close had deserted him—his actor boyfriend for a good-looking realtor with an income, his roommate for a fringe theatrical production in Riverside, and his agent, who had cut him loose three weeks ago with spurious sympathy and a brief observation on "the state of the business."

Fuck them all! He had a job. With dialogue. No billing, but maybe this could lead to something. He signed "Jackson McCauley" with a flourish. The girl provided a call sheet and directions to the location and the one-star motel where they would accommodate him during his week's work.

Done with the formalities, he took the crisp, new-looking script and hurried out of the office into the searing Southern Californian sun. He punched the air and shouted a joyous, "Yesss!" as he ran into the street to the shady spot he'd found to park his car.

The spot was there, but the car was gone.

*

3:52 P.M.

HE TRIED THREE payphones before finding one that worked on a dull stretch of Sunset. He had to shout to be heard above the traffic.

"Yeah, a 2004 Nissan!… *2004*!… I dunno why anyone would steal it either. But it's *gone*." The cop was either dim or just didn't give a shit. Jack figured the latter. "No, I can't come and make a report. I've got this job. I've gotta get to Flagstaff and—"

The cop interrupted, giving him a lecture on the necessity of filing a report. The pointlessness of the call occurred to Jack. The car was gone, period. No degree of complaint would get it back in a hurry.

He took a look at his watch. "Hey. I was gonna trash the fuckin' thing anyway." He slammed the phone down and took off at a sprint down the hill toward Santa Monica Boulevard.

Running in cowboy boots was hell, and by the time he reached West Hollywood, there were patches of sweat on his formerly pristine shirt.

Take a shower. Soon as I get in. Take a shower and change and…

And what?

No clear plan had evolved before he reached his apartment building. He climbed the stairs to the second floor. There, he was greeted by his landlord, a sullen Armenian who made himself clear in minimal English:

"No rent, no room." He dumped a backpack onto the floor by Jack's feet.

"What about my TV? My clothes?"

"You pay rent, you get." The landlord turned and started for the stairs. "I keeping safe for you."

Jack grabbed his arm. "Look, I've got a job. I'll be back end of the week. I'll pay you then."

"No rent, no—"

"I need my fuckin' clothes, man," Jack yelled. A couple of heads appeared from out of apartment doors. Jack tried to get past the landlord, but the man pushed Jack hard against the wall.

Jack's reflexive reaction was to lurch toward the landlord, who stepped back shielding his face with his hands.

"Don' you touch me!" he whined as he backed to the top of the stairs, teetered, seemingly in slow motion, then tumbled down the entire flight. He lay on the bottom step in a fetal position, quite still.

"Are you okay?" Jack called.

"Shouldna pushed him," one of the onlookers offered.

"I didn't touch him!"

There was a hearty scream from below, and Jack looked down at a large woman in a grimy green velveteen bathrobe inspecting the prone form of her husband.

"Call the cops!" she yelled to no one in particular as she ran back inside their apartment.

Jack grabbed his backpack from the floor and took the stairs two at a time. He knelt by the twisted figure and put his head to the man's chest.

"Get offa me!"

Jack jerked upright and the man scrambled to his knees, clearly no worse for the fall.

"Are you okay?"

The man winced as Jack helped him to his feet. "Assault!" he yelled. "I have you behind bars, asshole!"

Jack drew breath to protest his innocence, but from within the landlord's apartment, the wail of "Police! He kill my husband!" deflated him. He turned and ran blindly through the lobby and out into the smoggy West Hollywood afternoon.

Chapter Two

4:20 P.M.

JACK SHRANK BACK into the corner of the bus shelter as a police siren added shattering counterpoint to the dull hum of the passing traffic. He wondered if it was in response to the hysterical Armenian woman.

This stretch of Santa Monica Boulevard in WeHo was alive at any given time, day or night. People strolled, jogged; some had cell phones clamped to their ears, some were plugged into music, all gave the impression they had somewhere to go, people to see, lives to live. Unlike Jack, most were innocent of assault and battery, albeit alleged.

He sat this way for some time, his arms folded around the backpack on his knees, the finger and thumb of his left hand absently twisting a silver ring on the pinky of his right. No bus came, but that was the nature of public transport in Los Angeles.

Jack opened the front pocket of the backpack and sifted through the contents: A strip of photo booth pics of him and his defunct boyfriend; a few playbills for waiver theater productions he'd done in remote parts of LA, and for which the gas for his antediluvian car cost more than he was paid; and attached to these, neatly cut newspaper reviews in which the word most frequently aligned with the name Jackson McCauley was "promising." There were several unheeded warnings from AT&T, a couple of year-old head shots, some stapled script pages, the extent of his part in the soap in which he had a terminal illness and died a noble death right after the opening credits, and a copy of Uta Hagen's *Respect for Acting*.

The dull ache of despair deep in his gut intensified suddenly, and he took a few short, deep breaths. Was this the bounty of his twenty-three years on earth? A box of souvenirs?

He flicked through the pages of the Uta Hagen and two small photographs fluttered to the sidewalk. He picked them up and inspected them. The familiarity of the pictures infused his despair with a further layer of emotion that brought tears to his eyes. In one, a young woman stood at the door to a modest Toluca Lake house Jack knew but didn't remember as that in which he was born. The image was blurred, suggesting she'd turned away as the shutter opened, reluctant to be photographed. But her blonde hair was unmistakably of the same genetic material as Jack's. This was the only evidence he had of a mother—a mother who'd abandoned him and his father within a month of Jack's birth.

In the other picture, a handsome young man stood by a plain stucco wall, bent at the waist as he held the hand of a blond boy of twelve; with his other hand, he pointed to the camera urging the boy to smile. Pride in his child was glowingly evident on the man's face. The picture had been taken the day Jack and his father set out for a weekend drive to Big Sur. The drive led them onto a back road, a rotten wooden bridge, and into the ravine below—a drive that killed his father and spared Jack.

After the accident, Jack lived with a doting grand-mother who felt the loss of her son as keenly as Jack did his father. But when he was fourteen, she died, and he was given over to foster parents who, while not unkind, were distant, their care of Jack fueled solely by the financial set-tlement from the fatal accident.

As he moved from high school to college and a theater arts major, the emotional gap between him and his foster parents grew, and he kept his thoughts, his feelings, and his ambitions increasingly to himself.

Another year, and the dregs of the settlement money were spent on a reputable acting class in which he'd shone. Convinced that the world of entertainment was waiting impatiently for someone of his superior talent, Jack took a share in a cramped apartment with two other budding actors and started the rounds. Since then, he'd managed to make ends meet, but only just. The residual checks for the few TV gigs he'd had were small but regular.

The emptiness he'd felt in recent years was due in part to a career that was, so far, less than stellar. But this only toughened the shell he'd constructed in adolescence—the warm smile, the well-practiced congenial manner—all to conceal the gut feeling that he was somehow unworthy and undeserving of a brilliant career or a fulfilling relationship.

There had been occasions, though not many, when he trawled the lower depths of his psyche and admitted he'd erected his own barriers against such things as upward mobility, against loving and being loved. Once, and once only, he opened up to someone and admitted these self-imposed restraints. Two roommates ago, there'd been a USC student, a kid who'd studied psychology but yearned to be an actor;

he'd failed at both. But during their brief affair, his assessment of the root of Jack's inadequacy feelings was simple and, not surprisingly, derived from Freud: Jack felt he'd been denied the most basic of all human rights—a family.

He slipped the photographs into his wallet and counted the bills in it. With a jolt, he realized he'd left a small stash of residual checks under a mug in his room, now no doubt in the custody of his landlord.

The rest of the memorabilia, including *Respect for Acting*, he shoved into a trash can. He closed his eyes and reached absently for the silver ring and twisted it back and forth. It was the only possession of his mother's that his father had kept, perhaps in the hope she'd return someday to claim it. She'd left behind the cheap wedding ring when she bolted. Considering it fit Jack's little finger snugly, it must've been a snug fit on his mother's left hand, third finger. It was a flat band with a perched bird engraved on the upper surface, the work of an amateur. But to Jack, the ring was precious. She'd abandoned it on the kitchen table the night she left, and his father had worn it until the day he died. Then Jack kept it.

As almost an afterthought, Jack opened the script he'd been handed after the test. This he'd kept clutched as closely as a drowning man might a life preserver. He flicked through the pages of routine western jargon and found the first and virtually last evidence of his role. A couple of interiors of domestic bliss and one exterior scene working his gold claim in which his character assailed the villain over property rights, reached for his gun, and was shot dead by the bad guy. Thus ended his role. But, with even one closeup, he could make an impression, he knew it!

Okay, enough. Get your shit together.

He'd catch the bus to Highland, walk to the highway, I-101, and hitch. He'd hitched around California, he'd hitched to Vegas, to Tijuana. People always gave him a ride. With no hint of narcissism, he was aware of his looks; he knew the first impressions he gave to total strangers were of openness, honesty. His reliance on this perception was calculated, sure, but the mechanism was never evident; such was the actor's craft. If he could get as far as I-10, sure as hell a truck, a produce van, a biker, *someone* would be heading for Arizona. How long could it take, six hours? He glanced at his watch. He had seventeen hours to make his noon appointment in Flagstaff. He could do it.

As he turned to search for an approaching bus, a tall guy moved into his line of vision—a bunch of tanned muscles in shorts and a tank. The guy dropped his gym bag and sat, flashing a toothpaste-commercial smile at Jack.

"Hey, man, waitin' for the bus?"

Jack nodded.

"Look like you work out."

"Yeah, when I can," Jack said, not taking his eyes off the stream of traffic.

"In a hurry? Or can I buy you a drink?"

Jack smiled apologetically. "In a hurry."

The guy moved closer, and his knee nudged Jack's. "Sure about that?"

"I'm sure," Jack said affably. On any other day, he might've submitted to such an overture, welcomed sex just to alleviate tension, or boredom, or loneliness, but now he had priorities. "Got a job waiting for me in Arizona."

The musclehead laughed. "You're not gonna get a bus to Arizona from here!"

"It'll get me to the 101. I'll hitch from there."

"My car's in back of the gym," the guy said. "I could give you a ride to the freeway."

"Yeah?" Now Jack beamed *his* toothpaste-commercial smile.

"Maybe we could stop off at my place on the way. Whattaya say?"

"Hey, man, I'd really like to, but I got a deadline." He broadened his smile suggesting downright availability. "I'll be back end of the week. Why don't I give you my number?"

The muscled guy talked as he drove. He was a model. He'd done a couple of commercials and appeared in an episode of *CSI* as a naked corpse. He told mildly amusing anecdotes about working with stars, about dumb scripts, about the offers he'd had to do porn, about the wretched ordeal of squeezing his splendid shoulders into regular-sized jackets. The monologue of his glamorous life so fascinated him, he was reluctant to interrupt it when they reached I-101, so he took Jack all the way downtown to I-10 and dropped him at the ramp. They swapped numbers. The guy gave Jack three: home, agent, and cell. Jack, reeling from the guy's autobiographical onslaught, gave him the number for his recently extinct phone. Muscles gave a cheery wave as he drove off. In the thirty minutes it had taken to struggle through the peak hour traffic, he hadn't made any inquiry about Jack's life at all.

Chapter Three

5:10 P.M.

A TRACTOR TRAILER pulled over, and a face like tanned leather peered out of the cab. "Where ya headed?"

"Flagstaff."

"Take you as far as Barstow. That'll put you on I-40."

The truck driver's conversation was minimal, and once they'd covered the weather and touched on the way the country was being run, it pretty well petered out. He asked what line Jack was in. Jack told him. No further questions were asked.

An hour on, a red Mercedes convertible overtook them

and sped ahead into the evening gloom.

Jack held it in view for as long as he could. "You see that? Great lookin' car."

Fifteen minutes later, they overtook the same Mercedes.

"Yeah," the driver agreed.

*

6:57 P.M.

IT WAS ALMOST seven when the truck reached the outskirts of Barstow. Jack thanked the driver and jumped down from the cab. The red Mercedes roared from out of nowhere and pulled in just ahead of the truck. A young guy in a baseball cap got out clutching a map and brushed past Jack as he approached the truck.

"Hey," he called to the driver. "Think I'm lost. GPS is fucked. And my phone just died."

Jack paused by the car and inspected its gleaming perfection. He glanced back to where the young guy was holding his map up for the truck driver to inspect. He seemed around Jack's age but was clearly from a superior financial stratum. He wore designer jeans, an expensive leather bomber, and a Dodgers cap. A gold necklet glinted at his throat.

Jack took all of this in and made a determined effort to feel—nothing. It was the best way he knew to avoid a longing for things he might never have. He heard the truck driver's voice above his idling engine.

"You want Phoenix? I-10."

"What am I on?"

"I-40."

"Aw shit!"

Jack started for the freeway onramp looking behind him for a likely ride. Apart from the truck and the Merc, there wasn't a car in sight.

"You take 247 through Yucca Valley and Desert Hot Springs," the trucker droned, "then you head east past the National Park... Nah, wait a minute; you could take the 15 to 215, go through Highland till you get to Redland, and—"

"Jesus, is there an easier way? Like via Philadelphia?"

The guy's comically affronted tone caused Jack to turn back to get another look at him.

The truck driver droned on. "Lessee. Maybe you could stay on I-40 till Needles. Then you take 95 south through Lake Havasu City. Then you get onto the 10. You head east, and it's, lessee, about a hundred—hundred twenty miles—or you could take 93; that's just past Kingman. You head south, you reach the 74, you head east to I-17, then south on the—"

"Yeah, yeah, yeah, thanks."

The truck took off, and the guy headed back to the Mercedes swearing quietly to himself. He caught sight of Jack watching him.

"Wanna ride?"

"Which way you going?"

The guy laughed. "Fucked if I know. How about you?"

"Flagstaff."

"Take you far as I can. Any good at reading maps?"

"Sure."

The guy tossed a look at the Merc. "Brand new, and the GPS bit the dust."

I'll navigate." Jack ran back to the gleaming red car. "Can I put this in the trunk?" he asked, heaving his backpack off his shoulder.

"It'll fit right behind your seat."

Jack squeezed the backpack into the narrow space and eased himself into the leather luxury of the passenger seat. "Great set of wheels."

The guy shrugged and held out his hand. "Martin Brenner—Marty."

"Jack McCauley."

They shook, and the guy put the car into drive. It took off quietly, powerfully, and insinuated itself easily into the flow on the highway.

"So. Whassup in Flagstaff?"

"A job."

"Yeah? What do you do?"

"Actor. Got a part in a movie there."

"No shit! Have I seen you in stuff?"

Jack laughed. "Been trying to keep my career a secret."

"So this is, what, the big break?"

Jack shrugged. "Could be."

"What is it, a western?"

"Yeah. It's set in northern California during the gold rush."

"So they shoot it in Arizona."

They both enjoyed a chuckle at Hollywood logic.

"Guess you're good with horses," the guy said.

"Pretty good."

"Me? Dunno a thing about 'em. And I'm on my way to Phoenix to take over a ranch. Ironic, huh?"

"Yeah" was all Jack could muster by way of endorsement.

The stream of cars thinned as the miles accumulated. The desolate wilderness of the Mojave Desert flanked the dark highway, but the neat, new-leather-smelling interior of the Merc was cozy.

Jack had always found it hard to open up to a total

stranger unless it was for professional reasons. But Marty was easy to talk to. Jack told of his stolen car, his inflexible landlord—leaving out the bit where the guy fell down the stairs—his short relationship with his sleazebag agent, and his even shorter relationship with his— Here, he hesitated, unwilling to expose his sexuality to a stranger.

"Cheater?" the guy prompted.

Jack just shrugged.

"Sounds like my wife. My *ex*-wife. Caught her in bed with another guy. *No*, not just another guy, my own brother!"

"Your brother. Wow."

"Wanna know the two most beautiful words I ever heard in our marriage? 'Decree absolute.'" He let this sit for a while, then added bitterly, "Women, huh?"

A cell phone chirped the *William Tell Overture*. Marty hauled it out of his jacket pocket, flipped it open, and took a quick look at the readout. "Right on cue. Bitch never lets up."

"She calls?"

"Oh, yeah. Sometimes she cries, sometimes she just wants to tell me what an asshole I am, always she asks for money."

He pressed Talk. "Nicki baby!" He listened for a moment, then inclined a taut smile to Jack. "Yeah," he said wearily to the phone, "yeah, yeah, yeah, and fuck you." He disconnected and tossed the phone to Jack. "Stow it in the glove compartment."

Jack did so, snapping the door shut with finality. Neither spoke for a while. Jack felt obliged to resuscitate the conversation.

"So, what happened to your brother?"

"The great Scott Brenner! They got him for smuggling coke across the border—and who bailed him?" Marty released the steering wheel to thump his chest. "World's biggest sucker! Last I heard, he's hiding out somewhere in Mexico."

"He's older than you?" Jack asked, not really caring, but listening to someone else's woes was somehow soothing after the stress of the day.

"Younger. A year. Twenty-four. But he always came on like he was older. He was breaking into houses by the time he was twelve. Back then, he only took little stuff. Petty cash, a watch or two, that kinda thing. Later, he got into the big time."

Jack was silent.

Marty glanced at him. "Guess you never did anything like that."

"Guess not."

"Pack of cigarettes? Candy bar you didn't show at the

checkout?"

Jack felt obliged to confess to some minor misdemeanor but could only think of the crumpled Armenian at the bottom of the stairs in Los Angeles, and, after all, he never touched the guy. "No poker face, I guess."

Marty laughed. "You wanna make it in Hollywood? You need to cheat a little, man!"

*

9:11 P.M.

JACK DOZED. THE slowing of the car woke him.

"Gotta get some gas," Marty said as he pulled into a brightly lit gas station which was, as far as Jack could see, the only sign of civilization in a pitch-black world.

"Where are we?"

Marty laughed as he got out of the car. "Some navigator! Just this side of Needles."

Jack got out and stretched, then spread the map out in the light from the pumps. "So, are you heading south from Needles?" he asked when Marty returned to the car.

"What'd the man say? South on 98, east on 34, to hell and gone on some other fuckin' highway? You hungry?"

Jack glanced at his watch.

"We're makin' good time! Tell ya what, I'll get you as

close to Flagstaff as I can before I head off, okay?"

"Fine by me."

"Come on, let's eat."

The diner in back of the gas station had two other customers who might have been asleep or dead; it was hard to tell.

A few cheap prints of old masters did their best to ornament the walls, but offended Jack's eye. His fine arts class in high school had imbued him with a degree of taste—and the *Mona Lisa* above the pastry counter was surely not the real thing.

They settled into a booth.

"Gotta eat something, or it's nighty-night," Marty muttered as he inspected the menu. He looked up and caught Jack's puzzled glance. "Got this blood sugar thing."

"Hypoglycemia?"

"Gotta snack every couple hours, or I pass out." He shrugged and smiled.

The waitress approached their table. She was from Central Casting: around fifty, overweight, bleached hair, too much makeup.

"Welcome to nowhere, fellas. What'll it be?"

Marty closed the menu and handed it back to the waitress. "Burger, Coke."

The waitress noted this and turned to Jack, who made

as if he was inspecting the menu while doing a mental count of how much he had in his wallet.

"Maybe coffee, couple donuts…" he said.

"This one's on me, man," Marty said. "You want to keep up your strength for the big gig? *Eat!*"

Jack's smile hid his embarrassment, and he shrugged. "Okay. Cheeseburger, no fries, coffee."

The waitress winked at him. "Watchin' the figure, huh?" Then she took his menu and vanished into the kitchen where they heard her relay the order to the chef.

Marty spread the map out on the table.

"Okay, I-40 goes right into Flagstaff; then if I take this one… What's that say?"

Jack turned the map and read, "I-17. Look, are you sure?"

"Sure, I'm sure! I got the time, *you* got hair and makeup, that kinda shit."

"That's great, really. Thanks."

The waitress put the drinks on the table. "Coke for you, coffee for you."

"Coke's for me, coffee's for him," Marty corrected her, swapping the drinks.

The waitress looked from Marty to Jack and back again. "You two brothers?"

"Not as far as we know," Marty said.

"Check with your folks, sweetie." She ambled back into the kitchen.

Jack took a closer look at Marty. "I guess there is a similarity. Take off your cap."

Marty slipped the Dodgers cap off revealing sandy-blond hair. He leaned across the table to take a better look. "Weird!" he said, inspecting Jack's face. "Your hair's kinda the same color. And your eyes. You sure your mother wasn't fuckin' the mailman? Mine was. Maybe he made deliveries in your neighborhood. Hey! I coulda been in the movies!"

"Forget it!" Jack laughed. "This gig is mine."

Marty folded his arms behind his head and settled back in his chair, inspecting Jack's face. "Really weird," he said quietly.

Jack appraised him as he would another actor at a casting session—with a disarmingly uncompetitive smile. They were both around six feet and of similar build, solid and well-proportioned, though Jack considered himself in better shape than Marty and offered fleeting gratitude to the gym gods of unemployed actors. Marty's eyes were perhaps a darker blue than Jack's, his lips less full, his jaw a little less strong. Or, Jack wondered, was this just his take on someone who might be up for the same role? Marty's hair was lighter than Jack's and had clearly been subjected to the scissors of a better hairdresser, but overall, the similarities outweighed the differences.

The food arrived, and the waitress took another look from one to the other, then smiled and clicked her tongue as she walked away.

They ate, they talked.

"Your folks in show business?" Marty asked.

"My mother left my dad right after I was born."

"Women," Marty muttered with a mouthful of burger.

"And my dad—well, he died when I was a kid," Jack added to put a period on his biography. He moved the subject to Martin. "So, what do you do?"

"Advertising. *Was* advertising. Resigned coupla weeks ago."

Somehow, the subject shifted to the women. It seemed to Jack that Marty boasted his sexual prowess to alleviate the anger at his wife for abandoning him.

"Not like I need her," Marty said out of nowhere. "I got no trouble getting laid."

Jack felt no more than obliged to chuckle.

"How about you?" Marty asked. "Bet a good-lookin' guy like you has the gals lining up."

Jack just shrugged.

Marty's take reminded Jack of a cartoon light bulb bursting into life above a character's head. "Wait! You're into *guys*!"

Jack was not ashamed of his sexuality, but the cautions related to being a leading-man type in the movie business kicked in. How many "out" stars were there? How many who played straight roles as well as gay? Few. He remained still.

"No biggie!" Marty said. "I play for both teams." He leaned forward and offered Jack a very inviting smile. "No point going through life one hand tied behind your back."

Jack tried, and failed, to conceal a blush. He changed the subject. "Nice necklet."

"This?" Marty lifted it from his throat with a thumb. "Ex. Wedding present. Only thing of hers I kept. And only because it's twenty-four karat."

They ate in silence for a while. Jack appraised Marty in light of his revelation of bisexuality. Certainly, there was something animal about Marty, a sensuality in the way he swaggered as he walked, something that proclaimed his expertise in matters of sex.

Marty caught Jack assessing him and offered a smile that reeked of invitation. Jack had wrangled with others as sexually attractive as Marty, but he wanted more from an encounter than Marty seemed likely to offer. He wanted someone to reciprocate emotionally—an ideal he might never find in casual sex. Yet, given the circumstances, the lonely drive, the time to kill, the likelihood of never meeting Marty again…

The waitress dropped the check on the table. Marty took a wallet stuffed with bills from his jacket pocket and slipped one out. It was a hundred. He handed it to the waitress who held it as if it carried some contagious disease.

"Anything smaller?"

"Keep it."

"You kiddin'?"

"Take your boyfriend to dinner."

The waitress shrugged and smiled and walked back to the kitchen stuffing the note deep into a pocket.

Marty caught Jack's sober gaze at his wallet as he pocketed it. He grinned. "Long story."

Chapter Four

11:22 P.M.

THE HIGHWAY WAS deserted now. The Merc cruised smoothly, almost silently at a steady 80.

"There were three of 'em," Marty said. "Everyone in Phoenix knew them as the Dalstrom sisters—Amy, Loretta, and Geena. They were all born in the US, but their folks were Swedish immigrants. All great lookers in their day. Amy was the oldest and married this rich rancher, Edward J. Wyatt, old Uncle Ed. Tough old bastard. But Amy was tougher. She never took shit from him. Or anyone. She ran the ranch right along with him. Single-handed after Ed bit the big one. Then there was Aunt Loretta, but she was one of those women who turns down all the offers until she winds up a— Whattaya call it?"

"Spinster?"

"Yeah. She lived in the house with Amy and Ed all her life. And that brings me to my mom, Geena, world's greatest slut. My dad couldn't keep it in his pants either. Made himself scarce after my brother Scott was born. So, I used to go stay on the ranch with Amy and Loretta when Mommy dear was screwin' some new guy and didn't want me around. Then when I was about eleven, there was this big argument. Amy laid into my mom, called her all kinds of a whore, and gave her money to get outta town. So she moved to LA, and just to piss Amy off, she took us kids with her."

"Is your mom still alive?"

"Drank herself to death, happy to say. They're all gone now, whole family. Except Loretta." He caught Jack's sympathetic frown. "It's okay. I hardly knew any of 'em. Jesus, I haven't seen Loretta since I was eleven. Wouldn't know what she looks like now. And vice versa."

"You never wanted to go back? Not even when you were older?"

Marty shrugged. "You grow up, you let go of stuff." He stared at the visible stretch of blacktop ahead of the car for a moment as if reflecting on something long past, then turned briefly to Jack with a puzzled smile. "So, big surprise, few weeks ago, Amy ups and dies and leaves the lot to me—ranch, money, whole deal. That's why I'm heading for Phoenix, take a look at the old joint, maybe put it up for sale." He stretched and shook a crick out of his neck. "They say it'll get seven million easy. Money for nothing!" He laughed. "Not to mention the load she stashed away in some bank."

"Great break," Jack said without enthusiasm.

"Nah, *nice* break. The *great* break is, all this happened right after the divorce was final. Nicki won't get a cent."

They passed Needles, barely noticing there was a town there at all. On this stretch of the 40, it seemed they were the only car on the highway—perhaps in the world.

At Marty's urging, Jack gave the abridged history of his life in show business.

"They come on with, like, 'you got talent, you're gonna be a star.' What they *don't* tell you is there's one of you in every drama class in the country. So I did auditions, tests, got a couple gigs. Then it all seemed to run out at the same time. Everything."

Jack turned and gazed at the dark, distorted reflection of his face in the door window. "I'm twenty-three, for Chrissake. Jimmy Dean was a legend at twenty-four. Maybe you gotta die before—"

The Mercedes veered onto the gravel shoulder. Jack glanced at Marty. His head was back on the headrest, his eyes closed, his mouth open.

Jack grabbed the wheel and steered the car back onto the highway.

"Hey! Marty! HEY!"

Marty jerked awake, instantly aware of the situation, and braked. He then seemed to realize the dumb move and accelerated again to get out of the skid. The car swerved into the adjacent lane, narrowly missing a motorcycle ahead of them before finding the right lane again and coming to a stop on the shoulder.

"You okay?" Jack asked.

"Christ, I was out like a light."

Flashing lights told them the motorcycle they'd just missed was a cop.

"Fuck," Marty whispered. He opened his window as the highway cop approached the car.

"You okay, sir?"

"Yeah, just tired."

"See your license?"

Marty flipped down the sun visor and took his license from under the mirror. The cop took it from him and examined it under the glare of a powerful flashlight.

"I was better looking when that was taken," Marty said

with a wry grin. "Before marriage took its toll."

The cop didn't smile. He turned the flashlight beam first onto Marty, then Jack, then the interior of the car. Then he walked to the front of the car, took a cursory glance at the lights, and moved to the rear. He played the flashlight beam over the trunk.

Marty was completely still and kept his eyes on the rearview mirror, watching the cop. Jack noted there were beads of perspiration on Marty's upper lip.

The cop returned to the driver's window. "Had anything to drink tonight, Mr. Brenner?"

"Nothin' but Coca-Cola."

The cop leaned closer, perhaps to catch any hint of alcohol that might be on Marty's breath.

"Where you headed?"

"Phoenix. Via Flagstaff."

The cop considered this a moment, then handed the license back.

"I suggest you pull over, get some sleep. There's a rest stop a little ways up."

"Good idea. Thanks."

"Take it easy."

The cop walked back to his motorcycle, and Jack had the impression Marty was holding his breath as he watched him in the rear view. The cop mounted his cycle, stunned it into life, and rode off into the darkness.

Marty wedged the license back behind the visor and wiped his face with the back of his hand. "Listen. I'm not gonna make it to Flagstaff tonight."

Jack felt panic rise from the pit of his stomach, and it showed in his face.

"Hey, don't worry. I'll get you there! But I gotta get some sleep. Whattaya say we find a motel?"

"I don't know—"

"You gotta be there twelve on the dot, I know. We'll *be* there. I swear. I'll take you right to the door of your trailer." He turned a warm and blatantly inviting smile to Jack. "Meanwhile, maybe we could get to know each other better."

Chapter Five

11:41 P.M.

THE CRIMSON DESERT Motel stood alone, a wedge of light in a black velvet landscape. There was no gas station, no diner, no general store, just the ramshackle clapboard motel. A jittery neon faced the highway: POOL—BBQ—VACANCY. There were lots of vacancies. Just three other vehicles stood outside rooms, an old pickup truck at one, and two motorcycles at another.

"Wait here." Marty went toward the fluorescent brightness of the reception office.

"Get a wakeup call," Jack called after him. "Early!"

Marty gave him a thumbs-up and went inside.

A dusty delivery van was parked by the office. Its logo read BBQ EXPRESS.

Marty returned to the car with a room key and drove around the L of the squat motel to the room at the far end. He backed up close to door number 14, and they got out. Jack grabbed his backpack and slung it over his shoulder. Marty put the key into the door and then slumped against it.

"You okay?"

"Yeah, yeah. Just need to snack. There's a vending machine up by the office. Get some protein bars or something." Marty pulled out his wallet.

Jack raised his hand. "Hey, this one's mine!"

Marty grinned. "You say so. I'll bring our stuff inside."

Jack sprinted to the end of the long, low building, rounded the corner, and narrowly missed colliding with a squat man in a khaki shirt. The logo on his pocket read BBQ EXPRESS. He wheeled a dolly with four tanks of propane and gave a cursory grunt to Jack, acknowledging their avoided impact. Beyond him, by the door marked Reception, was the vending machine. Jack slipped two dollar bills into it and pressed the button. After whirring efficiently for fifteen seconds, the machine delivered—nothing. He hit the machine with the heel of his hand a couple of times, but the snack bars remained imprisoned.

The BBQ EXPRESS van driver returned with an empty cart. "Machine's screwed," he said as he headed for his van.

"I just put money in there."

"Howya think they make a profit in this shithole?"

The motel night clerk came out of the office.

"Your machine's out of order," Jack said.

"Give it a thump," the clerk said without looking at Jack.

"I did that, but..."

The clerk ignored him and confronted the van driver. "What's with all the gas?"

"Don't ask me. You ordered it."

The night clerk grabbed the order form from the driver and inspected it.

Jack returned his attention to the machine. He gave it a solid thump. The thing whirred and, miracle of miracles, deposited a bag of chips in the tray. Jack regarded it for a moment, then figured it was better than nothing and took it.

"We usually order one," the motel clerk said as he shoved the order form at the van driver. "One tank! That's all we need."

The driver shoved the form back into the clerk's hand. "Look at the invoice. One- zero! Ten!"

Jack headed to room 14, clutching his emaciated wallet and the chips. The argument at reception was absorbed by the still, dry desert air and faded behind him.

"I'm tellin' ya, we don't *need* ten!"

"Fer Chrissakes man, talk to your boss! It's after midnight. You think I like this gig? This is the order I got! It's paid for already!"

Marty was closing the trunk of the Merc as Jack approached. Jack held up the bag of chips. "Machine's out of order. This is all I could get."

Marty sighed patiently and went to the motel room door. "Air conditioning's fucked too. Let's go sit by the pool." He pulled the door shut.

"You gonna lock the door?"

"You got somethin' worth stealin'?"

Jack considered the contents of his backpack and shrugged. They trudged around the end of the motel and came to a paved area with a small pool lit from beneath. It looked incongruously upscale against the shabbiness of the motel. Marty sat at the edge, removed his shoes, and dipped his bare toes into the water, uttering an exaggerated sigh. Jack laughed and sat by Marty. He tore open the bag of chips, and for a while, the only sound in the still air was the munching of stale potato chips and the crinkle of the bag as they passed it back and forth.

Then Marty pulled his feet from the pool, shook water from them, and sat back, gazing up at the sky. Jack followed his gaze. Myriad points of light, brighter and more than Jack had ever seen, studded the black, black sky.

"The stars don't sparkle out here in the desert," Jack observed.

Marty's gaze swept the sky. "Too many fuckin' stars." He crumpled the chip bag and tossed it onto the ground by his feet. "Guess it's the same in your business."

Jack picked up the ball of twisted plastic, straightened it, then crumpled it again.

"You want to be a star?" Marty asked without turning to him.

"What actor doesn't?"

"Tough call, up against all the Depps and Pitts and Clooneys—and all the new guys with the pretty faces and miles of teeth." Now he turned to look at Jack. "Some rat race, huh?"

Jack shrugged.

Marty stared at the pool but rested his hand on Jack's thigh. Jack felt a stirring and realized he was looking forward to whatever Marty had to offer.

"You'd give it all up, wouldn't you?" Marty continued without looking at Jack. "If you had, say, the money?"

"I don't know." It was something he'd never considered until now, now that he was dead broke. Jack tossed the crumpled bag at a trash can. It missed and fell to the dusty paving.

"I couldn't wait to get out from behind that goddamn desk at the ad agency." Marty massaged Jack's thigh gently as he spoke. "Now I got money. No way will I tie myself to some no-win proposition. I'm gonna put my feet up and let some other loser break his ass."

Jack said nothing.

Marty turned to him and squeezed Jack's thigh, leaving no doubt as to what was on his mind. "Whattaya say we tangle?"

Jack smiled back. No commitment, no emotional investment, just what he needed to relieve the tension of the day—of his life. And there'd been no one since the actor abandoned him three weeks ago, not even a passing ship. "Sounds good to me," he said.

As they got to their feet, Marty stumbled and clutched at Jack to remain upright. "Fuck! This fucking blood sugar thing! Gotta eat something." He turned to Jack with a frankly lascivious smile. "I want to be wide awake when I get you naked. Listen, the clerk said something about a diner about a mile up the highway."

"I'm up for that."

Marty shook his head. "Could you go? Get a sandwich—get a couple." He took Jack's hand and deposited the car keys into it. "Turkey, cheese, whatever they got." He kept hold of Jack's hand and pulled him a little closer. "We can relax then. Take our time."

Jack was aroused, but sanity was still an option. "Are you sure? I mean, that's a pretty classy car."

"So? Don't scratch it."

"You don't even know me," Jack said with an incredulous chuckle.

Marty took his hand from Jack's and placed it firmly on his ass. "I'm gonna rectify that, soon as you're back." He fumbled in his hip pocket, took out his overstuffed wallet, and thrust it into Jack's hand. "Take some cash."

Jack looked down at the wallet and then back to Marty's smile. "I can't take this!"

"I trust you. You've got an honest face. I should know. I got one just like it."

Jack shook his head.

Marty sighed, reached around, and pulled Jack's wallet from his hip pocket. "Here. Gimme yours, makes you feel better."

Jack laughed. "Some swap! There's nothing in it."

"Just get back here with the *food*!" Marty leaned close enough to brush Jack's ear with his lips. "If I'm asleep, wake me."

Jack leaned his head briefly into Marty's lips, then sprinted to the Merc. As he pulled away, he glanced into the rearview mirror and caught a glimpse of Marty watching him from the door of room 14, smiling and massaging his crotch.

Oh, yeah, I'll wake him!

The car handled just as Jack expected it would. Just being in charge of the machine was exhilarating, and the grin on his face was the only really genuine one he'd managed since he signed the movie deal that afternoon. It stayed on his face for half a mile, and then he sobered.

Don't get used to it. Guys like Marty own cars like this. Movie stars own cars like this. I might never own a car like this. Unless…

Unless this movie paid off and led to another and maybe another. It was a big "unless," but it was a goal.

The diner was brightly lit and flanked by gas stations. Jack pulled in carefully, locked the car, and went inside. It was busy, and as he took in the variety of customers—truckers, locals, maybe a tourist or two—he wondered what the hell they were doing in this non-place at this time of night.

"Two turkey clubs on wheat, two Cokes. To go."

The girl behind the bar conveyed the order to the chef. Jack settled onto a stool, feeling the bump in his shirt pocket to make sure Marty's wallet was still there, still crammed with bills, still safe—and still not his. He took another glance around the depressing restaurant with something like relief that he wouldn't have to spend more time in it than the making of a couple of sandwiches. And with the impatience of someone who was eager to "tangle" with an indisputably sexy guy.

A distant, rolling *thump* rattled the plate glass window. A couple of the diners looked up briefly, then returned to their meals.

The weather-beaten guy on the stool next to Jack looked up from his newspaper. "What was that? Thunder?"

"More like a tremor," someone else said with a mouthful of food. They dwelt on their speculations for all of three seconds, then went back to newspaper and burger respectively.

The sandwiches were delivered with a routine smile and a polite demand for sixteen-fifty.

Jack took a hundred-dollar bill from Marty's wallet. "I don't have anything smaller." He reveled in being able to use the phrase and realized he'd never said those exact words before in his life. "Sorry," he said without any sincerity.

The waitress consulted the till, made a big deal of sorting through bills, and brought back change. Jack left a dollar on the bar.

The drive back was just as elating as the drive to but was qualified by Jack's awareness that the car went back to its rightful owner at the journey's end. A rightful owner who offered benefits with his gesture of friendship. *Yes, oh yes*, Jack thought, *I need this. I need a little release, a little mindless pleasure to get over my sorry goddamn life.*

He turned on the radio and found a classic rock station. He pushed the volume up, and the familiar sound somehow salved the sense of loss that was a constant in his life. The thought of Marty waiting for him prompted further pressure on the accelerator.

A bright orange glow lit the sky beyond the low hills ahead.

Dawn? He glanced at the dashboard clock: 12:24. *No way.* And anyway, he was heading west. *Aliens?* He laughed out loud at the thought. He rounded a bend in the highway, and the orange glow became a fierce, surging, undulating entity.

The motel was ablaze.

A highway patrol car, siren blaring, sped past Jack heading for the conflagration. Jack hit the gas and tailed the patrol car. He jerked to a stop inches from the night clerk who was yelling into a cell phone.

"You said you were on your way fifteen minutes ago!" The guy's voice was pitched high and broke with emotion. "The place is *burning down* for Chrissake! I need all the water you got!"

Jack stumbled out of the car, leaving the door open. The night clerk pushed past him and ran to the patrol car. Two guys in nothing but jockeys and tees stood by their motorcycles, which they'd moved far from the blaze. Jack ran to them.

"What happened?"

One man's arms were folded around his body as if he were cold, but sweat glistened on his face, and he looked dazed. "I dunno, I dunno, I dunno," he muttered.

No less dazed, "Gas tanks blew," the other said.

"Did everyone get out?"

The man shrugged. Jack started for the far end of the row of rooms and came to an unsteady stop when he saw the room at the heart of the conflagration—the room in which he'd left Marty, room 14. The walls of the room, front and back, were gone, and beyond this blazing gap in the building, Jack could see the motel pool, lit from beneath and glowing an incongruous, luminous blue.

Jack shielded his face from the heat and took a few steps forward. He was pushed aside roughly by a highway cop.

"Get back!"

"Did everyone get out?"

Another tank blew. This one took the cop down to the gravel and Jack with him. He lay there, stunned for a moment, before the cop swore and rolled off him.

Jack tried to rise and couldn't.

"You okay? Sir?"

A paramedic knelt by him on the grass. Against the glare of the fire, Jack could make out nothing of her face, but her glasses reflected his image in flickering duplicate.

"Can you hear me?"

"My ears—ringing."

"I'm gonna give you something to calm you."

Jack turned back to the horrific spectacle, mesmerized by the leaping, crackling fire. He barely felt the needle. A moment later, the thought occurred to him dimly that she should have asked if was allergic to drugs, or something like that. He turned, but she was gone.

Fire trucks arrived, sirens screaming. Hands grabbed at Jack's arm and dragged him across the lot to a mound of grass. He watched in a daze as firemen moved in with hoses, then tried to get to his feet.

"Don't get up! We need to see if anything's broken, okay?" Another paramedic, a man, was kneeling by him. The medic went to work, shining a flashlight into his eyes, testing joints, examining a cut on his chin, then back to his eyes.

"Had anything to drink tonight?"

"No."

"Any medication?"

"No. Oh, one of your guys gave me a shot of something. For shock, I think she said."

The examination was interrupted by a police officer, and the medic moved on to the bikers. "Got a couple of questions about your buddy," the officer said. "The clerk says you were traveling with another guy."

"Is he okay?"

The officer lowered his head, unwilling to reply for a moment. "I'm sorry."

Jack stopped breathing for a moment, then exhaled in a sob. "Oh God." He struggled to keep his eyes focused.

"Was he a close friend?"

"I never saw him before tonight. I just—I went out for some food and then—when I came back…"

Jack drew his knees up under his chin and wrapped his arms about them. His head fell forward, and sights and sounds blurred. The paramedic was back by his side.

"This guy's in shock!" he called to someone out of view and then to Jack: "We need to get you to the hospital." The cop helped Jack to his feet, and he and the medic eased Jack into an ambulance parked beyond the patrol cars.

The drug took over completely now. As his awareness of the chaos around him faded, all Jack could hear was the steady thump of classic rock blaring from the abandoned Mercedes.

Chapter Six

THURSDAY, JULY 14

A JANGLING OF metal on metal brought him to life. The curtain rings sounded like an alarm clock as the privacy screen at the foot of the bed was pulled aside. Beyond it, the room was in darkness. Another curtain to his side was hauled open and a light snapped on. A face appeared in the glow reflected by the white top of the bedside table.

It took him a moment to focus on a girl wearing a plain blue uniform. She was perhaps twenty and moved with brisk, professional efficiency. She was accompanied by a man in a long white coat over a sweat shirt and jeans, a stethoscope hung around his neck; his hair was unruly, and tired eyes peered from behind thick lenses. He inspected the chart the girl handed him, took Jack's pulse, then peeled back eyelids to inspect Jack's eyes with a tiny flashlight.

"Look left—right." He held up two fingers. "How many fingers?"

"Two." Jack's lips formed the word, though no sound came out of him.

The doctor pulled down the sheet and prodded a rib or two. Jack was too groggy to object but registered no pain. At this point, awareness kicked in, and Jack's fogged brain registered "doctor" and "nurse."

The doc scribbled on the chart and handed it back to the nurse. "Minor shock. That's why you were out so long. That and whatever they shot you with last night." He glanced at the nurse. "Diazepam?" She gave him a non-committal smile. He returned his weary attention to Jack. "No concussion. A few bruises." And he left the room. "You're in better shape than I am," he said as he went.

The nurse offered a practiced smile. "How do you feel?"

Jack managed a rasping cough and a nod. The nurse produced a glass of orange juice, and Jack raised himself on one elbow and drank it in one hit.

"Your clothes are here." She patted a neatly folded pile

on a chair. "We cleaned them up for you." She took a towel from a shelf and placed it on the end of the bed. "You'll want the bathroom." The nurse then indicated a narrow door. "And your personal items are all here." She tapped a cardboard tray on the table by his bed. "When you're ready, go to reception down on the first floor. They'll have some paperwork. Anything else you want to know?"

"Yeah. Where am I?"

"Lake Havasu General."

"Lake...what?"

"Lake Havasu City."

Jack's blank stare prompted her to append.

"Arizona."

He tried to compute the situation, but his head was stuffed with cotton.

The nurse went around the small room folding things. "Oh, and there's a policeman downstairs who wants to talk to you. We thought he might want you to identify the body, but..." She paused in her neat sweep of the room and looked faintly apologetic. "What I hear is there's not much left to identify."

Jack sat bolt upright and gasped loudly.

"Sorry! I thought— They said you didn't know the, uh, the victim. The deceased. Sorry."

Images and sounds came back to him in a rush, and he

remembered—the fire, the sirens, the chaos, the yelling, and, with a shudder, the fate of the guy who'd given him a lift. Marty. The fate that could've been his.

And the job!

"What time is it?"

She glanced at her watch as she went to a heavily draped window. "Five of twelve."

"Twelve? Midnight?"

She pulled open the drapes and daylight flooded the room. "Noon. Five to twelve noon."

Jack felt as if a bucket of ice had been dumped in his gut. "How far am I from Flagstaff?"

"Flagstaff?" She thought about this for a few seconds. "About two hundred miles." She glanced at her watch again and headed for the door. "Don't be too long, Mr. Brenner. We need the bed." She swept out of the room, a hint of antiseptic in her wake.

Jack slumped back onto the pillow and closed his eyes. There was no thought in his mind, just an aching mesh of loss and finality and helplessness. His big chance, his *only* chance—shot. Shot to hell. Guilt needled him faintly as he considered the fate of the guy, the affable, sexy guy who'd been kind to him the night before.

What now? Back to LA? To what? To whom?

Mr. Brenner.

Jack froze for a moment, and then suddenly galvanized, he scrambled to the edge of the bed, knocking the cardboard tray off the table and scattering its contents. The intensity of his heartbeat threatened to shatter his eardrums. He had to call the nurse—no, he had to go to someone in authority and put them straight.

He knelt on the cool floor to gather up the contents of the tray, and his hand came down on a thick, soft wallet. Marty's wallet. The one he'd taken to the diner the night before. Next to it were Marty's driver's license and a letter bearing the logo of a Phoenix legal firm. It was addressed to Martin Brenner.

Jack took his time in the shower, the first he'd had since the morning before. Haste was pointless. The script, the precious script with all the contact numbers was ash. Even if he got a lift, it would take him three hours, minimum, to get to Flagstaff. And even if he got there, someone else was probably learning his lines, wearing his costume, right at this goddamn moment.

He stood stock still, eyes closed, and let the water run over him. If he hadn't been on that particular freeway ramp, if Marty hadn't offered him a ride, if they hadn't booked into that particular motel… Bottom line? He was just as out of a job as he was yesterday morning—and a nice guy was dead. That last thought sobered him: Martin Brenner was dead. Jack McCauley lived and breathed. That was something to be going on with.

*

12:21 P.M.

JACK EMERGED FROM the elevator into the busy hospital lobby. He headed for reception, dodging visitors and nurses. An old man on a walker swore at him as he brushed past. A line of disgruntled people waited, growing more disgruntled as the receptionist took call after call, paged a doctor or a nurse, and punctuated these efficiencies by touching and smoothing her hair. Finally, Jack moved up to the desk and dropped the envelope and Marty's wallet onto it. The receptionist offered him a meaningless smile. He held out Marty's driver's license.

"There's been a mistake."

The squalling of a toddler competed with his halting delivery. He cleared his throat.

"There's been a mistake," he repeated. "They brought me here last night, after the fire, and…"

She glanced at the license, then shot an irritated frown at the screaming child and its heavily pregnant mother. "Oh, yes, the fire. Terrible".

"I need to talk to—"

"The police? There's a detective…" She referred to a notepad. "Millet, or Mullet. He's in the cafeteria. Just outside, turn left; you can't miss it."

"Fine, but—"

"We have all the information we need. The paramedic who brought you in took a look in your wallet and gave us your insurance, your home address—"

The shrill giggle of an obese girl in stretch pants joined the cries of the distraught child. The phone rang. The receptionist reached for it.

"Wait!" Jack clamped his hand over the phone. "Can you wait just a minute?"

The receptionist shot an icy glare from Jack's hand to the phone and back again. "Excuse me," she said, broken glass in her tone.

Jack pulled his hand away, and she brought the handset to her ear. "Lake Havasu General," she said with professional composure. She pushed a piece of paper across the desk to Jack. "Just sign."

Jack sighed in exasperation. The only remotely urgent action in the lobby was on a big-screen TV showing, ironically, a western. On the screen, a Technicolor horse skidded to a dusty stop and threw its rider to the ground, where he began to grapple with, presumably, the bad guy. No dialogue could be heard above the inane chatter of the girl on her cell phone, the yelling of the child, and the general echoes of conversation and coughs in the lobby. Jack looked away from the screen and closed his eyes.

Reflecting a long time later, he'd remember that the thought, the germ of the idea, the lunatic plan, occurred to him at that very moment. But it would be an expedient recollection, a lie he'd tell himself to support the outrageousness of what he was about to do. In reality, the idea had been at the back of his mind since he'd showered in the hospital bathroom. Yet later, he would truly believe he'd acted on impulse, here, at the reception desk of Lake Havasu City General.

He tightened his grip on Marty's overstuffed wallet as he studied the driver's license on the desk. Then carefully, but not too carefully, Jack took the pen and signed "Martin Brenner" on the release form.

He slid the form slowly across the desk. The receptionist placed it on a stack of similar forms without interrupting her call. Jack put the license into the wallet and pushed it into his hip pocket. Then he picked up the legal letter addressed to Martin Brenner and started for the exit.

"Sir? Sir? Just a minute!"

He turned back.

The receptionist dangled a ring of car keys from her hand. "Your car's in area three."

"My car?"

She jangled the keys impatiently. Jack walked back to the desk slowly and took them. He went out of the lobby into the desert-dry July heat.

He slowed as he approached the Mercedes in the parking lot. A thin veil of desert dust dulled its gleam. Jack walked around to the trunk, and after a moment, he inserted the key and opened it. Inside, there was a brown leather suitcase, which appeared to be brand new.

"Mr. Brenner?"

Jack slammed the trunk shut and spun around to a tall, lean man of middle age with a shock of steely-gray hair. He wore blue jeans and a light sport jacket; he smiled at Jack's mildly comic reaction.

"Sorry. I didn't mean to, uh…" The man sobered. "Guess you're a little shook up after the—after last night." He produced a badge. "Detective Keith Miller, Lake Havasu City Police Department." The man offered his hand. Jack's hand was clammy with sweat, and he wiped it on his jeans before placing it into the detective's.

Jack's gaze moved to the Mercedes. "How…?"

Miller gave the car a cursory glance. "We checked with the medics, found which hospital they brought you to. I had one of my officers drive it here. Given the circumstances, there was no point impounding it. And the motel is a charred ruin. So."

He waited for a response; Jack managed a nod.

"You're welcome," Miller said with an affable smile. Then he sobered. "I'm sorry about your friend."

"He wasn't my friend. I never met him before last night. He thumbed a ride. I didn't know him." Jack wiped his mouth to check the avalanche of words.

"Any idea where he was headed?"

"Um—Flagstaff. Yeah, Flagstaff. I think he said he had a job there."

"You know what kind of job?"

"A movie. He was an actor."

"An actor, huh? We found a burnt-up backpack we assumed belonged to this guy…" He snapped his fingers a couple of times to jog his memory. "McCauley. Jake McCauley."

"Jack."

"Excuse me?"

"He—said his name was Jack."

"Ah. Yes." Miller took a plastic ziplock bag from his jacket pocket. Inside, charred but instantly recognizable to Jack, was his own thin, worn wallet. He watched without blinking as Miller removed it carefully and opened it. The photograph of Jack's father, his only memory of the man, fluttered to the ground.

Miller picked it up carefully. The edges were brittle from the heat it had been so recently exposed to. Jack reached for it reflexively, but Miller slipped it back into the plastic bag. Then he opened the blackened wallet and withdrew Jack's charred driver's license carefully, with fingertip and thumb.

"Wasn't much left of the guy. Not at all. Nothing we could use for identification. The tanks went up right in back of the motel room and…"

Jack's stomach rebelled, and he made a determined effort not to throw up. He pulled a handkerchief out of his pocket and wiped his face.

"Sorry, Mr. Brenner. I know this is tough on you, but we'd like to find this guy's folks. We need all the help we can get. The address on the license is five years old—an apartment building in LA—and nobody there ever heard of him, no forwarding address. If there's anything you can tell us."

Jack took a deep gasping breath. "You know? I remember now— He said his folks were dead. I don't think he had any family."

Miller considered this, nodding slowly. "Too bad." He held out the license close to Jack's face. "This *is* the guy?"

Jack's picture was five years old, and thanks to the DMV's unique gift for portrait photography, bore little resemblance to him. He nodded.

"Anything else you can tell me about him?"

"No. I don't think so."

"Anything come up in conversation? Something about his friends, people he worked with? I presume you guys talked while you were driving."

"He slept most of the way. Then I got tired and suggested we should stop for the night. I checked in at the motel, then he went to a diner for something to eat."

"He?"

Jack realized instantly what he'd said but turned a querying frown to Miller. "Sorry?"

"You said *he* went to the diner."

"No, no, *I* went. *He* went to bed, and, uh—I went for food, and when I got back…"

"And you picked this motel at random?"

"Sure."

Miller turned to look at some far horizon that only he could see and was silent for a moment. He turned back to Jack with a smile. "Well, thanks, Mr. Brenner. Take my card. Just in case you think of anything else."

Jack pocketed the card. "Sorry I'm not much help."

Miller extended his hand to Jack, and as Jack reached for it, he dropped the letter he'd been holding. Miller picked it up. "If I need to talk to you again, where can I find you?"

"I'm not exactly sure…"

Miller glanced at the face of the envelope. "How about here? Adams and Finch Attorneys, Phoenix? This where you're headed?" He took a notepad from his pocket, scribbled the address and number, then handed the letter back to Jack. "Take it easy, Mr. Brenner."

Jack offered Miller a smile that was honest as the day. As Miller walked away, the smile faded, and Jack leaned against the car to steady himself.

The parking attendant gave him directions out of town and after negotiating streets, he came to a T-junction.

A sign pointed north to I-40, which would give him a choice of Los Angeles or Flagstaff. The sign also offered a route to Phoenix to the south via I-95. Ahead of him was the state park, and against a backdrop of seemingly painted mountains, Lake Havasu sparkled with reflected sunlight. The postcard serenity of the view did nothing to slow his heartbeat nor the thoughts racing through his brain.

He pulled the Mercedes over, close to a parked car, and let his head fall back onto the headrest. The impulse that had set him on this route was overtaken by panic. He couldn't possibly get away with—*with what*? He had no clear idea just what he was doing. Thought tumbled over thought.

I haven't seen Loretta since I was eleven. Wouldn't know

what she looks like now. And vice versa.

Maybe he could…

A sharp rap on the window by his head brought him bolt upright with a gasp. A guy in a Hawaiian shirt peered into the car. Jack lowered the window.

"You okay?" the man asked.

"Yeah, fine," Jack said with no conviction.

"Looked like you were—"

"I'm fine!"

He pushed the stick into drive, jerked the car into the stream of traffic, and turned at the intersection.

He'd been driving for twenty minutes before he realized he was heading south on I-95.

Chapter Seven

THURSDAY, JULY 14
4:59 P.M.

IT WAS NEAR five when Jack reached the outskirts of Phoenix, and the early evening freeway traffic was heavy. Behind him, the sun sat low in a clear sky, and ahead, to the east, its light gave the city a warm glow. High-rise windows sparkled like gem facets, and beyond the city skyline, low, purple-blue mountains stretched across the horizon.

During the three-hour drive from Lake Havasu, Jack had kept his mind barricaded against self-criticism and reason. Now, as he deciphered the highway signs and aimed for the city center, this barrier was breached by unease.

He left the freeway at 7th Street, doubled back to the Burton Barr Library as instructed in the attorney's letter, and parked. He read the letter once again. It spoke of the pleasure Adams & Finch, Attorneys at Law, took in providing the requested Mercedes along with five thousand dollars petty cash for "interim expenses." Upon Mr. Brenner's arrival in Phoenix, Mr. Adams would define the details of the will, which named Martin Brenner sole beneficiary, and set up the essential accounts, advise on credit, investment institutions, et cetera, et cetera.

The office of Adams & Finch was situated on the second floor of a squat, unprepossessing building on East Moreland. Jack stood on the sidewalk clutching the letter and stared at the polished brass plate for some time. He shuddered as a gust of cool evening air brushed his face. The shudder sparked alarm, and he turned back to the parking lot—but then he thought, *I've come this far...*

On the second floor, the door marked Reception bore an aged sign painted onto a frosted glass pane. At one time, it had read Adams & Finch. Now, masking tape covered the "Finch." But the light from inside the office shone through, and the name was still faintly discernible. Jack went inside.

A plump woman in a beige business suit stood at a desk straightening a stack of files. Her short, well-groomed hair was mostly gray, and she might have been in her sixties, but a round face subtracted a few years and gave her a genial appearance. She glanced up and offered an apologetic smile. "We're just closing up for the day."

Jack held out the envelope. "I, uh—I have this letter…"

The woman frowned, and then her eyes opened wide, and she put her hands to her cheeks. "Oh, my hat! Wait! Wait!"

She went into the inner office, and Jack could hear her joyous proclamation of his arrival. He glanced at a wall mirror, noted his ragged appearance, and did his best to smooth down his hair.

"Martin! Welcome home!" The voice was gravelly, old, but full of warmth. Harry Adams gave the impression of someone who'd spent most of his seventy-some years outdoors. Sunspots covered his forehead, and his pure-white hair looked as if he combed it exclusively, though not often, with his fingers. He wore an open shirt tucked into baggy pants, which indicated that while his girth might have fluctuated over the years, his tailor's measurements had not. He strode into the room and took Jack's hand in both of his and shook it heartily.

"You met Maggie," Adams said.

Maggie beamed at Jack. "Coffee or tea?"

"He doesn't want coffee!" Adams growled. "He's had

a long drive; he wants a good stiff drink, don't you son. What'll it be?"

Jack would've welcomed paint stripper. "Bourbon."

"Two," Adams ordered.

"Blood pressure..." Maggie started.

"Doubles," Adams said firmly as he put an arm about Jack's shoulders and led him to the inner sanctum. Inside, he took a sheaf of letters from a chair and pushed it toward Jack. "Sit down, sit down!"

At first glance, the office seemed chaotic. Files crammed the shelves, manila folders fat with papers covered two desks, and in the corners of the room, boxes sat stacked on the floor. Yet, there was a hint of order in the way these were arranged—Maggie's influence, Jack guessed. It was clear Adams resented her attempt to make sense of the disarray when he pushed a stack of papers aside and perched on the edge of his desk. Some of the papers drifted to the floor, but Adams made no attempt to retrieve them.

"Now, let's take a good look at you." The old man surveyed him, squinting, deepening the already profound lines at the corners of his eyes. "When were you last in this office?"

Jack swallowed. He had no idea.

"I'll *tell* you when! Not since you were ten. Or eleven.

And you want to know something? I would've known you *anywhere*. Yes, sir, you've grown into a fine-lookin' fella." The broad smile that creased the weather-beaten face cross-faded into a sympathetic frown. "I haven't even offered my condolences. Well, not since we talked on the phone. You were a tough man to track down! And to think, when we finally found you, it was to give you bad news."

Jack lowered his head, unable and unwilling to confirm the call. Adams apparently took the gesture to be borne of loss and modulated his tone accordingly.

"Hardly a day goes by I don't think of Amy and the awful way she ended it." Adams sighed heavily and stared in silence for a moment at the heavily speckled backs of his hands resting on his knees.

The awful way she ended it? Jack considered this but could only wait for Adams to expound.

"She worked all her life to keep that ranch going. After Ed's death, it was like an obsession. Then, to just—give up like that."

Jack looked up at Adams, who seemed to read query in the glance.

"That's what she did," Adams continued. "She gave up! Just let go of it all and took to her bed. And then to die that way, the very morning after she made the new will."

Adams turned his hands over and searched his palms

as if an answer might be found there. "Naturally, we all thought she'd leave the place to Loretta. But her intention was quite definite. I knew your aunt for fifty-seven years, and in all that time, I never saw her so determined. You were to be her sole heir. Sole."

He slid off his perch on the corner of the desk and rummaged in the congestion of paper on its surface. "It's here. Somewhere." He shouted in the direction of the office door: "Maggie!"

"Hold your horses!" Maggie yelled back.

Adams continued to rummage. "Place is a mess since old Charlie Finch passed on. You probably don't even remember him." He gestured briefly to the office's second desk, as chaotic as his own, then shook his head slowly and sighed. "You reach an age, all your friends just…"

A moment's reflection, and then Adams's mood shifted abruptly to good cheer. He pulled a small photo from the mess of papers, regarded it briefly, and thrust it at Jack. "Know who this is?"

The picture showed a small boy in a cowboy hat. He leaned against a white rail fence and looked so sad he might've been holding back tears.

"Amy gave me that picture, morning she signed the will." Adams took the picture back and inspected it. "I guess this was the last time you ever saw your aunt. She took this the day your mother upped and dragged you off to LA. Remember?"

Jack tried to nod but couldn't execute even so simple an action.

Adams shook his head. "Well, we don't want to go into that now." He dropped the picture onto the desk. "Under the bridge, eh? Under the bridge!"

Maggie came in bearing two glasses which contained more ice than bourbon. She gave one to Jack and one to Adams, who raised the glass briefly to Jack before downing the contents in one eager swallow. He shook the ice around and tried to drain a little more liquor from it, then deposited the glass on a stack of files.

"Any idea where the Wyatt papers are?" Adams asked.

Maggie lifted the glass from the files. "Right here. Where they've been all week." She made an elaborate point of blotting the ring left by the glass with a handkerchief before surrendering the file to Adams. He took a brief look at it and dumped it back onto the desk.

"Aw, hell, this can wait till tomorrow." He clapped Jack on a shoulder. "We might as well go right on out to the ranch. What do you say?" Adams took his suit jacket from where it hung shapelessly on a hook by the door.

Jack drained his glass and handed it to Maggie, who held the glasses between thumb and forefinger in a way that suggested if she had her way, they would never again contain anything more intoxicating than water.

The bourbon kicked in and injected a sudden clarity into Jack's mind. And with that clarity, shame.

I can't go through with this!

He jumped to his feet. "You know, it's getting late. Maybe I could stay at a motel tonight and—"

"A motel? *A motel*? You've got your own *house*." Adams managed to get one arm into his suit jacket and with his free hand, eased Jack into reception. "You busy right now?" he asked Maggie.

"Sure, I am," she said, helping his other arm into the jacket. "Brad Pitt's waiting for me down at Denny's."

"Follow me out to the Wyatt House. I'll ride with Martin. We've got some catching up to do." Adams turned back to Maggie. "Oh, better call Loretta, tell her we're on our way. Wouldn't want to walk in unannounced. You know what she's like." He opened the office door and followed Jack into to hallway. "Where'd you park?"

"Just up the block." Jack's voice was husky, almost inaudible.

"Red, right?"

"Excuse me?"

"The Mercedes."

"Oh, yeah."

"Cost of cars these days," Maggie said as she turned out lamps.

"It's the *gas*," Adams said. "*That's* what costs." He gave Jack a conspiratorial grin. "Anyhoo, won't make much of a dent in the final figure. Drop in the bucket, eh? Drop in the bucket!"

Maggie thrust a muffler at Adams who regarded it as he might a viper. "It's a hundred ten out there!"

Maggie ignored him and confided in Jack: "The temperature just plummets at sundown."

Adams snatched the muffler from her and herded Jack out of the office stuffing the muffler into his jacket pocket. "Woman won't be happy until I'm dead," he grumbled. "Then she can say I told you so."

As they walked the block to the car, Jack became aware his hands were trembling. He pushed them into his jacket pockets.

"So," he said casually, "Loretta is still at the house?"

"Don't think she's got anyplace else to go," Adams said simply. "I don't know what memories you have of her, but she's become kinda bitter over the years. Never know why she didn't marry. God knows she had offers, plenty of offers. She'll be glad to see you," he said cheerfully and then with less conviction, "I'm sure she will."

When they reached the Mercedes, Adams stopped and

inspected it as a man of his age might a beautiful woman of twenty—with admiration bordering on lust and the sad awareness that they would never quite look as if they belonged together.

"Mind if I drive?" he asked.

*

7:38 P.M.

THE SUN HAD gone, but the sky was still bright with just one star visible, unblinking in the still desert air.

"Had me a Caddy convertible, back in the day. Sixty-nine. Robin's-egg blue, white upholstery. That was a *car*." The broad smile took twenty years off Adams's weathered face. He glanced briefly at Jack and hope underlined his smile. "Wouldn't happen to have a smoke on you?"

"No, sorry."

He nodded resignedly. "Don't tell Maggie I asked."

They headed east and Adams took advantage of the sparse traffic to floor the car once in a while, glancing frequently into the rear view for any sign of the highway patrol. He caught Jack's expression during one of these bursts of speed and reluctantly slowed to eighty. They passed road signs to places with exotic names like "Paradise Valley" and "Shadow Mountain."

To Jack's relief, "catching up" meant Adams gave more information than he demanded.

"Loretta's a fine, strong woman, but no talent for running a place like the Wyatt ranch. None. There's money, God knows, but she has no business sense. The place is going to ruin. Not in small part due to her goddamn temper! Less than a week after Amy took to her bed, she had a run-in with four of the ranch hands, and they walked. Only one left is Diego. He's been with her five or six years now. He was in Afghanistan. Still has issues, I think. Very loyal. He manages best he can, does most of the work. Though how he puts up with her! No one wanted to work for her, so she had to sell off some of their best stock. Through all this, Amy just lay up there in that grand bedroom of hers, staring at the ceiling." Anger crept into his tone. "Damn-fool doctor. Shouldn't have left those goddamn pills where she could get at 'em."

He slowed at a sign which read Scottsdale and turned off the highway, drove through affluent if dense suburbs, and onto roads from which farmland stretched on either side. A little later, he turned onto a narrow road on which there was neither traffic nor streetlights.

"The old house will probably bring back memories. Even though you were a little tyke last time you saw it."

The night was warm, but Jack shivered. The uneasiness

he'd pushed into a far corner of his mind moved up to a more accessible region, but even if he'd had a plan B, it was too late to implement it.

They came to tall, wide wrought iron gates which stood incongruously alone, flanked by no fence. The name "Wyatt" was worked into the vast iron arch over the gates. Jack craned to take in the conceit of this as they passed through the gates and onto an even narrower drive. A sign just inside the gates stated that the road was private, and trespassers would be greeted with armed response.

For a time, the drive seemed to lead nowhere but into deepening scrub, but then it turned, and the way ahead cleared to reveal patterned lawns and carefully planned arcs of trees that fanned out to reveal the house.

Jack's first sight of it caused him to draw breath audibly.

Adams laughed. "No matter how often I come out here, the old place never ceases to surprise me either. Well, Martin, lad, it's all yours now."

The house was in no way related to the ranch houses they'd passed in the twilight. It was a vast Victorian monster, one of those houses that didn't quite qualify for historical significance but one that had been preserved stubbornly over the years as if to spite this oversight.

There were two floors of wood and brick and an

octagonal tower at one corner. A wide porch flanked the entire width of the first floor and the upper floor had a broad balcony that also ran the width of the house; both had balustrades of intricate wrought iron. Part of the brick façade had been invaded by ivy, massed around one of the downstairs windows. Jack counted six tall brick chimneys.

He searched the sullen architecture for elements that complied with his concept of "home," but his criteria related to sitcoms or movies, and he found few parallels. The house that towered over him was grand, spectacularly so—but there was nothing inviting about it.

Chapter Eight

ADAMS PARKED ABRUPTLY, skidding on the gravel, then got out of the car and gave it an affectionate pat before tossing the keys to Jack.

A gunshot startled both men.

"Loretta's idea of a warm welcome," Adams said.

They climbed three wide brick steps to the porch and crossed to the front door. Adams reached for the knocker and raised it, but the door opened suddenly, wrenching it from his hand. A short, round woman in her sixties stood in the doorway. Her black hair was pulled back into a tight knot. Though she stood in silhouette, Jack could tell she wore a simple black dress. Oversized felt polishing gloves covered her hands. Her small, dark eyes were fixed on him as she spoke.

"Miss Loretta, she—"

"I know where to find her, Consuela," Adams interrupted. "You remember Martin?"

Consuela's eyes hadn't moved from Jack. "I remember."

"Hi," Jack said.

Consuela responded by glancing conspicuously at the doormat. Both men wiped their feet thoroughly, and she stepped back to allow them to proceed into the lobby. Jack thought he could see a hint of his reflection in the high polish of the dark, wood-tiled floor, but it was probably imagination in overdrive. Ahead of him, an elaborately carved oak staircase ascended grandly to the floor above. They moved through a long hall, passing a library, a spacious living room, a dining room, and several closed doors before they came to a door which Adams opened.

Another gunshot. Jack flinched.

Adams laughed. "Come on. She's not gonna shoot you."

He led Jack through a glassed morning room, out onto the back terrace. Lawn stretched away from the house and eventually turned to red earth on which stood an imposing stable, bright white in the fading daylight. Beyond sat bunkhouses bordered by a white fence, and on the other side of them, rolling fields stretched off into low hills and the twilight shadows as far as Jack could see.

"Pull!"

Loretta stood at the far border of the lawn, a rifle to her shoulder. A powerful-looking Latino man in chaps ejected a clay pigeon that barely made it out of the catapult before it was shattered. The echo of the shot returned several times from distant hills, diminishing with each repetition. The daylight was almost gone, and Jack wondered at the woman's eyesight.

"Well done!" Adams shouted.

Loretta turned slowly and looked at the two of them for some time before ejecting the shell from the rifle. The big man hurried to pick it up. Loretta shouldered the rifle and walked casually across the lawn.

She looked to be in her early forties, a strikingly handsome woman with high cheekbones and sleek blonde hair pulled into a ponytail. She wore jeans, riding boots, and a neat checked shirt tucked in at a trim waist. Loretta regarded Jack with ice-blue eyes. "I expected you earlier."

Jack considered an excuse, but Adams made it for him.

"Traffic," he said, shaking his head sorrowfully.

Loretta's eyes remained on Jack. A hint of a smile lifted the corners of her mouth. "You've grown."

Jack's adrenaline was at a level he might've experienced on an opening night. He met her gaze and tried to match the temperature of her smile.

Adams glanced from one to the other. "Nice to see you two reunited," he said a little too jovially.

Loretta's attention didn't stray from Jack. "We missed you at the funeral."

Jack struggled to think of an excuse, but Loretta seemed not to expect one.

Adams piped up anyway. "We didn't quite know where to find—"

Loretta half turned to the terrace and yelled, "*Consuela*!"

Consuela stood solidly at the back door and yelled back a hearty, "*Whaaat!*"

"Did you get Mr. Martin's things from the car?"

"What I gotta get?" Consuela asked belligerently.

"There's just one case," Jack said.

Consuela marched across the lawn and held her hand out. Jack realized he'd had the keys clutched tight in his hand ever since Adams had thrown them to him. His palm bore white pressure marks from the keys. Consuela swiped them from his hand. "I get. If it ain't too heavy." She walked slowly back to the house.

"*Y más rápidamente*," Loretta called, but Consuela's

pace didn't accelerate at all. Loretta turned her smile to Adams and linked her arm through his. "How about a cocktail?"

"Good idea," Adams said with immense gratitude.

Loretta tossed the rifle to Jack who caught it clumsily and turned it over in his hands as they started for the terrace.

"This is a Winchester," he said, admiring its pristine condition.

She glanced briefly at Jack over her shoulder. "Still know your guns."

Jack felt as if he'd passed a test. In fact, he'd admired a replica of the Winchester on the HBO episode in which he'd merely stood beside the featured player who carried it.

They crossed the terrace to the row of sliding glass doors and went into the morning room, a mid-century addition to the old house. Loretta led them to a bar flanked with several armchairs.

"A toast," Adams said when they had their drinks. "Long life, happiness—and family." He raised his glass.

Jack hesitated for a split second, then lifted his glass.

As if this was her cue, Loretta raised hers to Jack and said, "Family."

Adams drained his glass and refilled it. Jack went to the windows and gazed out as the light went from the fields.

He watched the man pack up the clay pigeon equipment and marveled at his muscularity. The man obviously worked out. He glanced back at the house and caught Jack watching him. His face was more than merely handsome — Jack tried to think of the right word to describe it. High cheekbones and a square jaw suggested some Native American blood. His hair was black, sleek, and pulled back into a short ponytail.

Noble. That was it. There was *nobility* in the man's beauty. He remained still, expressionless, but seemed to be appraising Jack, who flushed under the scrutiny. Jack turned back to the room.

Loretta perched on a barstool, watching him. "Diego does most of the work here these days."

Jack nodded, faintly embarrassed to have been caught examining the man.

"Place has changed a bit since you saw it last," she continued. "Most of the stock has gone. Two mares, that's all that's left. And a couple of wranglers who don't know horse sense from horse shit."

Adams laughed, and when Loretta didn't, he switched swiftly to earnestness. "Well, now Martin's back, maybe he can help pull things together again."

Loretta swirled the ice in her drink slowly. "Last I heard, you wanted to sell up."

"I—haven't really thought about it," Jack said.

The tinkle of ice in Loretta's glass was the only sound in the room. Adams glanced from one to the other and was saved from bridging the silence by Consuela's appearance in the doorway.

"Miss Maggie outside. In a hurry. Date with Brad Pitt."

"Ah!" Adams said, relieved to be offered an exit strategy. He dragged the muffler out of his pocket and wound it around his neck, then shook Jack's hand. "You need anything, just call me." Adams gave Loretta a wave or a salute, Jack wasn't sure which. "See you at the memorial." And he fled.

The faint click of Adams's footsteps on the wood tiles of the hallway was followed by the distant sound of the front door closing, and there was silence.

"Memorial?" Jack asked casually.

"Tomorrow morning. We postponed until we knew you'd be able to make it." Loretta swiveled her stool to the bar and put a little more ice into her glass. "I knew you'd want to pay your respects. Considering how close you were to Amy when you were a child." She turned back to Jack. "And considering Amy's generosity."

She took her drink to an armchair and eased herself into it smoothly. Jack sensed a lithe physical strength, which controlled not only her body but every impression she wished to give to the world. He realized with some surprise that he not only understood this, he respected it. It was the same control, the same calculated manipulation, he'd employed professionally for that part of his adult life he'd labeled "career."

The daylight had gone, and the glass doors no longer offered a view, merely a reflection of the two of them. Jack leaned on the bar wondering if there was anything he should or could say that was relevant without being in any way revealing. But Loretta seemed comfortable in the silence. She drank deeply then surveyed the darkened windows over the rim of her glass.

"When we came in just now, I could've sworn Amy was sitting there," she said almost in a whisper, and Jack followed her gaze to a brown leather armchair by the windows. "After Ed died, she liked to watch the last light of the day as it crossed the fields and moved to the treetops, then the hills. She loved this room." She glanced about the room and up toward the ceiling. "She loved this whole antique heap of wood and bricks. This, and the land, and the horses."

A long pause, and then she added, "And Ed Wyatt." She turned to Jack and uttered a brief, wry chuckle. "There you have it—Amy's life by *Reader's Digest*."

"So why did she…?" As soon as he heard the sound of

his own voice, he wished he hadn't embarked on the question, and he let it hang. Loretta remained still for a moment, then stood and walked to the windows and gazed into the darkness.

"Why did she kill herself?" Her tone was matter of fact. "Why does anyone? If the choice is between the cold light of day and a good night's sleep…" She turned her cool smile back to Jack.

Jack managed a noncommittal nod.

"She always believed you'd survive your mother and your asshole brother and make something of yourself. She held on to that faith, long after you stopped writing. She was greatly saddened that you fell out of touch." She put her head to one side, inviting a response.

After a moment, Jack dredged up Marty's conversation of the night before—*You grow up; you let go of stuff.* He shrugged. "Life. Gets in the way."

"I heard you were married."

"Divorced."

"Harry Adams said you were in the advertising business. You must've given up a comfortable life, good friends, to come to this godforsaken dot on the map."

"Not really."

"I'd like to hear what you've been up to these last fourteen years." She walked her glass to the bar and deposited it, then went to the hall door. "I've opened up the dining room, in your honor. I thought we'd have supper in there tonight—and talk."

Jack felt a chill, and his mind went into overdrive. He'd have to talk about the past, Martin's past, Martin's life between eleven and— How old was Martin when he…? Jack had seen the driver's license. Twenty-five. A year older than his brother Scott. Two years older than Jack. How much could he invent? How convincingly? The divorce— He could talk about the divorce in abstract terms, about his wife's affair with his brother. But he didn't even know the name of Martin's wife.

He put his glass on the bar clumsily, spilling some of the liquor he'd barely touched. He grabbed a paper napkin from the bar and mopped the spill, pulping the napkin in the process.

"Leave that. Consuela can clean up."

"You know? I'm kinda beat. It's been a long drive, and I'm not really hungry."

When Loretta eventually responded, her tone indicated she knew he was dodging. "I'll have Consuela bring you a sandwich. We can catch up tomorrow night, or the night after. There's time. Unless, of course, you plan to take the money and run."

Jack smiled and shook his head as if this was a

ridiculous notion. "Tomorrow. Fine."

"You're in your old room."

He followed Loretta into the long hallway, the lobby, and to the staircase where she stopped and leaned against the elaborately carved newel. The top of the staircase was lost in shadow. Jack started up cautiously. At the top he paused to let his eyes become accustomed to the gloom. He was faced with a door and took a step toward it.

"I've left Amy's room just as it was."

He turned to Loretta, watching him from below.

"Just as it was when she died. Of course, now you're master of the house, you might want to rearrange things." If she intended irony, there was no hint of it in her voice.

"Everything's fine," he said feebly.

Loretta continued to watch as Jack turned to other doors. One of them opened suddenly, spilling light into the hall, and Consuela emerged.

"I don't change sheets every day. This ain't no motel." She dumped a heavy, folded bath towel into Jack's arms as she brushed past him and continued down the stairs.

Grateful for the lead, Jack went into the room and closed the door. He stood leaning against it for some time with no thought on his mind except that he was here, in Martin's room, in Martin's house; that alone seemed an achievement of some kind. The pounding in his chest subsided, and his breathing slowed.

Martin's suitcase sat open on a chair by a tall oak armoire, lit by a single lamp. Jack felt around the wall beside him and found a switch for the overhead light.

The room was neat and smelled of furniture polish but gave the impression it hadn't been occupied for some time. The pale-yellow wallpaper had a muted pattern of sepia roses, a theme repeated on the heavy velvet drapes at the tall window. A small fireplace of brick and wrought iron looked as if it had been freshly set with wood. By it, a door opened to the porcelain of a bathtub gleaming as if new, though the brass claws on which it stood indicated the era when it had been installed.

He turned and gasped as he saw a stranger in the room—then chuckled nervously, almost hysterically, as he realized it was his own reflection in the armoire mirror. He relaxed and took in more of the room.

Groups of photographs punctuated the rose-patterned wallpaper at intervals. One was a school photograph of a class of fifth graders and above it, a neatly framed certificate for Junior Horsemanship presented to Martin Brenner, aged ten.

At the foot of the single bed sat an oak chest with brass hinges that might have materialized from the pages of *Treasure Island*. Jack lifted the lid and found inside the kind of treasure a kid might indeed sail the seven seas for — a bat and mitt, a football, a neatly folded Cardinals sweater, an elaborate colored pencil set, DVDs of action movies Jack had seen when he was ten, kids' books ranging from science fiction through pulp westerns to champion horses, a stack of yellowing comic books, a small astronomical telescope, and a Lego kit for assembling a *Star Wars* fighter.

Jack closed the lid slowly, moved by this glimpse into Martin's early life and faintly disturbed by the zeal with which these childhood mementos had been preserved.

He sat on the edge of the bed and opened the drawer of the nightstand. It contained a single envelope addressed simply: "Aunt Amy." The envelope might have been a crisp white fifteen years ago. Now, the corners were yellowing, and it appeared to have been folded and unfolded many times. He took out a single sheet of paper written on both sides in a young hand.

It was the plea of a frightened and bewildered child who had no wish to be parted from his aunts, no eagerness to return to his loveless home or his indifferent mother, no desire to leave this sprawling antique of a house.

Surrounded by these relics of the past, and now that the headlong rush into another man's life had slowed, Jack suddenly felt an overwhelming sadness for Martin's lost life. And a profound exacerbation of guilt at having assumed it as his own.

He folded the letter and sat staring at it for some time before exhaustion triumphed, and he slept.

Chapter Nine

FRIDAY, JULY 15
6:35 A.M.

HE WAS ON stage—but in a play he didn't know, with players he didn't recognize, and under the collective glare of a silent, menacing audience. He struggled to find words, any words, to break the silence. And then he saw the flames. The theater was on fire! The audience was being consumed by a fierce, crackling inferno, but no one moved. He tried to shout a warning, to run, but he had no voice, and his feet were like lead weights. He wrenched himself out of the nightmare and opened his eyes.

A labyrinthine maze of diamond shapes filled his field of vision. He let his gaze drift lazily over this intricate pattern for a full minute before it occurred to him that he was looking at a pressed tin ceiling.

He was on top of the covers on a narrow bed, wearing only his shorts; he guessed he'd passed out from sheer exhaustion. He couldn't remember undressing—who'd removed his clothes? A tray bearing a sandwich and a glass of milk was on the nightstand—courtesy, no doubt, of the housekeeper in lieu of the dinner he'd missed.

Consciousness returned fully and, with it, panic. The cocooned security the yellow room afforded him the night before was gone. He rose unsteadily and parted the heavy drapes; blinding sunlight flooded the room. Inside the armoire, he found expensive, alien clothes hanging neatly— Martin's clothes.

It was seven by the time he'd showered and dressed in jeans and a plain white shirt. They were brand new, and he had to tear labels and exorbitant price tags from them, but both were a neat fit. He considered a pair of pristine designer sneakers, which appeared to be his size, but the phrase "dead man's shoes" passed fleetingly through his mind, and he opted for his own cowboy boots.

Since he'd opened his eyes, he'd heard nothing but the rapid thumping of his heart. He had to get out—out of the house, out of the city, out of the charade he'd begun without thinking beyond the first lunatic impulse.

A search for the car keys bordered on frenzy and turned up nothing. When did he have them last? Adams had given them to him, and he'd given them to... The housekeeper must still have them. He'd have to find her, hopefully without meeting Loretta and being forced to compound his lie.

Martin's wallet sat on the dressing table. After wrestling briefly with his conscience, he took a hundred note from it and slipped it into his pocket. He'd need gas and food to get to...where? Maybe Flagstaff. Maybe he could pick up a day's work on the movie. He'd lost the role, but in a conventional western, they could always use extras who were handy with horses.

Wait.

Everyone thought Jack McCauley was dead. And he'd signed Martin Brenner's name, stolen his car. Down the line, he'd have to explain his actions, perhaps as some kind of psychological aberration caused by the events at the motel. Yes, he'd call that detective and lie—no, *act*—his way out of this.

He listened at the bedroom door before opening it. The house was utterly quiet. He walked slowly along the hall, his tread absorbed by the thick runner of carpet at its center.

He stopped at the room he'd almost entered last night—Amy's bedroom—and listened, then turned the knob.

The heavy dark-green drapes were drawn, the room dim. The smell of polish indicated that everything had been cleaned meticulously only hours ago rather than in the weeks since Amy had died. Silver-backed brushes were lined up neatly on the dressing table with an elaborately carved open jewel box; faceted gems gleamed against its black velvet interior. The big, wide bed was neatly made, and an attractive peignoir lay carelessly over the cushioned silk cover as if it had been left in imminent readiness for its deceased wearer.

Jack closed the door quietly and descended the wide staircase. He stood at the bottom for a moment, taking in the old-world grandeur of the polished wood, the paintings, the ornate mirror reflecting the heavy front door, and the stained-glass panes flanking it. As in the room he'd just visited, the smell of floor polish was evident and almost overpowering.

A little way into the hall, wide double doors gave way to the room beyond, paneled in dark wood with a long dining table at its center. Jack counted eighteen chairs.

Across the hall from this, sliding doors led to another room. He parted them and slipped into a vast living room. He called softly "Carlotta?" then winced as he remembered her name was *Consuela*.

Colored light streamed into the room from a tall window, its panes of stained glass in an abstract pattern, but the dark, wood-paneled walls reflected little light. Two long chesterfields in dark leather dominated the space; oak chests held ornate glassware, and the walls, various works of art—a group of watercolors, a large oil of a horse in the style of Stubbs. On a marble plinth by the windows, a bronze cowboy sat on a rearing bronze horse—a Remington, Jack guessed.

Above the vast marble fireplace hung a portrait in oils of the efficient school rather than masterpiece. It depicted three pretty blonde girls, life size, perhaps in their early twenties. The tall girl at the center had strong features and a confident smile. Jack surmised this to be Amy, the eldest. At her left was perhaps the prettiest of the three, her lips parted in overt invitation—Martin's mother, Geena, he guessed. And at Amy's right, her long blonde hair tossed gently as if by a breeze, stood Loretta, younger, but unmistakably the woman who'd greeted him coolly the night before. Here, her broad happy smile gave the impression that the world was hers and her future bright and clear. What had happened, Jack wondered, to lower the temperature of that smile?

"No touch!"

He spun to where Consuela stood in the doorway wielding a floor mop as if it were a weapon. "I wax tables. Don't touch *nothin'*."

Jack held his hands up in surrender and offered a smile he hoped was reassuring but which Consuela did not return. She moved to him and pointed to the portrait with the mop handle.

"You mommy very young in that picture, very pretty." She paused for a moment as if reflecting on this, then added matter-of-factly, "Also big slut." She turned a disdainful glance to Jack. "I wash you smelly clothes." Then she started back to the door. "Coffee in the morning room. Breakfast when Miss Loretta say so."

"The car keys—I need the car—"

"I don't do no valet parking!" Consuela snapped. "I give to Diego."

Jack waited until he was sure she was busy in another room before he went back out into the hall and continued to the rear of the house, to the room where they'd toasted "family" the night before—the morning room. He searched the bar top, the ashtrays—no sign of the car keys.

He squinted against the clear, dazzling light. Beyond the terrace, near the stable, a man in a wide-brimmed hat did his best to stem the encroachment of shrubbery with a scythe; another sat on an idling power mower, gazing vacantly at the overgrown field.

There was no sign of Loretta.

He crossed the terrace, the lawn beyond it, then the dusty bare earth, and went into the stable. Clearly, Consuela didn't do stables—there was no sense of care in here. The stalls were unoccupied and hay was strewn untidily over the earthen floor. Jack stepped on something rigid and metallic, and it shot up from the floor. He dodged in time to avoid being swiped by the handle of the pitchfork he'd stepped on.

Oldest gag in the book, he thought as he stood it against the wall. The tines glinted in a shaft of light.

The door at the far end opened to the fields, and he started for it. Large tiles paved the central area of the stable, and Jack kept to these to avoid stepping on any other implement that might attack him. He glanced into empty stalls where harnesses hung abandoned. A gentle *snort* caused him to pause. A horse peered at him over the farthest stall door. Its coat was a uniform chestnut except for cream-colored "socks" and a wide, white blaze on the nose. It watched Jack with keen, liquid brown eyes.

He stroked the horse's nose and the creature responded by lowering its head to accommodate him. Jack glanced up at two blue ribbons with elaborate rosettes and a framed certificate fixed to the frame of the stall.

"Guess you're a little lonely, huh?"

The horse nuzzled his cheek.

Jack welcomed it with an encouraging murmur. "What's your name?"

"Her name's Duchess."

Behind him, Loretta sat astride a sleek, dark horse at the stable door. "Duchess of Piccadilly. She's rare, as I'm sure you can tell by the brindle pattern." She dismounted. "This is her mother, Majestic Maisie."

"She's beautiful."

The man he'd seen dispensing clay pigeons the night before entered the stable and proceeded to unbridle Loretta's horse. Mud caked his boots, and his shirt and jeans were grass stained.

Loretta's eyes stayed on Jack as she introduced the man. "Diego, this is Mr. Martin."

Jack said an affable "Hi," but the man merely nodded and turned to loosen the horse's cinch.

"You'll have to excuse Diego. He's not being impolite — he doesn't speak. He was a prisoner of war in Afghanistan. They treated him very badly."

Diego continued without any indication he'd heard her description of him. But Loretta glanced at him as if to make sure he was within hearing range as she continued.

"He suffered the tragic loss of someone very close to

him—"

Now Diego swung around to face Loretta. He fixed her with a steely glare, yet there was no anger in his expression; if anything, pain.

Loretta relented somewhat. "They say the condition is psychological."

Diego's expression didn't change, nor did the steadiness with which he held her eyes, but Loretta continued regardless.

"Who knows? Maybe he'll find his voice again one day," she said evenly. "But we understand each other."

Diego turned a quick glance to Jack as if embarrassed, then led the horse away to a stall. Jack was riveted to the coordinated musculature of this breathtakingly good-looking man as he took a bucket and sponge and began to clean the horse's mouth gently.

"Sleep well?" Loretta dragged Jack's attention back to her.

"Fine."

"I'm sure that room brings back memories."

Jack sidestepped. "The horses are in good shape."

"We give them a little exercise, when we can. But as Harry Adams probably told you, we're running on empty these days. Not for want of money. As you can see, we're in need of organization."

Jack searched his brain for something relevant, something Adams or Martin had said that might constitute conversation. He couldn't ask for the car keys outright without raising suspicion.

"Why did Amy let the place go like this?" Jack perceived the silence that followed as awkward, but when Loretta answered, her tone was light and even.

"Amy was deeply affected by your uncle's death. He wasn't the easiest man to live with—as I'm sure you remember. But he had a good business head on his shoulders. Which I don't." A graceful sweep of her hand embraced the entire property. "Patently obvious." She regarded Jack for a moment. "How about you? Do you have a head for business?"

Jack laughed. "If I did, I'd be rich."

"But you are rich," she said with a smile.

Jack sobered and said nothing. The brindle horse whinnied and scraped its forehooves on the ground impatiently. Jack stroked its nose.

"Why don't you take her out?"

Jack hoped she couldn't see the panic he felt—the car keys! He had to get out of here. Fess up and tell the truth further down the line, but get out now.

"I—haven't been on a horse in a long time."

"I don't think she'll mind." Loretta nodded to Diego,

who abandoned the towel with which he was drying Loretta's horse and began to saddle up the brindle. When he was done, Loretta led the filly to the open doorway and turned to Jack. He mounted awkwardly and turned the horse toward the open fields. Without warning, Loretta gave the horse a resounding slap on the rump. It took off at a gallop.

The initial shock of instantaneous speed almost threw him from the horse. Then, reflexively, from his trifling riding experience, Jack loosened the rein, flexed his leg muscles, and lifted his backside above the saddle. But these basics of how to cope with a horse in what seemed an uncontrollable gallop did nothing to lessen the terror of the ride.

A low fence loomed.

"Whoa! Jesus! *Stop goddamnit*!"

The horse continued, and Jack braced for a feat he'd never tried let alone accomplished—jumping a fence at forty miles per hour.

Far behind him, there was a shrill whistle.

The horse came to a stop so suddenly Jack nearly took the fence solo. But he held fast. He glanced over his shoulder to where Loretta stood, watching him with amusement. Diego took his thumb and forefinger from his lips, but otherwise, there was no indication he'd given the whistle.

Jack leaned forward and stroked the horse's neck as he

spoke gently. "You're dealing with a tenderfoot here." The mare nodded several times as if she'd understood every word, and in spite of the ice-cold terror in the pit of his stomach, Jack smiled. "Let's take a little ride, and you'll never see me again after today. I swear." He sat upright and touched his heel gently to the horse's side. They started across the fields at a light canter, gradually increasing speed.

He headed for the far end of the fields. He rode over a rise, past a pristine cabin of a much later vintage than the main house, then on into a narrow valley. A rundown wooden shack crowned the far hillside. Jack aimed for this, enjoying the clear, clean air, the speed, and the sensation of being in charge.

At the top of the rise, he brought the horse to a halt, dismounted, and looped the rein over the porch rail. The unlocked shack door creaked open to reveal a floor strewn with dead leaves. Though no more than one large room, the shack had a small open kitchen and a tiny bathroom. Jack twisted a corroded faucet over the kitchen sink, and after a rebellious clanging, rusty water flowed.

Furniture covered with dusty sheets had been pushed against the walls. He uncovered a long chesterfield, its leather upholstery old and veined with cracks. Jack thought this must've once been a neat place for privacy and retreat. For whom though? Amy, Loretta or Martin's mother, Geena?

He went to the shack door and stood gazing out at the open fields and the rim of mountains in the distance. He inhaled deeply and felt something he couldn't name immediately, a feeling that had been absent from a great part of his adult life.

The name came to him—contentment.

The glow lasted no more than a few seconds before he was assailed by a powerful rush of adrenaline.

Okay, enough. Go back, get the car, get the hell out of here.

Loretta was inspecting Maisie's hooves when Jack cantered up to the stable. She didn't look up as he approached. "You're a little soft in the saddle these days."

Jack dismounted and disengaged the saddle straps. "I'll rub her down."

"Diego can take care of that." Loretta started back to the house, then turned back to wait for Jack. He had no choice but to follow.

"Great sense of humor, that Diego," he said with some irony. "He might not talk, but he's a great whistler."

Loretta's voice was even and earnest. "Diego has a sense of loyalty absent in most of the human race. If he decides to become your friend, there's nothing he won't do for you." She aimed an oblique look at Jack. "*If* he decides to be your friend."

Jack looked over his shoulder at Diego, who was

absorbed in tending the horse. He almost laughed with relief as he considered the resolve he'd come to while riding. The dubious joy of being crowned with Diego's friendship would never happen.

"You need some breakfast."

"I'll settle for coffee," Jack said.

"You'll wish you had something more substantial in your stomach when you're sitting at the memorial."

Jack's step faltered. *The memorial.*

"Do you—have the car keys?"

"Diego has them safe."

Chapter Ten

8:52 A.M.

BREAKFAST WAS SERVED by Consuela while Loretta sat opposite Jack and sipped at a cup of coffee.

To Jack's relief, the conversation was minimal and covered such things as the weather in LA, a subject on which he was well versed. His relief was tempered by the knowledge that he could find no reasonable way to excuse himself from the memorial.

He dressed in the most appropriate clothes he could find in the armoire—dark shirt, jacket, and slacks. All were a perfect fit. He overcame his feeling toward the shoes and tried a pair. They were brand new, the soles entirely unscuffed, and they too were a perfect fit. If he felt unease at his matching Martin's measurements so precisely, it took second place to the frenzy of planning his escape.

Jack examined himself in the mirror and felt the kind of nervous anticipation he experienced before stepping onto a stage or a movie set. Perhaps he was beginning to enjoy this. He shook his head violently to get rid of the notion. His eyes fell on the childhood letter from Martin to his aunt, on the nightstand where he'd left it the night before. He picked it up.

A sharp knock at the door startled him, and he shoved the letter absently into a pocket as Loretta opened the door and looked in.

The rancher he'd seen just an hour ago was transformed into a smartly dressed and strikingly beautiful woman. She wore a simple black dress that might have come straight from Chanel.

"We'll go in your pretty red car."

*

9:37 A.M.

"ANYONE EVER TELL you that you drive like a maniac?"

"Sorry." Jack slowed down.

"Nervous?"

Jack shrugged.

"You should be. There'll be a bunch of folks there want to get a good look at you." They drove in silence for a while, then Loretta said reflectively, "I wonder how Scott feels about all this."

Jack dredged up the limited information he had on Scott—Martin's no-good brother.

"That's if he feels anything at all about anyone or anything," Loretta continued, interrupting his thoughts. "One thing's for sure, he'll be pissed as hell he's not getting a cent of Amy's money."

Jack considered this, then asked carefully, "Do you know why she left everything to Mar—to me?"

Loretta didn't take her eyes from the road ahead. "Yes," she said simply. And that was the end of conversation for the rest of the ride.

The Mountain Preserve Reception Center, a squat, white building, nestled against a barren hill.

An attendant directed Jack to a parking space directly in front. From the car, he could see maybe a hundred people gathered on the wide terrace. He recognized Adams and Maggie, she dressed colorfully in a flowered blouse, Adams in the same baggy pants he'd worn the night before and an ill-matching jacket. Consuela and Diego hovered nearby.

Jack got out and walked around to the passenger door to help Loretta out of the car, aware that all eyes were on him.

Loretta made a considerable show of easing out of the low seat, setting high- heeled black shoes on the pavement carefully and making sure everyone got more than a glimpse of leg before taking Jack's hand and allowing him to help her up. She took her time straightening her skirt, with a cool smile firmly in place, then linked her arm through Jack's as they mounted the steps and joined the others.

A few people greeted Loretta; some merely cleared the way. Loretta joined Consuela and Diego, Consuela dressed in a patterned burgundy dress with a turquoise brooch at the shoulder and Diego in pristine jeans and a sport jacket. His black hair, released from the ponytail of the night before, framed his face now. Jack had difficulty wrenching his eyes from Diego, who made no attempt to release Jack from his own piercing gaze. Jack excused himself to join Adams and Maggie.

Adams shook Jack's hand. "Martin, lad! How're you settling in?"

"Fine." Jack turned to take in the throng. "Big crowd."

Adams followed his gaze and sighed. "Amy was loved, no doubt about that."

A tall, thin man with a professionally mournful expression approached. Adams took his elbow and guided him to Jack. "Reverend Carnley, this is Martin Brenner. Reverend Carnley conducted the funeral service for your aunt."

The reverend offered a sympathetic smile that wasn't really a smile at all. "Your aunt was an exceptional woman."

Jack nodded with appropriate gravity.

An attendant appeared at the entrance and announced that the guests would be welcome in the North Room. They started into the center.

Jack held back. "Maggie?" Maggie paused by Jack, allowing the others to pass, and he continued, "I was wondering; have you heard anything from Scott?"

"*That* lowlife!" This was vehement enough to turn a few heads. Maggie lowered her voice. "I'm sorry, I know he's your brother, but he's a piece of work. And that's not just my opinion. Have you spoken to him since Amy died?"

"No."

"He hasn't tried to harass you in any way?"

"No."

"About the will? The money?"

"I thought he was hiding out in Mexico." Jack was running blind and wanted out of the exchange. "Maybe we'd better go in." He turned to see Loretta approaching.

Maggie's voice went down to a whisper, her tone

conspiratorial. "There are certain things Loretta needn't know. She's got enough on her mind. Call me at the office when you've got a minute. I'll tell you all about your *brother*." She injected enough venom into the word to assure Jack that whatever she had to impart would be juicy. Loretta took Jack's arm, and they went in.

In the North Room, waiters directed the guests to attractively laid tables where they examined place cards, and sat.

Loretta, Jack, Maggie, and Adams were seated at a table up front by a wooden lectern. Loretta allowed Jack to help her into a chair facing the room, but once in it, she adjusted it so that her back was to the guests. She crossed her legs elegantly, smug in the awareness that she and Jack were the center of attention.

Adams fumbled in his breast pocket and took out a page of notepaper, which he held upside down.

Maggie turned it right way up. "Where the hell are your reading glasses?"

Adams gave an exasperated sigh and searched his pockets. Eventually, he found his glasses, rose, and went to the lectern. The murmur of conversation in the room trickled away, and Adams cleared his throat.

"Good morning, good morning, everyone." He nodded to various areas of the room and a few "good mornings" came back to him. "I know most of you, you know me, so I won't bother to introduce myself. I'll just welcome you all to this very handsome reception room."

Maggie sighed audibly, and Adams took the hint and referred to his page of notes.

"This is a sad day and a happy day. Sad in that we bid farewell to a beloved friend—happy in that we come together to celebrate a life of achievement, community service, of love, generosity, and loyalty to all who knew her."

Jack took a sidelong glance at Loretta, but she was inscrutable and stared ahead rather than at Adams.

"Let's begin with a word, a *brief* word"—there was hope in his emphasis on brevity—"from Reverend Carnley."

Carnley moved to the lectern and surveyed the guests with an expression designed for the occasion: eyebrows knit in sorrow, thin lips straining for the smile of one convinced that Amy was in a better place. "Let us offer a prayer for our dear Amy's salvation and her eternal life." He raised his head to heaven. "Lord, let not Amy's abandonment of your holy laws cloud the record of a good life, nor obstruct her path to the glory of the afterlife. Accept from us everything we feel for our dear departed friend, give us strength to meet the days to come without her, and open wide your arms to welcome her into your kingdom on high."

The gathering murmured, "Amen". Loretta uttered

only a sigh, either of accord or boredom, Jack couldn't tell.

The reverend relinquished the lectern to Adams, who inspected his notes.

"Amy Wyatt was born Amy Eleanora Dalstrom on May fourteen, nineteen fifty-seven, here in the city she loved so much. She was the daughter of Swedish immigrants who instilled in her their love of horses, and Amy made the breeding of champions her life. In her late husband, Edward Wyatt, she found her soulmate."

He paused and removed his glasses. "I was just seventeen years old when I met Amy. She was two and the cutest kid I'd ever seen. My father represented her father's legal interests, and when I opened my office, it was my honor to become Amy's attorney."

Loretta glanced down at her hands, clasped loosely in her lap. She turned one over slowly and inspected her nails.

"Amy always regretted that she never had children. But, as many of you know, there was a child she loved dearly. He's now a fine young man—a man Amy would've been proud of."

Jack dropped his gaze to the floor as he felt heads turn in his direction.

"I know that many of you here today wish to offer tributes, but first, we might have a few words from one who, while absent from our community for so many years, was never far from Amy's heart—her beloved nephew, Martin Brenner."

Jack flushed. Of *course* he'd have to speak.

He should've seen it coming.

He sat frozen for what seemed an eternity, then rose and moved awkwardly to the lectern, acutely aware of the stillness in the room and Loretta's attention, now quite focused—on him.

If he lied, he'd stumble; he knew that. He dredged up whatever advice he'd gleaned from Uta Hagen and projected sincerity. And dodged. "I—I feel like an outsider. But being here, with all of you, helps me to understand the sense of loss you feel." His audience was quiet and still. His mouth was dry. He swallowed hard and put his hand briefly to his throat, then thrust the hand into a pocket—and found a crumpled paper. He withdrew it, grateful for the providence that had directed him to place it there carelessly. He stared at the paper for a moment, then opened it out.

"Let me read a letter from an eleven-year-old boy who knew Amy Wyatt well." He smoothed out the sheet. "Dear Aunt Amy, I had a real great time at the ranch with all the horses. Daddy won't let me have a bike even. Since I cut my arm, he says I am accident prole."

Someone chuckled, many smiled, and one elderly woman dabbed daintily at the corner of an eye with a small handkerchief.

"I haven't met Daddy's new girlfriend yet, but Scott says she got juicy melons. I sure hope she sends us one before the summer is done."

The chuckles were encouraging.

"I miss you so much I cry every night. I wish I could stay with you at the ranch all the time. You are my best favorite aunt. Why don't you ask me to live with you? If you did, I'd be good all the time and help with the horses. I'd even let Aunt Lorrie hug me whenever she wants."

Loretta's gaze didn't waver.

"I love you, and I hope I see you real soon. Your nephew, Martin."

Jack folded the letter and, bathed in the warmth of a collective smile from the gathering, sat down by Loretta, her expression unreadable.

Various people of various ages and in various states of emotion spoke glowingly of Amy, and finally, Adams turned to Loretta. She shook her head slowly, indicating an unequivocal disinclination to speak. There was a faint murmur in the room, which might have been disapproval. It was silenced by Adams's invitation to toast Amy.

Afterward, when they'd moved outside the venue, many of the gathering shook Jack's hand and most nodded respectfully to Loretta. Facing these people and accepting their condolences, it seemed to Jack that the word "fraud" was written above his head in neon. Eager to get away, he took the car keys from a pocket.

"Great group! Hold it!"

A flash startled Jack, and he turned to a man in jeans and an open shirt. The man lowered his camera to reveal a tanned face split by a toothy smile. He was accompanied by a neatly dressed young man wearing sunglasses, who stepped forward and held out his hand to Jack.

"*Arizona Republic*. We need a few words. You know, sadness about your aunt, how do you feel inheriting—"

Loretta turned a quick glance to Diego, who moved between Jack and the reporter. Diego towered over the man, who took the hint and backed up. Loretta took Jack's hand and eased the keys from it, then gave them to Diego and said, "I have a few things to discuss with Harry Adams. Diego will drive you."

Diego took his elbow and led him to the Mercedes. As they got in, the reporter found the courage to approach again.

"Look, all we want—"

Diego drove off without acknowledging the man.

Chapter Eleven

THEY DROVE IN silence, Diego's eyes fixed on the road ahead. They passed parkland with various signs proclaiming that refreshingly unspoiled acreage was soon to become a luxurious country club or golf course. Considering the number of country clubs he'd passed on the way out to the memorial, Jack wondered if the city could accommodate the leisure overload.

He took a sly glance at Diego from time to time and marveled at the physical strength the man exuded without any conscious attempt to impress by it, countered by his inability to conceal it. From the intense focus he applied to the commonplace task of just driving the car, Jack assumed that strength, in its every connotation, was an essential part of Diego's being.

Given Diego's inability to speak, conversation wasn't an option, but Jack felt obliged to break the silence. Almost overwhelmed by the power of the man beside him, all he could manage was "Guess you work out." Jack was instantly embarrassed by the banality of stating the obvious.

Diego nodded solemnly, and Jack bumbled on.

"You inspire me to work harder."

Diego kept his eyes on the road, but he took his right hand from the steering wheel and briefly touched his lips as if to apologize for the absence of a verbal response, then tapped his chest and turned the hand, palm up, toward Jack.

"You'll help me?"

Diego nodded.

Jack warmed. He relaxed suddenly after the tension of his memorial subterfuge, and this easing of the mental pressure caused him to reconsider his eagerness to escape. What would be the fallout of his return to LA, admitting what he'd done? There'd be a charge of fraud. And even if he talked his way out of that, then what? Begging acquaintances for a loan to see him through to the next badly paid bit part? Then there was the Armenian landlord who'd claim Jack had pushed him, the unpaid rent, and his few possessions, which had probably been trashed.

They passed under the wrought iron arch and onto the overgrown drive to the Wyatt mansion, and he was reminded of what this new life could offer. Here, there was care, kindness, generosity, and comfort he'd seldom known in his twenty-three years. Money? Yes. But money wasn't important, nor was it a deciding factor.

As Diego pulled up by the entrance to the house, the muffled chirping of a cell phone ringing the *William Tell Overture* broke the mood. Jack realized with alarm that the sound came from the glove compartment.

Martin's phone.

Diego turned to look at Jack and then to the glove compartment. He reached over and popped the button, and the door sprang open. Jack had no option but to take the phone out.

Diego sat watching him as he answered it.

"Hello?"

A shrill female voice, loud and clear: "Hey asshole. We've got some talking to do!"

Jack froze.

"Are you there?"

"I'll—call you back."

"No, you won't, Martin. I know you. You listen up. You don't get rid of me like some—"

Jack shut off the phone and held it as he might a

venomous snake. He turned to Diego, who watched him coolly. After a moment, Diego pointed to the third finger of his left hand, mimed slipping a ring off, tossing it over his shoulder, and raised an eyebrow to Jack.

Jack managed a feeble smile and nodded, then flinched as *The William Tell Overture* burbled out of the phone again.

Diego regarded the phone for a moment and gently took it from Jack's trembling hand. He opened the car door, got out, dropped the phone onto the gravel, and stepped on it with the heel of his boot, shattering it. Then he walked around the car to open Jack's door.

Jack sat, stunned for a moment by this gesture of — what? Support? He stumbled out of the Merc and watched as Diego got back in and drove off to put the car wherever he kept it.

What of his plan to make a run for it? Hadn't he, just this morning, determined he would get the hell out of town? That he would somehow extricate himself from the lie? Now, he'd elaborated on his deceit by playing for sympathy at the memorial; moreover, he'd dragged innocent people into complicity: Adams, Maggie, Loretta.

And now, Diego.

The shrill voice on the cell phone echoed in his mind. The ex. Natalie? Nita? What the hell was her name? Martin said she'd been harassing him since the divorce. Presumably, she was in LA. He could ignore her, perhaps get Adams to slap a restraining order on her. There'd be hurdles, certainly. But no more than he'd encountered in improv sessions—convince yourself, and you'll convince your audience.

It was as if someone had shouted "action," and there was no backing out until he heard "cut."

Chapter Twelve

WEDNESDAY, AUGUST 10

AUGUST PROGRESSED FROM hot to hotter. Jack had fallen into a routine. He rose with the ranch hands and, under Diego's silent supervision, helped clean out the stalls, exercised the mare and the filly, checked fences, organized repairs where repairs were necessary, and generally kept busy in this way until six in the evening, when he'd return to the house, his shirt and jeans soaked with sweat.

Introspection was something Jack never submitted to willingly. There were too many negatives in a life he'd spent fighting to find positives—the mother he never knew, being robbed of a father, the obstacle course in chasing his dream of being an actor, the succession of short-lived lovers who found fault in him or in whom he found fault. Added to these was the tragic death of a man who'd befriended him, a stranger who, by coincidence, looked like him. A man who barely knew him yet had trusted Jack with his car, his money, his life history. A man who'd wanted him sexually—perhaps more—he'd never know. Now Jack was living a lie based on that tragedy.

Guilt should've been primary in Jack's emotions, yet in the few weeks since arriving at the ranch, he'd fallen, automatically, uncontested, into a position of leadership. And he found, with no little surprise, that he enjoyed these days more than just about any he could remember. Had his so-called career meant less to him than he'd believed? He'd enjoyed no great heights as an actor, but as a part of this ranch, this family, he found he not only had an aptitude for the work, he had a life, a rewarding life.

As he reorganized the workings of the ranch, Loretta watched with what might have been approval or curiosity, her face as unreadable as ever. She neither questioned Jack nor advised him. They dined nightly in the formal dining room, just the two of them at one end of the long table, and discussed no more than the details of running the ranch.

Diego was supportive of his every move, and Jack had

begun to understand, with astonishing clarity, the sign language Diego used to express himself. At the end of his second week, Diego had led him to his residence at the eastern edge of the property. Diego's cabin was out of the 1980s. Unlike the main house, it had large clear windows, light having been considered some kind of blight in the era of Victorian architecture.

To the north of the cabin, the hills rolled on to the property line of the adjacent dairy farm, two miles away. At the southern side of the cabin, a diverse vegetable garden flourished. Wire mesh covered some items that passing critters might deem desirable. Diego clearly tended this garden with care and dined on its produce. It occurred to Jack that similar plantings might be made on a much larger scale to profit the ranch.

The cabin had two spacious rooms, a separate bathroom, and an open kitchen, all furnished modestly but attractively and with obsessive order. Diego conducted a proud tour of his domain and watched Jack, who was impressed by what he saw.

The kitchen, part of the open plan, revealed the expected microwave and cooking implements, and a wood stove.

In the bedroom, twice the size of the living room, a king-sized bed of roughly hewn oak dominated, and which

Diego indicated he'd built himself. There was also more than adequate room for a sleek multi-station gym, a bench, a leg press, and racks of free weights. Diego showed the equipment to Jack with a degree of pride.

As Diego busied himself making coffee, Jack inspected the living room. Art relieved the minimal furnishings, with a couple of representational figures, a still life, and a "Wild West" painting over the fireplace that looked like Remington. It was impossible to tell if it was an original or an extremely good copy.

A floor-to-ceiling bookshelf was built into a wall by the fireplace, crammed with books, hard and soft cover. Jack was surprised at the variety of reading, some in Spanish, most in English, ranging in extremes from the *Meditations of Marcus Aurelius* and Plato's *Symposium*, to popular American novels of the early twentieth century—Tarkington, Dreiser, Steinbeck.

A sole photograph, simply framed, stood on the mantel over the fireplace. In it, a handsome young man in his twenties smiled generously at the camera. He wore US Army camouflage, had light-brown buzzed hair, and appeared undeniably athletic. Jack peered closely at the picture and made out the faded ink of a date written at a bottom corner—2014—and an inscription in fading ink: "*El que con lobos anda, a aullar se enseña.*"

Jack wracked his brain for the minimal Spanish he'd acquired in his twenty-three years in Los Angeles and made a rough guess: *He who walks with wolves will learn to howl.*

Diego came into the room with mugs of coffee on a tray and hesitated as he saw Jack inspecting the photograph. Jack turned to him and detected something stark in Diego's usually stoic countenance. His expression resolved in a moment, and Diego continued to the plain wooden coffee table and deployed the mugs.

Conversation, some of it signed, some written on a thick notepad, ranged from the upkeep of the ranch to general current politics—tricky ground for a military vet, but Jack was delighted they were on the same team here as in so many other topics.

Jack indicated the bookshelves. Diego pointed out books he treasured and those he read for pleasure. Both had read Plato, both had read Steinbeck, both had a taste for art—Jack for the impressionists and surrealists, Diego for the traditionalists; and yes, his prized piece was indeed a Remington, a gift from Amy.

Discovering their mutual interests warmed Jack. It also surprised him that in this man to whom the physical seemed intrinsic, there was a taste for the aesthetic.

Diego produced a calendar, circled dates, wrote "M" on these, and stated times of an hour apiece to these days. Then he pointed to his arm and flexed a bicep. Jack nodded enthusiastically.

Diego smiled—a grace, Jack surmised, he bestowed on few people.

*

DINNER WAS ALWAYS a quiet time, and to Jack's relief, Loretta never asked about his past—about Martin's past. Instead, she'd settle back and listen as Jack enthusiastically described the work he'd done that day, or how this or that part of the property could be improved, or how he respected and admired Diego's work ethic and the intense gym workouts Diego subjected him to.

Early every evening, seemingly unwearied by the day's housework, Consuela prepared and served food. Jack always congratulated her on her cuisine, which was superior. Consuela would nod, careful not to mar her expression with anything like a smile, and after a few weeks, offered Jack seconds—a grand gesture, he figured.

Exhaustion followed dinner closely, and Jack would retire to the enveloping comfort of the yellow bedroom and sleep dreamlessly until dawn. On only one night did Loretta express a desire to extend the evening with a nightcap.

In the cozy, oak-paneled comfort of the den, an adjunct to the vast living room, they sat in the enveloping leather armchairs and sipped shots of cognac in silence. Over the fireplace hung a large portrait of three fair-haired preteen girls smiling out from the canvas, younger in this than in the grand painting in the living room. After some time, without taking her eyes from the painting, Loretta said simply, "Time's a bitch."

A silence followed which, emboldened by a second cognac, Jack broke. "Can I ask you something personal?"

Loretta shrugged. "Shoot."

"Why didn't you marry?"

"None of your goddamn business."

On Jack's startled reaction, she smiled in warm amusement at his discomfort.

She downed her brandy then sighed. "Why didn't I marry." A statement, not a question. "God knows I didn't suffer from a lack of choice. Or opportunity." She gazed into her empty glass. "There was only one man who really mattered. And for him, marriage was out of the question."

"I didn't mean to be nosy."

The cool smile returned. "You have every right. After all, you're family."

At a gentle knock on the door, it opened to reveal Consuela. "I go to bed now. You want anything?"

Loretta shook her head. "No Consuela. *Dormir bien.*"

Consuela nodded and just before she closed the door,

offered something akin to a smile to Jack.

"Goodnight, Consuela," he said as she vanished from sight.

Consuela occupied the small bedroom atop the octagonal tower at the front of the house and was always first up and last to bed. Twice a week, one or another of her many nieces would come to help with the considerable chores of cleaning, polishing, dusting, and generally maintaining the interior of the vast house in museum condition.

"She's a pretty remarkable woman," Jack observed. "I've never met anyone like her."

Loretta raised her eyebrows. "After all the time you spent here as a child?" There was bemusement in her tone.

Jack kicked himself mentally. "A lot has happened since I was a child," he ventured. It wasn't strictly a lie.

"She's been the anchor in this house for forty-six years, spiritually, morally, and until Diego came along, physically. Under the chub, she's all muscle. I've seen that woman lift things half her weight."

"Didn't she ever marry?"

"At eighteen. To a drunk who left her pregnant when she was nineteen. She miscarried. I think she channeled all the love she might've given her own child to us, the three of us girls, here. And to you."

"She seems—I don't know—cautious around me."

"She hasn't seen you for a long time. None of us have," Loretta said easily. "But take my word, she's loyal beyond any standard you can imagine. She was to Amy; she is to me. She will be to you. And she's been like a mother to Diego. He was a broken man when he came to us. Consuela nurtured him, helped him to become the man he is now." She turned a meaningful glance to Jack. "The man we all admire."

Chapter Thirteen

MONDAY, SEPTEMBER 26
12:30 P.M.

MAGGIE CALLED JACK to set up an appointment with
Adams; there was paperwork concerning the will, accounts
to be established—and had he forgotten she'd promised to
spill the dirt on his brother, Scott? She suggested lunch.

The Arcadia Café was in the Phoenix Art Museum and
favored a "business lunch" clientele. The warmth of the dé-
cor was conducive to easy discussion.

"So, honey, how's life on the ranch?"

Jack could reply to this one honestly and effusively.

"It's good. Everything seems to be working out fine. There's stuff to do of course—the place is still a bit run down. But I'm working on it."

More than just politely pleased, Maggie seemed relieved that he was so earnestly involved. "Second nature, I guess. Considering all the time you spent out there when you were a kid." She reached across the table and covered Jack's hand with hers. "It's good for Loretta to have flesh and blood with her. She may not show it, but she's real glad you're here."

"In spite of Amy's will?"

"Maybe *because* of it. She made a big thing of telling Harry she had no intention of contesting the will in any way. She *wanted* you at the house. Badly." Maggie relinquished Jack's hand and smiled. "She thinks she's so cool, but I can see right through Miss Loretta Dalstrom." There was affection in her tone.

A waitress took their order—Jack ordered a club, Maggie a small salad. "I'll bet you're the kind of guy who never puts on weight. Me?" She sighed and patted her hips.

They ate in silence for a few minutes, and then Jack said, "Tell me about Scott."

Maggie pursed her lips and was silent for a moment, but only for dramatic effect. Clearly, she couldn't wait to tell all. "It's not my place to create divisions in families—but I feel it's my duty to warn you about that guy."

"Warn me?"

"I'm not telling you anything you don't know if I say Scott's no good. I mean, if he ever shows his face back here in the US, he'll probably spend the rest of his life behind bars. And yet, he was willing to risk that…"

She left this sentence hanging and glanced about the restaurant as if to make sure no one was listening. She lowered her voice dramatically. "He did something so disturbing, something so *driven,* so downright dumb, that he just might do something like it again." She leaned forward. "He'd heard about Amy's will, and he walked into the office, bold as brass, and pretended he was you."

Jack's appetite suddenly vanished.

"Now sure, there's a slight similarity. But what he didn't realize is that we had the newspaper piece about his arrest on file. The mug shot from, like, a year, year and a half ago. Unmistakable. I wanted to call the police, but Harry's an old softy. He just told him never to come back. Slipped him some money, which he thinks I don't know about."

"Do you think he will? Come back?"

Maggie shrugged. "All I know is he's trouble." She sat back, then smiled at Jack and shook her head. "Who could imagine two brothers could be so different?"

Driving back to the ranch, Jack tried to think through the variations of damage Scott could do him, but physical harm was not uppermost on the list. Jack's principal fear was exposure. And curiously, less for the consequences to himself than for what it might mean to Loretta. But Scott was on the run. It was unlikely he'd try anything. That was if he risked returning to the United States. And that was what Jack told himself to ensure a good night's sleep.

*

FRIDAY, OCTOBER 7

REGULARLY, ON THE appointed days, Diego ushered Jack into the cabin for a workout.

Given the various traumas of the last weeks, Jack had all but forgotten what attraction to a male body meant. Memory returned like a battering ram when Diego removed his shirt to work out. The man seemed to Jack like a god, physically perfect, in total control of his body and his emotions, and capable of projecting these strengths to anyone in his orbit. His skin was the color of milk coffee and shone during these workouts, muscles rippling as they extended and contracted. A tattoo covered most of his right shoulder: a rose in faded reds and blues. At some past time, it seemed that a name had been inked in script under the rose. Now, starker, more recent ink had reworked the script into the rose design. But the name was still apparent: Aaron.

During these intense, sweaty workouts, Jack tried not to stare too much, but even when he did, and was caught doing so, Diego's staid expression never changed. When he was pleased with Jack's progress, he signified it by signs. Never allowing Jack to rest on laurels, he urged further effort, greater progress. Far from exhausting Jack, the effort paid off in improved appetite, physical wellbeing, muscularity, and mental acuity.

*

FRIDAY, OCTOBER 21

ADAMS PORED OVER a stack of papers. His reading glasses were fixed to a delicate chain that Jack had never seen before. He guessed it had been provided by Maggie after the memorial.

Maggie eased her way into the office with a tray bearing mugs and a plate of cookies. "Coffee for you honey," she said, offering a mug to Jack, then to Adams, "and herbal tea for you."

"I hate that shit!"

"I'm thinking of your stomach."

"She can't get her mind above my stomach," Adams

said grimly to Jack.

"Ulcer," Maggie declared and turned to go.

"Wait, wait," Adams demanded impatiently and waved a paper at her. "We need some documents drawn up. Martin wants to set up a financial trust for Loretta."

Maggie shot a triumphant glance at Adams. "What'd I tell you?"

"Well, don't go blabbing to Loretta, for Chrissake. It's supposed to be a surprise. Just get the goddamn papers."

Maggie beamed a warm smile at Jack and hurried from the office. Immediately after the door closed, Adams took a hip flask from a drawer and poured a good deal of its contents into the tea.

"I don't know if you've considered making a will," he said, stirring his tea with a pencil.

"Why should I do that?"

"Well, the way thing stand in Amy's will, in the event, the *unlikely* event, anything should happen to you, everything goes to the state." He removed his glasses and considered the middle distance. "No idea why Amy made no provision for Loretta." This stated, he replaced his glasses and turned to Jack. "You could rectify that in a will of your own."

"Do it," Jack said without hesitation.

"We're talking 'ifs' here." Adams chuckled. "*If*, heaven

forefend, anything were to happen to you. *If* you're not a married man by then."

"Unlikely," Jack said without further explanation.

"Oh, I'm sure the right woman is just around the corner." Adams said. Jack saw no point in disabusing him.

"Do whatever you must with a will," he said. "I just want to make sure the money, the property, the house—everything—is in Loretta's name while I'm alive and kicking and after I'm gone."

Adams regarded him with curiosity for a brief moment, then brightened. "Okay, Martin my lad, let's talk horses. They're not chicken feed, you know. What you're proposing is upward of a quarter of a million."

"Can we spare it?"

Adams frowned. "Well, let's see—that'll leave about twenty-three million in the kitty, give or take a few bucks. Do *you* think you can spare it?"

Jack laughed. "Okay! What do I have to do?"

"Nothing. I'll take you to the auction, but *I* do the bidding." He raised his mug to Jack. "Cheers."

Chapter Fourteen

SATURDAY, OCTOBER 29

SATURDAY WAS PRODUCE day for Consuela, a day of relaxation for Jack and Diego. Mornings, Consuela raided the markets for food and supplies. Saturday afternoons, Jack and Diego had fallen into the habit of a leisurely ride over the hills and across the valley to the shack Jack had seen on his first day at the ranch. He relished the time he spent exclusively in Diego's company. How could he not be drawn to this man? This proud, loyal man in whom the adamantine Loretta placed such trust? And Diego had become supportive of Jack's every decision for the advancement of the ranch.

Their conversations—Diego's partly signed, partly written hastily on a notepad—had become enjoyable discussions about mutual likes, dislikes, their favored philosophers, composers, art. The awkwardness of communication with a mute had vanished long ago. Conversation was just that—conversation. Greatly anticipated by both, enjoyed mutually, and easy, so easy.

Jack wondered about the man's sexuality. Diego had never mentioned a partner of either sex. The only indication of anyone who mattered to him was framed and on the mantel. He never mentioned anyone of importance in his life and seemed content with his solitary existence.

At the shack, they tied the horses and sat on the splintered porch. Diego broke out lemonade Consuela had prepared for them, and they took turns drinking from the flask and contemplating the distant hills. If Jack had felt contentment on his first view of this landscape, the peace he now felt had multiplied a hundredfold.

Diego knew nothing about the shack, who'd occupied it, or why it was still standing. Jack posited that the land on which it stood was of more value to the ranch than the rotting wooden boards. It should come down.

Diego shifted focus to Jack. He indicated Jack's bare third finger on his left hand and turned to him for elucidation. So comfortable was he in Diego's company, Jack spoke from his heart.

"No. There's no one. There never was," he said, unaware of the carelessness of the statement.

Now Diego pointed to the silver ring on Jack's right hand.

"This? It was my mother's wedding ring," Jack said, turning the ring so the engraved bird was uppermost. He uttered a bitter chuckle. "She left the ring on the kitchen table and just—vanished. I never knew her. I have no memory of her at all. I was, like, a month old, so I really have no idea who she was, what she looked like."

Diego offered a grin and with his forefinger, drew a frame around Jack's face.

Jack laughed. "Well, yeah. I guess I inherited her hair, her eyes. My dad was darker. He kept the ring. Until his accident—until he died. Then I kept it."

It occurred to him with a jolt, that he'd just given an entirely different life history to that of the person he was supposed to be. He took a sidelong glance at Diego, who gazed into the distance as if seeming to weigh this information. After a moment, Diego reached down, took Jack's right hand, and held it up so he could take a closer look at the ring. Then he turned his gaze to Jack's eyes—but kept hold of his hand.

Jack's breathing sped up a little, and he found it impossible to take his eyes from Diego's. Eventually, Diego lowered his eyes, as if somehow, he'd overstepped some line. He released his hold and took a drink from the flask, then passed it to Jack, who did likewise.

Both men sat staring across the fields for some time, simply enjoying the afternoon, the quiet broken only by birdsong as they watched the lazy progress of wisps of clouds crossing the sky.

On their return to the house, Jack saw Loretta standing by the door of the stable. A man stood with her, in trim blue jeans and a sport jacket. Jack recognized Detective Miller from Lake Havasu.

"Someone to see you," Loretta said, stating the obvious as Jack and Diego dismounted.

"Nice to see you again, Mr. Brenner," Miller said, extending his hand.

Sweat seemed to go hand-in-hand, literally, with Miller's presence, and Jack felt obliged to wipe his palm on his jeans before shaking the detective's hand.

Loretta took the reins from Jack. "We'll take care of the horses." She and Diego led the horses to the stable.

Jack and Miller started toward the house.

"I just wanted to check a few details about that motel fire," Miller said.

"Sure."

"You say you never met the deceased, uh…"

"McCauley."

"You never met him prior to that night?"

"That's right."

"We managed to trace him through the Screen Actors Guild, and we found his boyfriend. His ex-boyfriend, that is."

"Uh-huh," Jack said as casually as he could.

"The guy was sorry to hear about him. Not *too* sorry. Seems McCauley was a bit of a loser."

Jack pressed his lips into a thin line.

"We finally found out where he lived," Miller continued. "He had a run-in with his landlord the day he left town."

"Yeah?"

"Landlord says McCauley pushed him down a flight of stairs."

Jack suppressed an urge to put the story right.

"Was talking pressing charges—until we told him McCauley was deceased. After that, all that interested the guy was clearing McCauley's possessions out of storage so he could use the space."

Miller surveyed the house. The sun had just dipped below the hills, and the vast hulk of the house had taken on a diffuse, warm glow in the early twilight. "Nice place. Hear it's yours now."

Jack looked at the house and then back to Miller, waiting for him to get to the point.

"Mind if I ask you a personal question, Mr. Brenner?"

"Shoot."

"You take drugs?"

"No! I never have."

"The hospital report at Lake Havasu mentioned a high level of—" Miller reached deep into his jeans pocket and took out a crumpled piece of paper. "—Diazepam in your blood."

"I don't even know what that is."

"It's used as a relaxant, a pain killer, in times of stress."

"Oh, yeah, yeah. A paramedic shot me with something at the fire. I don't remember much after that."

Miller smiled. "We have to check out everything."

Jack nodded and tried for a smile. "Sure," he managed.

Miller examined the ground around his feet before he spoke again. "Can you think of any reason someone might've wanted to kill this McCauley guy?"

Jack was startled by the question. "Why should I think that? I mean, I never even knew the guy."

"We're just looking at loose ends," Miller said affably. "Got to in a case like this."

Jack nodded solemnly as if to acknowledge that a policeman's lot was not a happy one, but he remained silent.

Miller was happy to expound. "Like, the order for all that propane. Night clerk says he ordered one tank the night before the fire. Next day, another ten turn up."

"Yeah," Jack offered. "I saw the delivery guy wheeling the tanks."

"The way the night clerk tells it, this was a prank by a guy he'd fired. The former employee denies it. But the credit card record says otherwise."

Miller stared off across the lawn and took in the distant hills as if he envied the peace they suggested, then turned back to Jack with a defeated smile. "Burn victims don't give us much to go on, any time. In this case, the fire was so intense there was practically nothing left. We found bone fragments but nothing we could get reliable DNA from. Even if we could, we'd have no reference point. This McCauley was a nobody. No family, no close friends, no dental records."

A hollow, physical pain invaded Jack's gut to hear his life reduced to untraceable elements. Had he meant so little in the world he'd inhabited for twenty-three years? He turned to see Loretta approaching from the stable and, unwilling to let her hear the discussion, he put a hand on Miller's shoulder and guided him into the house. They walked slowly up the hallway, passing Consuela who stood in a doorway, beady eyes watching curiously.

Once in the lobby, Jack cleared his throat and asked, "Why do you think someone might've wanted to, you know, kill this guy, uh, McCauley?"

"We recovered shards of some of the propane tanks that blew. The valves were faulty. Faulty in a way that could lead to an explosion. Coincidence maybe. The manufacturers have a good safety record, so no answers there. But there's gonna be lawsuits, sure as hell—motel against the BBQ guys, BBQ guys against the tank manufacturers—you know how it goes. Anything else you remember about that night?"

"I went to get a snack from the vending machine. Delivery guy said it was out of order. That's why I went out for food. If the machine had worked..." He suppressed a shudder.

Miller smiled. "Another coincidence. Lucky one for you. You might've been plastered all over the countryside like, uh..." But the name evaded him again.

I was a human being! I had feelings! A life! A future!

"McCauley," Jack blurted, trying hard to strip his tone of bitterness.

"McCauley, yeah." Miller considered this for just a moment, then smiled. "Well, I guess that's all."

"Sorry I can't be more helpful."

"You think of anything, give me a call. Still got my card?"

"Uh, I…"

"Here, take another one. Got more than I need."

Jack took Miller's card and opened the front door for him. Loretta entered the hallway but stayed at the far end. Miller looked over Jack's shoulder and gave her an affable smile.

"Thanks, Ms. Dalstrom," Miller called. Then he shook Jack's hand. "Take it easy, Mr. Brenner."

Loretta strolled to join Jack and watched as Miller got into his car and drove off. "Everything okay?"

Jack kept his tone light. "Sure. Fine. There was this fire. The motel I stayed in on the way out here. He just wanted a little information."

"I saw it on the news," Loretta said. "Someone died."

"Yeah. Guy I was traveling with."

"Did you know him?"

"No!" Jack said a little too sharply. "Hitchhiker. I just— I don't really want to talk about it." He turned and started up the stairs. "Gotta clean up."

He went into the yellow bedroom. There, he stood against the closed door for some time. The drapes were closed, and the room dim, but he didn't turn on a light.

Eventually, he walked to the framed school photograph on the wall by the tall window and inspected it. The unhappy face of eleven-year-old Martin Brenner stared back at him.

Chapter Fifteen

THAT NIGHT AT dinner, he felt that Loretta was scrutinizing him, more closely than she had in the past weeks.

"Glad you're hitting it off with Diego," she said eventually.

Jack smiled in as noncommittal a way as he could manage. "Hitting it off" barely described his inability to wrench his eyes from the man.

"He's had a troubled past. Someone like you—someone *grounded*," she said, pointedly, "can only be good for him."

Grounded?

Jack took a deep breath but said nothing.

"And who knows? Maybe it works both ways," Loretta added lightly.

Were his glances at the man so obvious?

Stick to Martin's story. The wife, the career in advertising.

They ate in silence, with Consuela refreshing dishes, clearing, and serving coffee.

Loretta seemed in no hurry to leave the table. She glanced conspicuously at the wine decanter; Jack took the hint and topped up her glass and then his. She watched as he did so, a faint smile at the corners of her lips.

Jack struggled to find the courage to ask, "So, Diego. He…um, he's…?"

Loretta took the cue instantly. "He's a fine man." She let this settle on Jack before continuing. "He was disowned by his family when he was young. Did he tell you?"

"No, no, we never discuss his, well, his history, his background." Jack realized with a stab of anxiety just how much of his *own* background he'd revealed to Diego.

"It's unlikely he ever will open up about himself. Until he's entirely sure of you."

"I don't want to pry."

"Yes, you do," Loretta said, not unkindly. She settled back in her chair and contemplated her wine glass for a moment, then said quietly, "Diego Manuel Perez. From an affluent, socially visible family, strict Catholics, intolerant assholes. He was an exceptional student as a kid. Made it to Arizona State University but defied his father's demand that he study economics and majored in philosophy, with a minor in ancient history. I'm sure you've inspected his bookshelves."

Jack nodded, faintly embarrassed to admit it.

"His degree did nothing to impress his father who refused to admit him back into the family."

"How come?"

"A personal issue." She left Jack to ponder this as she sipped her wine. "Unable to find remunerative employment with such—esoteric credentials, he took menial jobs simply to eat, and to support his gym regime. And you've seen the result of that."

Again, Jack was coy in acknowledging Diego's spectacular physique and nodded again.

"He enlisted to fight in Afghanistan. Mostly for the income. He made a close friend in his unit."

"Aaron, "Jack ventured.

"They were both captured by the Taliban, who tortured them for military information. Neither would give them what they wanted. So, aware of how close the two men were, they forced Diego to watch as they hacked Aaron's tongue from his mouth and allowed him to choke to death on his own blood."

"Oh my God!"

"You know the result of that. Diego suffered psychologically. He lost the power of speech. It's there somewhere, the voice, but the link between his vocal cords and his brain is broken."

"After what he saw —"

"He was rescued, hospitalized while they tried to figure out the problem." She shifted her gaze from Jack to her glass as if uncertain how to continue. But when she did, her tone was matter-of-fact. "He left the hospital in the dead of night, stole an AK-47 from a stash of captured weapons, a few magazines, and walked barefoot three miles to a heavily guarded Taliban base." She lifted her eyes to Jack. "He slaughtered every last man he found there. When he was done, there were more than two hundred bodies."

Jack found himself unable to comment, to query, to express shock or admiration, or to make any observation at all in the wake of this information. He'd never underestimated Diego's strength, physical or moral, but the man's capacity for revenge was beyond his comprehension.

"He was court-martialed. They found him not guilty of a war crime but, nevertheless, discharged him without benefits. He couldn't return to his family in Nogales, so he answered an ad in the *Republic* and came here looking for work."

Seemingly satisfied with the effect she'd had on Jack, Loretta drained her glass. "There's more. A lot more. Maybe he'll tell you himself one day."

Jack detected a faintly smug smile as Loretta rose from her chair. She'd imparted shocking information and was happy with Jack's reaction.

She headed for the door and turned back to him brightly. "I think," she said as if it had just occurred to her, "the legion of Amy's friends and admirers should get to know you better. We'll give a party."

Almost as an afterthought, she added, "Ask Diego to help you organize it. Turn out the lights." And she was gone.

Jack sat for some time gazing at the flickering flames of the table candles, thinking, but not clearly, about his every encounter with Diego. Beyond his inability to speak, there was no indication of turmoil in the man's easy, cool command of himself.

Eventually, he extinguished the candles and went to the door. He turned out the lights, and as the room became dark, it hit Jack with astonishing clarity: he was falling for this man.

Chapter Sixteen

SUNDAY, NOVEMBER 6

THE DAY WAS fine and warm with little hint of fall.

Under Diego's supervision, the ranch hands strung colored lights across the terrace and rigged speakers to trees. Consuela had been in a frenzy of preparation for days, grouching volubly about how much work she had to do and how little time to do it. But beneath this, she reveled in every pastry she baked, every silver salver she polished.

Jack bought new clothes for the event and spent as much time on his appearance as he would for an opening night. He made a last-minute inspection of the waiters

Consuela had hired and checked the food and drink.

Jack went into the entrance hall and made sure the flower arrangements met with his approval, tweaking a flower here and a fern there until he was satisfied.

Consuela stood sentinel by the front door. She was resplendently spherical in a red dress with turquoise beads at her throat. Jack complimented her on her appearance and hugged her, which flustered her into a fit of giggling embarrassment. He followed up with a wolf whistle.

"I hope you've saved one of those for me."

Jack turned to see Loretta standing on the stairs in a strapless cocktail dress of deep blue silk, which highlighted the intense blue of her eyes. Her hair and makeup were perfect, and she seemed more like a movie star than the woman Jack had seen for weeks working the horses. Jack gave her an extended whistle that implied both admiration and surprise. Loretta's usually cool smile broadened into something warmer.

Headlights swept the Tiffany panels flanking the front door. Jack started for the door, but Consuela beat him to it.

"*I* do welcome to guests! You and Miss Loretta *hosts*!"

Jack reacted with mock alarm and extended his arm for Loretta.

*

BY EIGHT, SEVENTY people had gathered on the lawn at the rear of the house, talking, laughing, eating, and drinking. Loretta's attitude was never less than aristocratic, and the guests responded with apposite respect.

Adams and Maggie arrived. She was dressed smartly in something just a fraction too tight, and while Adams had made an effort with his appearance, his suit still looked as if he'd taken the pants from one model and the jacket from another. He patted the breast of his jacket.

"Got all the papers here. Just need your signature."

Jack smiled and nodded. Maggie tried to say something, but emotion robbed her of speech. She kissed Jack on the cheek, leaving a scarlet smudge, and as she took a handkerchief from her purse to wipe his face, Adams sighed impatiently.

"Why don't you get the kiss-proof kind for God's sake?"

"He can't get his mind off my kisser," Maggie confided drily to Jack. Adams rolled his eyes.

Jack led them into the throng. Most of the guests were eager to get a good look at Jack, and after brief conversation with him, curiosity was displaced by warmth.

Diego had dressed smartly in jeans, a midnight-blue shirt, and a gray tweed sport jacket, none of which made a secret of his physique. Jack took him a glass of punch and brought him into the mass of people.

Loretta took over the introductions, describing Diego's vital importance to the ranch. Her eyes flicked over Jack as she proclaimed, "None of us could manage without Diego."

Music played subtly from the speakers in the trees and the throng was alive with animated conversation. Loretta took Jack's arm.

"Some party," she said with more than a hint of approval.

"Oh, you ain't seen nothin' yet." He disengaged himself and ran up onto the terrace and struck the dinner gong as Consuela held it, according to his instructions.

"Everybody? Hello! Could I have your attention?" Jack called out. Conversation petered out, and everyone turned to him. "I want to thank you all for coming, and I want to offer a toast." He raised his glass. "To Amy Wyatt."

The guests all uttered a ragged, passionate, "Amy," and drank.

"And I want you all to know something," Jack continued. "The Wyatt Ranch is up and running again!" This was greeted with a hearty murmur of approval and applause from the guests. Jack came down from the terrace, and as he passed Adams he winked. When he reached Loretta, he tried to read her face, but couldn't.

"I have a surprise," he announced to the guests, then

added directly to Loretta, "A surprise for you."

"I wonder if you could surprise me," she said evenly.

"I'll do my best. Close your eyes."

"Oh please!"

"Just close 'em!"

Loretta sighed and closed her eyes. Jack took her shoulders and turned her slowly away from the guests.

"State fair this week. The ranch should be represented."

Loretta opened her eyes.

"No peeking!" He put his hand over her eyes.

Ahead of them, Diego cleared the guests to reveal a horse trailer. He opened the trailer door, and Jack lowered his hand. Diego led a sleek, nervous black stallion from the trailer. The guests gasped in unison.

Loretta was absolutely still, and no one on the lawn uttered a sound. After a long time in which the beating of Jack's heart belied the calm with which he'd introduced his gift, Loretta turned slowly to face him. She swallowed hard and bit her lip to stem its trembling, and then she took a deep breath and smiled at Jack.

The guests erupted into enthusiastic applause. Loretta walked to the stallion and stroked its nose and whispered into its ear. The horse raised its head high and whinnied, stamped the ground once with a fore hoof, then nuzzled Loretta's cheek and gave itself over to her body and soul.

Some of the guests pointed cameras, and flashbulbs lit the still night air like lightning ahead of a storm.

Jack turned and caught Diego watching him with a wide, warm smile. That was the capper on the evening, Diego's approval. At that moment, the past became just that—the past, and happiness became a tangible thing for Jack. He returned Diego's smile and was about to thank him for his part in securing the gift to Loretta, when he was interrupted by a curt, "'Scuse." Consuela pushed her way through the throng. She stopped a few feet from Jack, her face grim.

"Everything okay?"

Consuela opened her mouth but couldn't form words. There was confusion and a little fear in her eyes.

"Consuela?"

"Your wife—she is arrive."

Jack laughed. "My *what*?"

Consuela turned to the terrace. Jack followed her eyes to the woman standing there.

She was in her mid-twenties and attractive in a brassy way. The red highlights in her short, stylishly cut hair implied artifice, but it wrapped around a face that featured green eyes, and full scarlet lips. Her dress, a little too low and a little too short, sparkled here and there, and perhaps it had first seen the light of day in a Beverly Hills boutique; here, surrounded by conservative suburbia, it seemed garish.

The woman scanned the crowd until her eyes fell on Jack. There, they rested for quite some time, and then she walked slowly down from the terrace. Five-inch heels compelled her to seek out the paved path rather than risk the freshly mown lawn.

Jack stood frozen to the spot.

The woman stopped inches from him and gave him a warm, assured smile. Then she leaned forward and kissed him on the lips, too affectionately and too long.

Loretta cast a blatantly critical eye over the newcomer. The woman turned to Loretta and met her gaze with an equally critical inspection.

"You must be Loretta. The old maid."

This categorization had never been applied to Loretta's face in so many words; it was enough to hush the curious murmur of the guests. The only sound in the night air came from the speakers—Sinatra singing "One for My Baby."

"I'm Nicki, Martin's recently ex-wife," the woman said, extending her hand to Loretta.

Loretta ignored it and turned to Jack. He realized he was holding his breath.

Unfazed, Nicki turned to the hushed guests. "So! What are we celebrating?" She linked her arm through Jack's. "I mean, wow! Colored lights, champagne, gotta be something important, or you wouldn't all be here, dressed to the nines." She gave a couple of the female guests the once-over. "Maybe that should read dressed to the eights."

She laughed, a husky sound with no warmth and snuggled up to Jack. "So, what is this, a sendoff for dear old Auntie Whatserface?" Jack tried to withdraw his arm, but Nicki held firm. "Why don't we make it a double celebration?"

She addressed the crowd in a loud, clear voice. "Hey! Marty and I have something to tell you." She glanced at Jack with a playful smile. "We've been so miserable apart we figured we might just as well be miserable together. So. We're gonna tie the knot again."

Jack felt as if ice had been poured into his gut.

The guests were quite still, watching, each of them waiting for someone else to react to the announcement.

Jack caught a glimpse of Diego, his warm smile now replaced by a grim glare at the smug, garish woman. Jack's look to Diego begged for support, and he opened his mouth to seek it. But support for what? His deception? His lies to these people who now mattered to him? Who trusted him?

Nicki tightened her grip on Jack's arm. "We've got some talking to do," she said just loud enough for him to hear. "In private." Then she turned and addressed the crowd. "Marty and I have a bunch of things to discuss. Excuse us."

Diego took a step toward Nicki, but Loretta grabbed his elbow and restrained him. They watched as Nicki led Jack into the house. Consuela barred the way, but under Nicki's determined glare, she moved aside to let them into the hallway.

Nicki peered into a couple of rooms before finding the living room. "This looks cozy," she said, urging Jack inside. "Makes Grand Central look like a cubbyhole." She closed the door and ambled around the room, taking in the luxury of it, nodding approval at the Remington, the portraits, the soft leather of the sofa and chairs, then turned to Jack who stood riveted to the spot at the door. She made an appreciative inspection of him, head to foot. "Money agrees with you."

Jack closed his eyes briefly in an attempt to marshal his thoughts, but his mind was in chaos. "I'm not Martin," he blurted.

Nicki continued to look at him, smiling.

"I'm not Martin Brenner." Jack said, his voice breaking.

Nicki widened her eyes a little. "Duh. I coulda told *you* that."

"Martin…" Jack took a ragged breath. "Martin's dead."

The smile never left Nicki's face. "Couldn't happen to a nicer guy."

"I'm serious!" Jack said.

Nicki laughed. "You sure are babe, you sure are."

"There was an accident, a fire…" He sank into a chair and buried his face in his hands. "God, I don't know how to explain."

If Nicki was interested in an explanation, she gave no sign. She merely continued her appraisal of him. "Same hair, same eyes, build, same deer-in-the-headlights look. Great act. I can see why everyone bought it. Does anyone else know who you are? Or rather, who you're not?"

Before Jack could reply, the door opened, and Loretta stepped into the room. She glanced briefly at Nicki, then turned to Jack. Aware of the query in her eyes, he doubled in the armchair in agony.

"The guests are leaving," she said. "I thought you might like to see them off."

"We're having a private conversation here," Nicki said with steely insistence. "You mind, dear? Shut the door on your way out."

Loretta continued to watch Jack for a moment, then turned and walked out of the room, leaving the door wide open.

Jack leapt from the chair. "I'm going to tell them!"

Nicki's smile vanished. "Tell *who—what*?"

"Everyone. This is crazy. I have to tell them the truth."
He started for the door, but Nicki beat him to it and

slammed it shut.

"I don't think so."

She stood close to Jack. There was something repellant about her too perfectly applied makeup, her too sweet perfume. And there was something dangerous in her coldly confident eyes. Jack took a step back as if she might spring at him. She smiled sweetly. "Whoever the fuck you are, buddy, however the fuck you got here, if you fess up now, you'll lose the lot. Bad idea."

"It's the best idea I've had since I got here. I'm signing everything over to Loretta anyway. The papers are all drawn up."

Nicki widened her eyes ingenuously. "What name are you gonna sign?"

Jack mumbled, "This isn't about the money."

"*It is to me.*"

Jack regarded her with disgust. "Jesus, no wonder he divorced you." He pushed her aside and reached for the door handle.

"So what did you do to Marty? Did you kill him?" Nicki asked coolly.

"No!" Jack said, appalled. "No. There was — it was an accident and—"

"Look around, mister. Look at where you live, how you spend. You've got every motive to get rid of him. So fess up.

Did you kill him?"

"I swear I didn't!"

Nicki dismissed any further explanation with a sly smile. "Tell you what." Nicki strolled up close to Jack, who stood rigid, his hand clamped on the doorknob, knuckles white. "I'll make a deal. You lead me to the altar, and soon as the sound of wedding bells fades, you can do what the fuck you like with your stupid life. Just so I get my cut. As for Marty, if you don't tell, I won't."

A knock brought Jack to life. He opened the door to reveal Adams, who held a thick envelope. Adams glanced nervously from one to the other and looked as if he'd rather have walked into a bear pit. "Sorry to interrupt, sorry, sorry. The papers. The estate papers, et cetera, et cetera. Um. I need your signature—"

Nicki snatched the envelope from him. "We'll take care of it."

"Well, actually—" Adams started.

"We'll take care of it!" Nicki repeated as if to an idiot schoolboy. She pushed the door shut, and Adams had to step back into the hall to avoid being hit by it. She crossed the room to a table lamp and pulled a page from the envelope, scanned it briefly, and raised her eyebrows. Then she looked at Jack and shook her head in amused disbelief. "I've met some dumbos in my time…"

She tore the page in halves, then quarters, then took another document from the envelope and did the same. One last document comprised several stapled pages. Nicki inspected it with an incredulous grin, which she turned to Jack. "A will! What's the bet you don't mention me in it?" She kept her eyes fixed on Jack's as she slowly tore the document into several pieces.

Jack wrenched the door open and stumbled into the hallway. He leaned against the wall to get his breath, ignoring the curious glances of the departing guests.

Nicki emerged from the living room and thrust a small ring of keys at a grim Consuela. "Get my stuff outta the car. It's the SUV right in front."

Consuela didn't move until Loretta abandoned the guests and joined her. She assessed the situation, nodded, and Consuela snatched the keys from Nicki and went to the front door.

Jack stumbled to the morning room and stood with his head against the sliding glass doors, eyes closed. He heard Nicki walk up the hall to the lobby, avoiding the thick carpet, choosing instead the border of wood tiles, which made the going easier for her stilettos. Then, the clack of the heels on the oak treads as she started up the grand staircase.

"Which is the best room in this heap?" he heard her demand. "This one?"

Loretta's reply was grim. "That was Amy's room."

"Now it's mine."

When he heard the door to Amy's room open and shut, Jack took a broken breath, pushed the glass door aside, and fled into the deserted yard where the colored lights now seemed incongruous. He stumbled between tables that bore the debris of the party and ran until he found himself standing outside Diego's cabin.

Before he could evolve a plan, a lie, a plea for comfort or understanding, the door opened, and Diego stood in silhouette watching him take heaving breaths. After a moment, Diego stepped forward and wrapped Jack in his arms. They stood this way until Jack's breathing had steadied, and then he led Jack inside and sat him on the small sofa in the main room. Jack was unable to meet Diego's eyes for some time, yet when he did, there was no disapproval in them, not even query, just the calm, steady assurance of unqualified support.

He leaned back and closed his eyes. As he drifted into exhausted sleep, he was faintly aware of a hand stroking his hair.

Chapter Seventeen

MONDAY, NOVEMBER 7
5:15 A.M.

LORETTA WAS UP, showered, and dressed in jeans and a flannel shirt by five-fifteen. The house was dark and quiet. She paused by Jack's door and listened for a moment before she knocked gently and opened it. The room was empty, the bed undisturbed.

She went to Amy's bedroom. After a cursory knock she went in. Until yesterday, the room had been a shrine to Amy, pristine and inviolate. Now, it looked like a garage sale. Hangers sporting designer clothing had been hooked onto any likely support—doorknobs, chairs—and the dressing table had been cleared of Amy's treasured silver-backed brushes to accommodate Nicki's makeup. There was no sign of Nicki.

Loretta went downstairs, and as she passed the kitchen, she heard the clatter of plates and Consuela complaining to herself in Spanish. Loretta continued to the morning room. A solitary light illuminated the bar where coffee had been brewed. A cigarette butt floated in a half-filled mug.

Before anything more, she needed to talk to Diego.

The predawn light was clear, the air moist, and clouds hung over the hills as Loretta strode across the lawn where workers dismantled the party tables and cleaned up the leftover food and drink.

She didn't knock, just opened the door and went into the main room. She wasn't surprised to see Jack stretched out on the sofa, asleep, still fully dressed—all but his shoes, which sat by the foot of the sofa. A blanket had been placed over him. She stood watching his steady breathing for a moment. She'd encouraged his friendship with Diego and was relieved to know he trusted and confided in the man.

Loretta went silently to the bedroom, where the bed was neatly made, and Diego's smart jacket from the night before hung on the door hook.

She crept from the cabin, careful not to wake Jack, and

headed for the stable. She caught sight of Diego standing at the entrance. He put a finger to his lips, warning Loretta to be quiet, then to his ear—listen.

Inside, Nicky sat on a wooden crate, unaware she was being watched. She wore an expensive-looking silk robe and slippers, her candy-pink cell phone clamped to her ear. Her voice was shrill, urgent.

"I think you're pushing it!" A pause, and then she went on quietly but with some apprehension apparent. "Okay, I'll be there in thirty minutes... *Thirty*. I want to put on some fucking makeup!"

She glanced up at Loretta and Diego watching her from the doorway.

"Later," Nicki said to the cell and disconnected. She met Loretta's gaze and raised an eyebrow. "You mind? I wanted a little privacy. God knows I can't get any in that heap of a house with the Mexican bitch spying on—"

"I don't want you anywhere near the horses," Loretta said with sufficient menace to wipe some of the smugness from Nicki's face.

She strode along the row of stalls and went to the black stallion. She inspected it in silence, then turned and leaned against the stall door to take a good look at Nicki. "So, when's the happy day?" she asked easily, politely.

"What's it to you?" Nicki rose from the crate.

"You might need a maid of honor. An 'old maid.'"

Nicki slipped the cell phone into the pocket of her robe and turned her attention to the stallion. "How much does a horse like that cost?"

"I couldn't say. It was a gift."

"Marty's kinda free with his money. I'll have to talk to him." She reached up to the horse's nose. The horse reared, startling Nicki, who stumbled back and fell to the floor.

Loretta regarded her coolly. "Horses are great judges of character. You'll find out. If you're here long enough."

Nicki got to her feet and inspected her robe to make sure she'd sat in nothing more than hay. "I hope this one came with a return policy." She strode out of the stable, colliding with Diego at the door. "Get outta my way!" She pushed past him. "Dumb spic!"

Diego's eyes narrowed and followed her progress into the house. Then he turned and lifted his head to sniff the air. Loretta caught this and was suddenly alert. The acrid smell of burning overtook the general scent of the horses. A smoldering cigarette butt on the floor had touched off a little of the dry hay. Diego stamped out the embers, picked up the butt, and brought it to Loretta, who inspected it and strode for the exit.

"I need to talk to that bitch."

*

6:05 A.M.

THE AGONY OF a cramp in his left leg woke Jack from an instantly forgotten dream. He extended his leg and massaged the knotted calf. He glanced at his watch, then became aware of where he was.

"Diego?"

No response. He stumbled to the bathroom and peed. Then the events of the night before flooded his consciousness, and briefly, he considered throwing up. He went to the kitchen. A tall glass sat on the counter, filled with one of Diego's protein smoothies. Next to it, a scrap of notepaper read: DRINK

Jack did so, gratefully filling the void in this stomach.

He stumbled out of the cabin into the clear, cold air and regarded the ranch in the hazy fog of the early morning. No plan of action occurred to him. If he'd been reluctant to return to the house last night, he was more so this morning. Should he call Nicki's bluff? Who would the authorities believe if she accused him of murder? Given the suspicions of the detective from Lake Havasu, Jack couldn't be sure of his ground. Could he confide in Loretta—and perhaps lose her trust after doing so much to gain it? And Diego, whom he respected above all, and with whom he believed he was falling in love—what would he think of Jack's great lie? How would he convince *anyone* that the emotional value of his stolen life was infinitely greater than its financial value?

He walked across the lawn and wove his way between the workers and onto the terrace. The back door flew open, and Consuela emerged.

"You gotta come quick! Big trouble!"

He could hear Nicki's voice long before he went into the morning room.

"I don't take orders from you!"

Both women turned as Jack entered—Nicki flushed with anger; Loretta, ice cool.

"What's going on?" Jack asked.

"She's not gonna tell me what I can do, what I can't do," Nicki yelled. "It's not like it's her fucking house."

"If it burns to the ground, it won't be anybody's house," Loretta said. "No smoking—anywhere on this property. *Anywhere*. Understand?" She walked out onto the terrace and started across the lawn.

"Fuck you," Nicki said under her breath. She dragged a pack of cigarettes out of her robe pocket and considered it angrily before shoving it back again. "It'll give me great pleasure to kick her ass out of this dump." She pushed past Jack to watch Loretta heading for the stable. "Well, as of tonight, it's *my* dump."

"Tonight?"

Nicki turned to Jack with a humorless smile. "I've decided I can't live without you another day." Her tone was a mix of honey and acid. "It'll be a simple ceremony—just you, me, and a justice of the peace."

"I'm not going to do it," Jack said quietly.

"Really?" Nicki said with exaggerated surprise. "Then I'd better go tell Loretta you're a phony!" She started for the terrace.

Jack grabbed her shoulders and twisted her around so violently that she gasped in shock. "Okay. *Tell* her. Tell *everyone. Then* what? If I go to jail, you won't have a hope in hell of getting your hands on this house, or the money!"

Nicki eased out of his grasp and massaged her arm. The smug smile reappeared. "Your choice, babe. There's a big difference between a sentence for fraud and life for murder. I've got enough on you to make it stick, believe me." She crossed the room and disappeared into the hall.

He caught a glimpse of Consuela as she darted out of sight into the kitchen. Had she been listening?

In the distance, Loretta's voice rang out, raised in anger, a sound he'd never heard before. He turned to the windows to see Loretta urging the stallion out of the stable. Diego was with her, trying to calm the horse. The rage Loretta had kept in check while confronting Nicki erupted, now directed at the startled Diego. She'd mounted the stallion, but Diego seemed reluctant to hand the reins over. Loretta wrenched them from his grip and took off across the fields at a gallop.

As she approached the low fence that Jack remembered well from his first day on the ranch, Loretta leaned in preparing for a jump, but the stallion didn't accommodate her and came to an almost instantaneous halt just feet from the fence, throwing her. She landed heavily on her back, her left foot caught in the stirrup.

Jack and Diego ran to where Loretta lay, her left leg twisted at an ugly angle. The stallion, breathing rapidly, stood quite still as if sensitive to the situation. Jack knelt by Loretta.

"Leave me alone. I'm fine," she yelled. But as Diego released her foot from the stirrup, she cried out in pain. Jack tried to remove her boot, but Loretta winced and sucked breath between clenched teeth.

"Stay here. Don't let her move," Jack said as he started back to the house.

Loretta called after him, "If it's broken, bring a goddamn gun and shoot me!"

Chapter Eighteen

CONSUELA AND DIEGO hovered solemnly at the living room door while Jack stood at the end of the long sofa watching the doctor bandage Loretta's ankle.

Dr. Emil Verne was eighty-five and looked every minute of it. He grimaced when he knelt and again when he rose, grabbing for the back of a chair to steady himself each time. His work was thorough, but Loretta's expression indicated weary tolerance rather than appreciation. Verne muttered once or twice about the inconvenience of "coming all this way on a busy Monday" and "not many would make house calls." But his tone had no ill feeling.

He beckoned to Jack and produced a small plastic vial.

"Painkillers," he said, rattling it as if to establish the veracity of his claim. "These are the only ones I have with me. They're potent, so one every four hours, no more." He patted Loretta's hand, which she promptly removed from his reach. "I've prescribed a mild hypnotic to help you sleep. Consuela can collect it in Scottsdale." Loretta clicked her tongue impatiently.

Verne stood and eased himself into a vertical position, grasping briefly at his lower back. "You should be mobile by Wednesday. I want you in my office first thing for a complete checkup."

"It's a sprain, for Chrissake," Loretta said. "Nobody died of a twisted ankle."

"You haven't been to see me for quite some time. Your blood pressure is through the roof. I want to take a good look at you."

"First time a man's said that to me in a while."

The doctor's deadpan remained firmly in place as he packed his bag. "Show a little respect for the fellow who brought you into the world. No point telling you not to walk, I suppose, but if you must, use a cane."

"Fuck you."

"And you," Verne replied pleasantly. Consuela showed him out.

Loretta turned to Diego. "Don't you have work to do?"

Diego turned to Jack for his order.

"We'll take the mares out. Enrique and Charlie can do the stalls."

Diego turned to go. Jack took his arm.

"Thank you," he said. "For taking care of me last night."

A faint smile crossed Diego's face; he nodded and left the room.

Jack watched him go, turned, and flushed when he realized Loretta was watching him watching Diego.

He sat on the chair by the sofa. Loretta looked vulnerable for the first time since he'd met her, and he realized with an unexpected rush of emotion how much he cared for this woman. She allowed his sympathetic gaze for just a moment.

"I don't need a sitter."

Jack smiled and shrugged. "Okay." He got up from the chair and went to the tall window, taking a tumult of thoughts with him.

Loretta didn't take her eyes from him. "So, where is she? The bride from hell."

"I don't know. I heard her car."

"Have we got time to change the locks?"

Jack smiled, and then the weight of Nicki's threats settled on him again, and he sobered and turned back to the window.

"Big step, marriage," Loretta went on casually. "Bed and ten thousand breakfasts, as the wise guy said. Though I get the distinct feeling Nicki won't hang around for breakfast once she gets her hands on the loot."

Jack stared out at the lawn, hoping Loretta's needling wouldn't goad him into either lying to her or telling her the truth. When he turned back to her, Loretta's ice blue eyes were fixed on him.

"What's she got on you?"

Jack was still.

"Can't be she's pregnant. Anyhow, she looks like the type who'd eat her young."

"I have work," Jack said as he hurried out of the room.

As he ran up to his room to change into dungarees, he saw Consuela through the open door of Amy's bedroom. She stood surveying Nicki's chaos, swearing quietly but passionately in Spanish. He darted into the yellow bedroom, opened the drawer of the nightstand, and grabbed his wallet. A small white business card lay atop it: Miller's card. He stared at it for moment, then pocketed it.

As he emerged from the room, Consuela caught sight of him.

"You ex-wife *es un cerdo.*"

Jack nodded, unable to disagree. He hurried downstairs to get on with the day's work.

At a break, he left Diego in charge of the horses while he went to check on Loretta. He met Consuela in the hall. She wore her cleaning gloves and put a felt finger to her lips.

"She sleeping."

"Where is—?"

"The bitch?" Consuela shrugged *"Quién sabe?"* She tiptoed to the rear of the house.

Jack went upstairs and looked into Amy's bedroom. The bed was made, Nicki's makeup was corralled at one end of the dresser, and Amy's silver brushes had been reinstated. Every surface was clean, and the room smelled almost nauseatingly of disinfectant.

Back in the enveloping warmth of the yellow bedroom, he sat on the edge of the narrow bed and stared at the rose-patterned wallpaper. Ten minutes passed in which he didn't move a finger. Then he took his phone and gazed at it. Another fifteen minutes passed in which Jack remained immobile, cell phone in his hand. Finally, he took the business card from his jeans pocket and keyed the number on it.

"Lake Havasu Police Department."

"I want to speak to Detective Keith Miller."

"He's busy right now," the officer said. "Is this urgent?"

"Yes, very," Jack said. "How long will he be?"

"I'll see if I can get him. Who's calling?"

"This is—it's uh…" Jack struggled to pronounce his own name. "Tell him Jack…"

A single knock at the bedroom door, and Consuela put her head in. "I gotta go visit my niece in Glendale. She in labor."

"One moment," Jack said to the phone and then, "Go!" to Consuela.

"Dinner in the fridge, okay? Just for you and Miss Loretta," she added sternly. "Nobody else."

"How's Miss Loretta doing?"

Consuela rolled her eyes. "Boy, what a temper she got today." She glanced at her watch and started out of the room, then turned back. "I give her pills and a shot of scotch."

"You *what*?"

"Is what she want," Consuela said with a shrug, and she vanished from sight.

Jack heard the phone say, "Hello?"

"I'll call you back." He disconnected and ran downstairs into the den.

Loretta lay on the sofa, covered by a quilt, her eyes closed.

Jack knelt by her and took her hand. "Loretta?"

Loretta's eyes flickered and opened. She took a moment

to focus, and her eyes moved to Jack. He felt her forehead.

"You're feverish. Maybe I should call the doctor."

"Like hell you will," she said faintly. She tried to turn and winced in pain.

"How many pills did you take?" Jack asked, and when Loretta looked faintly surprised, repeated "How many?"

Her eyes narrowed. "How many do you think I took?"

"I don't know. Consuela said you had whisky and—"

Loretta uttered a short laugh. "Jesus, kid, give me a break. I took two pain killers and a shot of scotch to wash 'em down. And they've made no frigging difference."

Jack was relieved and faintly embarrassed. "I'll help you up to bed."

"I'm comfortable here."

"You sure?"

"Sure I'm sure. Don't fuss."

Jack adjusted the pillow behind her head and tucked the blanket under her back. "You want me to keep you company?"

Loretta glanced at the portrait over the fireplace with a wry smile. "I have all the company I need."

Jack leaned over and kissed her gently on the forehead.

"Don't get sloppy, kid. I was just getting to like you." This was accompanied by a small, affectionate smile.

Jack got to his feet as Consuela entered the room,

puffing from the exertion of running after him.

"I forget. Message for you. Urgent!" She handed over a crumpled page of notepaper. "Someone called Jack. I dunno no Jack!"

Jack glanced at the note scrawled in Consuela's over-sized caps.

> JACK
>
> 651 WEST SHERMAN 2C
>
> <u>URGENT</u>

He was momentarily frozen with panic.

"I tell 'em wrong number, but they swear a lot. So. I go to my niece now." And she vanished from sight.

Jack tried to keep his voice steady as he turned to Loretta. "I have to go out. You sure you'll be okay?"

"I'll be asleep," Loretta said, "with any luck. Don't do anything dumb!" Loretta called after him with some urgency as he started for the door. "You hear?"

Jack drove steadily, never above the limit. The day was autumn-short, and heavy clouds had gathered, speeding the fading daylight. His stomach reminded him he hadn't eaten since Diego's protein smoothie.

He found the address in a sad, dimly lit part of the city where low-rise industrial buildings alternated with trash-strewn vacant lots.

The dingy, wooden motel had two floors and looked not just deserted, but as if it had been long abandoned. Paint peeled from every visible surface, and here and there, wood was clearly rotting. There was no light at the door marked "Reception," but Jack glanced up at a dim, yellow glow in one window on the second floor. He locked the car and started up the unstable wooden steps, which hung off-angle from the side of the building.

The door to 2C was open a few inches. It creaked as he pushed it all the way, and he stepped into a small room with one grubby, unmade bed. A reading lamp lit a bottle of vodka and a glass by an open laptop on the surface of a battered desk by the window. Beside these, ominous in the dim glow of the lamp, a new-looking Glock 17 glinted. In the shadows by the desk, he made out the high back of a dilapidated swivel chair.

"Nicki?" There was no sound beyond the distant hum of traffic on the freeway. He took another step forward. "I'm here. What do you want?"

Thunder rattled the rotting boards of the motel. The swivel chair turned slowly. The figure sitting in it leaned forward into the light and smiled.

It was Martin Brenner.

Chapter Nineteen

LOS ANGELES
WEDNESDAY, JUNE 1
3:05 P.M.

MARTIN BRENNER STARED at the layouts tacked to the wall of his so-called office, one of a row of soulless cubicles, each scarcely big enough for a desk and two chairs. The day was hot, a record for June according to the *Times*, and the air conditioning at Stannard and Burke Advertising, Beverly Hills, was feeling the strain.

He pondered the varying degrees of allure offered by the designs before him. The assignment was for a publisher bent on thrusting a volume of classic stories by Cornell Woolrich onto a hopefully eager if minority readership.

Several minutes passed before he realized that staring was all he was doing; none of the promotional designs had sparked a single neuron in his tired brain. The routine dullness of his life had anaesthetized him against sensation of any kind, and no small part of that dullness was his marriage. Such was the state of indifference that had grown between them that Nicki had forgotten his twenty-fifth birthday just over a week ago. He hadn't bothered to remind her.

He sighed and slammed the palm of his hand onto his desk. His secretary put her head around the door and lowered her glasses. "Everything okay?"

Martin grabbed a thick file and pushed his chair back from the desk. "I'll take this home with me."

"They need it by eleven tomorrow."

He lifted his jacket from a hook and slipped it on, then shoved the file into his briefcase. "Tell Groener he can reach me there if he needs anything." He started out of the office, easing past the girl, then reconsidered. "No, don't tell him anything."

The drive from Beverly Hills to Hollywood was slow. It seemed everyone in greater Los Angeles had decided to leave work early and take to the streets. Martin cranked the air conditioning in his SUV a little higher and turned on the classical station. Something soothing and mathematical by Bach lulled him for five minutes, then with no warning but a faint *pfft*, the air conditioning died. He sighed and opened the windows, letting the smog-laden Los Angeles air in. The sounds of traffic, helicopters, and distant sirens over-whelmed the Bach, so he turned the radio off. An hour later, he pulled into the basement of his Los Feliz apartment building.

Cinder block walls bordered his double parking space. Nicki's Mini Cooper usually occupied the second space but was mercifully absent. Prefab shelves, anchored to a wall, held a few boxes of old tax files and a kit of car tools. Sweating, and too tired to curse his disabled car or the heat, Martin dragged himself along a corridor of parked cars, trying not to inhale the exhaust fumes hanging in the air. He took a deep breath only when the door of the elevator closed.

A neatly dressed kid in a baseball cap got in at the lobby and regarded Martin with the silent suspicion instilled in him by paranoid parents.

"Los Angeles neighbor" is a contradiction in terms, Martin thought.

He left the elevator on the third floor and slid the key into his apartment door.

The air was on, and it was cool and silent inside. He detected a faint hint of stale cigarette smoke, which he detested. Just when he'd talked Nicki out of smoking in the apartment, Scott had turned up, and his heedlessness of Martin's aversion to cigarettes prompted Nicki to light up whenever she felt like it.

Nevertheless, he was glad to have the place to himself tonight. Nicki would still be at some casting session and wouldn't be home until six, maybe seven or eight—or nine or ten; he really didn't give a shit. He wasn't in the mood for company, particularly that of his wife.

Or his brother.

Scott had arrived unannounced six weeks before, having crept across the Mexican border and made it to LA without attracting the attention of the FBI. If he had registered on their radar, he'd be cooling his heels in a cell right now.

The brothers bore a resemblance to each other that might have made them closer at a time in their itinerant childhood, but at the pivotal moment, their sensibilities diverged: Martin embraced liberalism and logic; Scott mastered cunning and manipulation. The remaining similarities were purely physical.

They both had the thick blond hair common to their mother and her sisters and the same steely-blue eyes, but Scott's eyes were set deeper and shadowed by drugs; and while Martin's gaze was direct, Scott's never quite rested on anyone or anything and gave the impression he was constantly on the alert for someone who might take him down—legally, physically, or perhaps, mortally. And now Scott was a resident in the apartment. Martin had allowed him to stay in the guest room against the hostile opposition of Nicki and his own better judgment.

Marty, bro, it'll just be till I can get outta the country. Martin sniffed scornfully at the memory.

And just as he had bailed Scott out when he was arrested for smuggling drugs—a bail he'd forfeited when Scott fled to Mexico—he agreed to finance a phony passport to get Scott into Canada. Or better yet, some country far beyond North America, Martin fervently hoped. Now, the initial wracking of nerves at harboring a fugitive had given way to downright impatience, for in six weeks, Scott had made no move to secure the counterfeit passport.

Martin dropped his office files onto the hall table, went straight to the kitchen, and pulled a beer out of the fridge. He let the fridge door close with a heavy thud. A gasp from somewhere in the apartment echoed the thud, and Martin realized he wasn't alone. He went into the hall in time to see Nicki's bare ass vanishing into the bathroom.

Martin walked cautiously to the door of the guest bedroom and eased it open. Scott lay stretched out naked on the bed smiling, arms folded behind his head, his erection brazenly evident.

"Hey, bro."

Martin turned and walked briskly back to the living room and crossed to the window. He stood there for a moment, staring at the traffic on Los Feliz Boulevard, then raised the bottle to his lips and drank deeply. He went to the bar and took a good look at himself in the mirror above it.

What did he feel? Betrayal? Anger? Disappointment? It occurred to him distantly, dimly, that he felt none of the above. If it was possible to feel a vast, dull nothing, that's what he felt.

What he saw in the mirror was the gold necklet he'd worn since the day he was married. Nicki had given it to him as a wedding present long ago when he thought they loved each other. He reached for it, searched for the clasp, and was about to remove it when Scott came into the room and flopped into an armchair. He wore a pair of Martin's shorts.

"So. Whattaya doin' home so early? They fire you or something?"

"How long will it take you to get that passport?"

"Wanna get rid of me?"

Martin turned to face him as Nicki appeared in the doorway, flushed and bound in a towel. He looked from one to the other.

"I want to get rid of both of you."

*

NICKI HAD A friend in Wardrobe at Fox who was out of town on a movie; her Hancock Park apartment was free for a month, and Nicki took up residence there. Scott joined her. Martin reveled in their absence and hoped it would be permanent.

A lawyer acquaintance guaranteed a quickie divorce and set the wheels in motion. Martin carried on with his mind-numbing routine at the office. At night, he returned to his empty apartment, glad to the point of euphoria that he was now its sole occupant.

He spent a little time, though not much, of his first week alone pondering Nicki's choice. Was it just a physical thing? Was the sex better? Did danger enter into it? Did love enter into it? Nicki's love for Martin had always seemed more like a business arrangement than a match and had dribbled away well within the first year of their marriage. At the outset, they were an attractive couple, high on everyone's Hollywood party list, and both seemed to be on the way up in the world—Martin as a budding young advertising executive and Nicki, a tough casting director for movies and TV. Then, the sheen of coupledom dulled. Martin's career went into neutral, and Nicki found more and more reasons to work late. He knew she was screwing some guy at the casting office—whatever, whoever, it was okay. He was glad to be rid of her. One day, soon, when he could find the mental energy, he might start playing the field again.

June progressed into July with no fanfares, just higher temperatures. The divorce was headed slickly for its final phase when one night, the phone was ringing as Martin let himself into the apartment. He let it ring and slipped out of his shoes. He'd muted the answering machine weeks before to avoid Scott's frequent requests for money. Eventually, the ringing stopped only to start up again ten seconds later. He glanced at the ID—it was a number with a Phoenix code. Curiosity kicked in, and he picked up.

"Hello?"

"Is this Martin Brenner?"

"Who's calling?"

"This is Maggie Wallace. I work for Harold Adams, Adams and Finch Attorneys in Phoenix, Arizona?"

It sounded like a question rather than a statement, but the name meant nothing to Martin.

"Harold Adams?" Maggie repeated. "Perhaps you remember him? He knew you when you were a small boy and—"

Memory returned with a flood of related childhood

associations. "Mr. Adams! Yes! I remember!"

"Well, as you know, we represent your aunt, your late aunt, and—"

"My aunt died?"

"I'm sorry to be the bearer of sad tidings—"

"Which one? Aunt Amy or Aunt Loretta?"

"Your aunt Amy. We'll all miss her—"

A gruff male voice butted in. "Here, give me the phone!"

"Okay! Don't grab!"

"Martin?"

"Mr. Adams?"

"We've had the devil of a time finding you, my lad."

"I'm sorry to hear about my aunt."

"She was a fine woman, a fine woman. But we didn't know where to find you, so we laid her to rest last week and…"

Adams went on listing his aunt's many virtues, but Martin barely heard. Memories of his childhood, the only fond memories he had of his early life, inundated him. His Aunt Amy had been like a mother to him—more so than his own mother, who was indifferent to him at best. She'd dragged him from the protective care of his aunts at the ranch out of spite, not love—certainly nothing like love. At first, it was she who'd denied him access to Amy, the aunt he adored. Then the years of adjusting to adult life, a career, and lately, a ragged marriage had widened the gap, and Amy Wyatt had become a distant memory.

The woman's voice on the phone brought his attention back to the call.

"Jesus, Harry, just *tell* him!"

"Thing is," Adams said, "your aunt made a will—a will that names you sole heir to the ranch, the estate."

Adams left a pause for this to have the maximum effect on Martin. His aunt, whom he'd not seen since he was eleven years old, was well off. No, she was rich, extremely rich. He took a deep breath and exhaled slowly before he could speak again.

"*Sole* heir? But what about Loretta?"

"Your aunt Loretta has made it clear she wishes to abide by Amy's decision."

Adams rambled on with the details punctuated by Maggie's interjections. If Martin could present himself at the office in Phoenix, the paperwork could be attended to. Meanwhile, a small amount of cash would be deposited into his bank account for expenses and whatever else he felt necessary for interim expediency. Martin asked if a new car might fall into that category and instantly felt ashamed asking favors so soon. Adams was unfazed by the request and said a car could most certainly be arranged.

"There'll be a memorial, of course, but we'll hold fire on that until you get to Phoenix. So if you can consult your calendar…"

After he'd disconnected, Martin did indeed consult his calendar. He also called his lawyer and found that the decree absolute was imminent. With something amounting to glee, he was aware that Nicki would be entitled to no part of his inheritance.

The next morning, he called Adams and told him he'd be in Phoenix the following week. Then he called Nicki and suggested she should take her remaining belongings from the apartment immediately as he was selling up and moving to Arizona. He didn't tell her why, but as soon as he disconnected, he regretted this disclosure. Nicki knew he had family there, and she'd delve.

He opened his laptop, surfed the Arizona news, and found Amy's obituary. It was accompanied by a picture of her that triggered warm memories for Martin.

An accompanying news article read:

WYATT NEPHEW INHERITS 24 MILLION

Legal representatives for the late Amy Wyatt are searching for her nephew Martin Brenner, who has been named sole heir to the fortune amassed by Wyatt Enterprises.

Yes, Nicki would see this and hound him for money. Well, tough luck. She and his lowlife brother were on their own now.

Chapter Twenty

TUESDAY, JULY 5

MARTIN'S JOY AT the prospect of sloughing off his wife without a cent was short-lived. The phone calls began. Nicki called him at his office, his apartment, his cell phone, at first cajoling, then begging, and finally demanding money to which she felt she was entitled. Martin reminded her of the terms of the divorce that allowed neither party to benefit from the other's assets, at first with smug enjoyment and then with decreasing patience until finally, he refused to answer her calls.

Martin's final day at the agency was marked by neither

tribute nor fond farewell, just a modest hug from his secretary and a cursory handshake from one of the partners—the other was in a meeting. He gathered up his personal possessions, crammed them into a filing box, and left the building without a glance over his shoulder.

He drove back to Los Feliz in the usual sluggish stream of traffic, but today he didn't mind one bit because he drove a new car—90,000 dollars' worth of new car—a Mercedes convertible, Torch Red and gleaming in the smoggy afternoon sunlight. Given the freedom of choice Adams had offered, he could've bought a brand-new Porsche, a Jag, maybe a Ferrari, but his heart had been set on the Merc.

He stopped briefly at his bank on Sunset and Vine, where the manager ushered him into his office and handed him a letter from Adams & Finch Attorneys, along with a larger manila envelope. The manager urged him to count the contents. Martin counted five thousand dollars in crisp, new, one-hundred-dollar bills. Then the manager slid a sheaf of papers across the desk as if they'd been blessed by some holy order.

Martin parked under his building with only a fleeting glance at his crippled SUV in the adjoining parking space. The night before he collected the Merc, a front tire of the SUV had deflated before his eyes. He'd gotten out the spare, jacked the car up, then thought—fuck it. He left the car tilted drunkenly on the jack, with the spare and the tire iron aban-doned on the concrete floor. A call to a charitable organiza-tion assured him the car would be towed, restored, and given to some needy institution; in return, Martin would be rewarded with a proportionate tax deduction.

He let himself into his apartment and went straight to the kitchen, where he dropped the car keys and the enve-lopes from the bank onto the counter before heading to the fridge for a beer. Here, at least, there was a stool to sit on. Nicki had taken or junked most of the rest of the furniture. And that was fine. He'd be out of this place in a matter of days and on his way to another state, another life.

"Hey, bro."

Martin swung around to where Scott stood in the kitchen doorway. "How did you get in here?"

Scott dangled a key ring from a finger. "Musta forgot to return these."

"What do you want?"

Scott affected an affronted expression. "Just wanted to wish my brother a fond farewell as he heads off for the good life, that kinda shit."

"You want money, forget it. I've already given you five times what you wanted for that passport."

"I'm not thinking of me."

"Really?"

"I'm thinking of Nicki. I mean, fuck, man, the years you two were together, doesn't that mean anything to you? You're worth a freakin' fortune now. You wouldn't miss a few bucks to take care of your wife."

"My *ex*-wife."

"Okay, but c'mon, man—"

"Point one—I don't get anywhere close to the 'freakin' fortune' until I sign a bunch of papers and jump through a few legal hoops. Point two—I wouldn't piss on that bitch if she was burning in hell. Okay? Now get the fuck out of here."

Martin stood by the window overlooking the street, watching to make sure Scott left the building. Below, he recognized Nicki's car at the curb. Scott leaned over the driver's window and said a few words accompanied by a shrug. The car door opened so abruptly it nearly knocked him down. Nicki got out and slammed the door. She turned to look up at the apartment window, and Martin shrank back against the wall.

The last thing he needed now was Nicki and her shrill demands. Was this to be a serial occurrence now that he had money? He left the apartment and took the emergency stairs down to the basement parking garage. He was reaching for the door of the Mercedes before he realized he'd left the keys in the kitchen.

He turned to the crippled SUV. He was stuck. Maybe he could just get out onto Los Feliz Boulevard and walk down to the busy row of stores on Hillhurst to avoid Nicki. But before he reached the street exit, Nicki marched into the garage, followed by Scott.

"Wait a minute, you prick!"

"Look, stop bugging me! I'm sick of this!"

"I talked to the attorneys at the office and—"

"I don't give a shit *who* you talked to. You're not entitled to a cent. *Nothing. Nada.* Even if you were, I'd burn it before you got your hands on it!"

"Well, you're not burning *this*!"

Nicki held up a manila envelope, the one Martin had been given at the bank, the one that contained five thousand dollars, the one he'd left on the kitchen counter with the car keys.

"Give that to me."

"Fuck you. This is just a start."

Out of the corner of his eye, Martin could see Scott leaning against the cinder block wall that divided his parking space from the next, smiling, enjoying the scene. This only served to intensify Martin's anger. He pushed Nicki, and she stumbled against the derelict SUV. "Give it to me!"

"Get your hands off me!" She swiped at him with the stuffed envelope, enabling Martin to snatch it from her.

"You make me sick to my stomach. You and my slime-ball brother," he said with a quick glance at Scott, who was still smiling. Nicki grabbed for the envelope, but Martin held it out of her reach and, with his other hand, pushed her so hard onto the SUV, it took some of the breath out of her. "What if I tell the feds where he's holed up? Huh? How will that look to your fancy Hollywood friends? They already know you're a slut. What if they find out your boyfriend's on the run from the law? Huh? *Huh*?"

He pushed her against the car again. Her knees buckled, and in an unpremeditated but deft move, she grabbed the tire iron from the floor and swung it at Martin's head.

Chapter Twenty-One

THE BLOW CRUSHED Martin's skull above his left ear. There was no reaction, no cry of pain, he simply dropped to the ground. His feet moved in violent spasms three or four times, and then he lay still, his eyes open and staring, the pulp of brain matter visible beyond the infracted bone. Blood seeped slowly onto the oil-stained concrete floor.

"Jesus. Jesus Christ," Scott said in a whisper. He fell to his knees by the body, careful not to touch the widening pool of blood.

He looked up at Nicki, who hadn't moved. She still held the tire iron aloft like some grotesque clock tower figure waiting to strike the hour. The flush of anger had gone, her face now paper white beneath the rouge, giving her the appearance of a badly painted doll.

An agonized grinding of metal on metal echoed through the basement as the street gate opened slowly. A car could be heard idling, waiting to enter.

"Nicki!" Scott's voice was an intense whisper. "*Hey!*"

Her eyes shifted to him.

"Get something to cover him!"

Nicki dropped the tire iron; it clanged loudly onto the floor. She darted to a shelf with stacked boxes of files and auto accessories and found a folded tarp under one of them. She pulled it free, scattering old tax returns and stumbled back to Scott as the waiting car revved and entered the basement. He tossed the tarp over the body.

As the elderly man drove by Martin's parking space, he braked and wound down the window. "Having trouble?"

Neither spoke.

The man squinted. "Is that you, Mrs. Brenner?"

Nicki stared at him with her mouth open but said nothing. Scott nudged her, and she offered a feeble, "Yes."

"Flat tire?"

"Yeah," she said faintly. Scott surreptitiously smoothed out the corner of the tarpaulin that covered Martin.

"You'll get your pretty dress all dirty if you're not careful," the man said to Nicki. "I'll give you a hand."

She opened her mouth to object, but the car took off to the far end of the basement and parked.

Scott grabbed Nicki's arm viciously. *"Talk to him!"*

She seemed not to hear. He slapped her face hard. She gasped and focused her attention on him.

"Talk to the guy," he repeated. *"You know him."*

The old man ambled around the corner of the parking space and stood peering down at the bare tire rim. "I'll need my glasses—my *other* glasses." He chuckled. "Got glasses for every occasion. They're upstairs. I'll just—"

"There's no need," Nicki said. "We can manage. We're nearly done."

"You sure?"

"Yeah. Sure."

"Thanks anyway," Scott said.

The man nodded affably. "Any time. You've had a lot of trouble with that car, Martin," he said as he walked off toward the elevator.

Neither Nicki nor Scott moved until the elevator door closed, followed by the whir of the machinery that took it aloft.

Nicki spoke without looking at Scott.

"He called you Martin."

*

7:39 P.M.

THE EVENING INFLUX of tenants began, and as each car passed, Scott and Nicki busied themselves in the subterfuge of changing a tire. No one else offered to help. Color returned to Nicki's face in uneven blotches. Her hands shook, and her lips were pressed into a grim line.

Scott, on the other hand, was all business. After making certain the coast was clear, he moved the tarpaulin covering the body to a clear part of the concrete floor, then directed Nicki to take Martin's shoulders, while Scott took his feet and they lifted him onto the tarp. Scott wrapped the tarp around the still malleable body. Nicki performed the exercise with eyes squeezed shut.

Scott considered the patch of blood that had pooled around Martin's head, about two feet wide.

An inspection of the shelves high on the wall of the parking space revealed a six-pack of paper towels, auto detergent, car wax, cans of motor oil. Scott thought briefly of the many times he'd mocked Martin for his "Mr. Be-Prepared" Boy Scout attitude. Now he was grateful for the values he'd ridiculed.

He took down the paper towels, and a dispenser of engine degreaser and proceeded to mop up the blood.

After containing the mess, he hissed at the frozen Nicki,

"Get your shit together!" He thrust wads of blood-soaked towels at her and indicated the stack of file boxes. She stuffed the red, sodden paper into these delicately, obviously desperate to keep from staining her dress. Scott sprayed the contaminated concrete with degreaser and wiped the floor as clean as he could.

Toward eight, the tenant traffic eased, and he peeled back the tarp and went through Martin's pockets. He extracted a cell phone and Martin's wallet. Its contents were unremarkable—license, insurance card, two credit cards, a couple of stubs from a Beverly Hills parking valet, and fifty dollars in assorted bills.

A gold necklet glinted at Martin's throat, the wedding gift from Nicki. Scott undid the clasp, slid it from Martin's neck, wiped the blood from it with paper towel, and turned it over in his hand.

"Always wanted me a pretty gold chain." He pocketed it along with the wallet.

Martin's right hand still clutched the manila envelope. Scott released it and checked the bills inside—they were dry. He wedged the money into his jeans pocket along with Martin's cell phone; the envelope, he consigned to the box of bloody paper towels.

"We'll have to burn all this stuff," he observed quietly, then returned his attention to Martin's hand. "Take his wedding ring off."

Nicki looked up at him, eyes wide.

"Take it off!"

She peered at the hand for a moment before lifting Martin's hand delicately between her forefinger and thumb.

Scott watched impassively, but with a hint of enjoyment, as she struggled to slide the wedding ring off the lifeless finger. He made no effort to help when the hand slid from her grasp several times. Eventually, the ring came free, and she wiped her bloodied hands absently on her skirt. He took the ring from her and pocketed it. With the remaining degreaser, he cleaned as much of the now coagulating blood from the tarp as possible. He glanced around the space. "I'll come down here tomorrow, hose this down. Right now, we have to get him upstairs."

"Upstairs! Can't we just, like, drive him somewhere and—well, make it look like an accident?"

"Does this *look* like an accident? You did a fucking good job of making it look like anything *but* an accident. We dump him now, they come right to us." He contemplated the mute plastic cylinder containing his brother's corpse. "We keep him upstairs a couple days, then we figure out what to do, where to do it."

He took Martin's shoulders and braced himself against the brick wall. "Get his legs, bend his knees up as far as they'll go and—"

"*What?*"

"*Listen.* In a couple hours, he's gonna go stiff. It happens to dead people. And he's gonna stay that way for about three days. If you think you can get six feet of him into the bathtub like that, fine. I'll let you figure it out."

"Okay, okay." Nicki's voice was small and frightened.

Between them, they eased Martin's body into a fetal position—and waited.

It was past nine when they dragged the body to the far-too-well-lit elevator. Scott waited with the concealed body in an adjacent alcove while Nicki summoned it and made certain it was unoccupied. She held the door while Scott dragged the tarpaulin inside. Scott pressed 3. The elevator slowed and stopped at the lobby, but Scott kept one thumb firmly on 3 and the other on the Close Doors button. The door opened an inch. Scott jabbed at the Close Doors button repeatedly, and the door shuddered closed again. They heard a muffled expletive outside as the elevator continued to ascend.

As they hauled the tarp across the third-floor hallway, one-liners from a popular sitcom punctuated by inane canned laughter seeped out of an adjacent apartment. Nicki ran to Martin's apartment and opened the door wide. Scott pulled the tarpaulin across the hall, checking the floor to make sure no blood had escaped, and once inside the apartment, he shut the door and put the latch in place.

Both of them sweating profusely, they hauled the body to the bathroom and into the tub.

"Oh God!" Nicki wailed. Scott looked up to see her inspecting the blood stains on her skirt. "This cost a fortune!"

"Burn it."

"I'll have to send it to—"

"Burn the fucking dress," he yelled.

Nicki shut her mouth tight.

Scott flipped open the laptop in the apartment's token office and clicked though various search pages. "Ice—ice…" He noted a number and called it. "Yeah, I need some ice. Recyclable. In a hurry. Around a hundred seventy pounds. …I *know* it's a lot! I'm throwin' a party, for fuck's sake! …Yeah! Now!" He gave the address, Martin's credit card number, and disconnected.

He went to the fridge and opened the freezer door. "Get the food outta there. We change the ice every day."

Nicki removed packs of frozen meals, vegetables, and ice cream and put them in the sink. "How long do we have to—keep him here?"

"As long as it takes to figure something out," Scott said irritably. "You go back to work tomorrow as usual—"

"I don't think I can."

He grabbed her arms so tightly she gasped with pain. *"You go back tomorrow."* A wheezing sob escaped her. Scott ignored it. "Then, when I figure something out, *we* take him out of here. You and me. *Together*." His tone made it clear this was not negotiable.

Nicki nodded glumly and started out of the kitchen. She paused by the kitchen counter and turned back to him. "I'm sorry," she said in a barely audible whine, which made the apology sound as ridiculous as it was.

The phone by her elbow rang. She cried out and stumbled back against the door. Scott grabbed the phone ready to do battle with the ice company if they had a delivery problem.

"Yeah?"

"Martin?"

Scott remained still and said nothing.

"Harry Adams here."

The name didn't register. Then Scott caught sight of the envelope addressed to Martin on the kitchen counter. The return address read Adams & Finch Attorneys. Reference points went off in his mind like flashbulbs—the Wyatt lawyer guy, the one who provided the payoff when Amy kicked his mother out of town fifteen years ago.

"Adams, sure!"

"How are you, lad?"

"Good, good."

"Forgive me calling so late, but we were wondering if you've come to a decision. Sooner you get yourself out here, the sooner we can finalize things, get the will sorted out, plan the memorial. Now you said you were aiming for this coming Thursday, the—um—"

"Fourteenth!" a woman's voice said impatiently.

"I can read!" Adams said.

Wheels turned in Scott's brain and clicked into gear.

You've had a lot of trouble with that car Martin…

"Hows about I'm there first thing Monday morning?" Scott said.

"Splendid. Splendid." Adams effused. "It's been a long, long time, lad. We all look forward to seeing you. Driving or flying?"

"Uh, driving."

"In your smart new car! Well, we'll book a room for you at—" There was a muttered conference between Adams and the woman. "—the Hilton Suites on Thomas Road."

"Great."

Adams offered more condolences, more goodwill, more eagerness to see the "lad" and hung up.

Scott disconnected and stared at the wall ahead of him. Nicki glanced from his face to the phone and back again. "Who was it?"

"Shut up," he said without taking his gaze from the wall.

Nicki backed out of the kitchen. A moment later, Scott heard the bathroom door close, and it crossed his mind that far from mourning, Nicki was in there trying to get the blood stain out of her skirt.

Chapter Twenty-Two

SUNDAY, JULY 10

SCOTT CONSIDERED TAKING the Merc, but it was showy—a risk he was not prepared to take, even with Martin's wallet and license in his pocket.

He wore Martin's wedding ring in the traditional manner—third finger, left hand. It was a tight fit, but he could live with that for as long as this little exercise took.

He replaced the tire on the SUV using a brand-new tire iron and stashed the bloody iron out of sight, but not too far out of sight, careful to keep his fingerprints from it while leaving Nicki's intact. If his plan didn't work out, the evidence pointed to Nicki.

He set out at dawn, aiming to be in Phoenix midafter-noon. He wore new jeans and an Abercrombie and Fitch shirt from Martin's wardrobe and had rearranged his hair to reflect Martin's expensive cut.

The traffic out of LA was sluggish and delayed him, and as he reached the heat of the Mojave Desert, he cursed the SUV's defunct air conditioning. He stopped briefly on a bleak stretch of the highway for gas and a sandwich, and it was nearly four when he approached Phoenix.

He pulled into the Hilton Suites on East Thomas Road and tossed the keys to a valet. At reception, when asked for ID, he flashed Martin's license. It was accepted with no more than a cursory glance at his face.

The suite was cool and spacious. Scott dumped his overnighter onto the king bed and stood at the center of the room, wallowing in his surroundings. This minor luxury was just a start. He contemplated all the extravagances 24 million bucks could buy—then the thought soured at the prospect of sharing the bonanza with Nicki. His anxiety about the state of the corpse outweighed his growing detes-tation of her, and he took Martin's cell out of his pocket and jabbed in her number.

"I'm here. I'll go see Adams tomorrow and—"

"I thought you were seeing him today," Nicki whined.

"It's Sunday. The office is closed."

"Can't you go to the farm, or whatever? See that aunt? Talk to her?"

"I can't risk it."

"But she hasn't seen Martin since he was a kid. You fooled the guy upstairs. You could—"

"I know what I'm doing."

"I just—I don't like being alone with—"

"Jesus. Get your shit together. And keep those ice packs cold." He disconnected and said, "Fucking women!" between clenched teeth as he headed for the bathroom.

He showered, dressed in a pair of smart, casual slacks and a light cotton shirt with no more than a passing thought about his brother's good taste, and sauntered down to the bar, where he ordered a double shot of vodka with a wedge of lime.

An attractive woman was settled elegantly on a stool at the far end of the bar. She wore a simple beige linen skirt and a pale-green blouse. The transparent pink Cosmo she held seemed to be more accessory than cocktail.

Scott took a good look. Why had he thought all the women in Phoenix would be dogs? This one was not only gorgeous, but he got the distinct impression she was putting out. He returned her smile, then took his drink and relocated to the vacant stool next to her.

"Do I know you?" she asked.

"Do you want to?"

The woman smiled and accepted Scott's offer of a drink. A couple of Cosmos later, she wrote her phone number on a cocktail napkin.

He took the napkin and held it against his crotch. "I'll keep this close to my heart," he said with a lascivious grin.

Fifteen minutes later, he was screwing the brains out of her.

*

MONDAY, JULY 11
7:52 A.M.

SCOTT WOKE JUST before eight, refreshed and pleased with himself. The woman had left sometime during the night—a bonus for someone of Scott's sensibilities. He'd climaxed twice in the space of an hour and would've aimed for a third if the woman hadn't pleaded exhaustion. The sex was great for Scott—and judging by the noise she'd made, the chick thought it was pretty hot, too, but her pleasure was a minor consideration.

His thoughts ran briefly to Nicki as he showered; she was nowhere near as wild a fuck as he'd enjoyed last night. If only Nicki would pack up and leave for—anywhere, just get the hell out of his life.

Maybe, when his plan had seen a financial return, he could do something about getting rid of her.

For good.

As he slipped into Martin's slacks, he found the cocktail napkin with the blonde's scribbled phone number in the pocket. He screwed it up and dropped it into the trash.

It was a little after ten when he ascended the stairs of the office building on Moreland, slowly, going over every memory he had of his brother—his manner, his speech, his walk, his smile. He entered the outer office without knocking.

Maggie Wallace looked up from her desk. "Help you?"

"Yeah. Martin Brenner. Adams called about the will and stuff."

Maggie's gaze remained fixed on Scott's face for a moment, then she gave him a professional smile. "Wait here." She went into the inner office. Minutes passed before she returned with Harry Adams in her wake. Scott stood, but Adams didn't greet him with the effusion he'd expected.

"So," Adams said without taking the hand Scott proffered. "You've grown since I saw you last."

Scott shoved his unshaken hand into his pocket. "Guess I have," he said with something approximating Martin's bonhomie. Adams gestured for him to sit and pulled up a chair close to him. Adams glanced down at the newspaper cutting he held and then up at Scott, who smiled back at him. Adams frowned.

"You have any ID on you?"

ID? Scott stiffened. "Don't you remember when I was a kid? I used to see you out at the ranch."

"I remember indeed," Adams said. Scott glanced at Maggie, who watched him with unwavering solemnity.

"So!" Scott said jovially. Maggie's and Adams's fixed expressions didn't relax one jot. He reached into his jacket pocket for the official letter from Adams addressed to Martin, but before he could withdraw it, Adams held out the news cutting.

"Maybe you should take a look at this."

After a momentary hesitation, Scott took it. He recognized it at once. It was the mug shot from his arrest for smuggling drugs. It was unmistakably him. His self-preservation machinery went into full gear. "Can't blame a guy for trying," he said to Adams with what he hoped was an embarrassed smile. "I've had a run of bad luck and —"

"Where's Martin?" the woman asked.

Scott looked at her and blinked.

"Is Martin *all right*?" Her tone was full of implication.

"Hey, Marty doesn't know I'm here. I swear!" He looked from one to the other to see if they were buying it.

Maggie picked up her phone. "I'd better call him."

Scott rose from his chair. "Look, I'd appreciate it if you didn't tell him about this." Maggie's finger was poised above the keypad. "He's planning to be out here, like soon. When did he say? Thursday? I thought— I dunno *what* I thought. Maybe I thought I could beat him to it." He lowered his eyes and strained to look ashamed. "Please. Don't tell him."

Maggie started to key a number. "I'm calling the police."

"No, don't do that!" Adams said. "No need for that. I don't think Scott's going to make any trouble, are you, lad?"

Scott shook his head and stumbled out of the office. "Hey, I'm sorry; I'm real sorry." He'd started down the stairs to the street when he heard Adam's voice.

"Scott?"

He turned as Adams took a furtive glance back toward his office before approaching.

"Take this." Adams held two fifties. "It's not much, but it might help out."

Scott nodded and frowned in a facsimile of embarrassed gratitude. He took the money and hurried down the stairs. *Fucking old idiot,* he thought as he reached the street door.

He sat in the car for some time reflecting angrily on the

encounter. He'd blown it. He'd shown his face to the wrong people, and that was the end of any chance he had of impersonating his brother. At least he hadn't compounded the blunder by showing them Martin's official letter. That, or Martin's driver's license would've raised questions about Martin's well-being far beyond the curt *"Where's Martin?"* He started the car, revving it unnecessarily, and the tires squealed as he drove off.

On the outskirts of the city, Martin's cell rang with the galloping *William Tell Overture*. Scott examined the caller readout before pulling over and answering. "Yeah?"

"Where are you?" Nicki sounded breathless.

"I'm on the highway. Out of Phoenix."

"What happened?"

"They didn't fucking buy it, that's what happened!" he shouted.

"Well—duh—I guessed that," Nicki shouted back. "That woman from the Adams office called."

"You picked up?"

"I thought it might be *you*."

"What did she want?"

"She knew about the divorce—Martin must've told them. She wanted to know what I was doing in the apartment."

"Jesus. Fuck."

"I told her I was getting the rest of my things."

"You didn't say anything about me."

"Give me a break. I told her Martin went to a movie. I said he didn't want to be here while I was packing."

Scott cursed under his breath.

"Are you coming back now? I really hate being stuck here alone."

"Well go out!" Scott yelled. "*Take a walk*. Nobody's got a fucking warrant out for *you*. Just keep your fucking mouth shut." He disconnected and yelled, "Cunt!" at the windscreen.

Nicki was starting to piss him off bigtime.

Chapter Twenty-Three

3:22 P.M.

SCOTT STOPPED FOR gas outside Blythe and relished just being able to pause, to do nothing but stand in the dry desert air, anonymously, not to have to think of the next ploy, to rush to the next razor edge of decision.

The junction of I-95 was just beyond the gas station, and he decided to take it, to drive north to the 40. It meant adding a couple of hours to the journey, but maybe a hit of the old Route 66 and the emptiness of the Mojave would clear his head.

He passed signs pointing to Lake Havasu City, noting

only that it was there and that the highway traffic was a little more congested. The words "London" and "Bridge" passed through his mind but were gone just as quickly.

*

5:15 P.M.

SCOTT PULLED OVER at the junction of I-40. Needles was fifteen miles to the west, and thirty more miles north on I-95 would get him to Vegas. The remains of Martin's five thousand bucks were burning the proverbial hole in his pocket, but throwing big cash around in the wrong places was not a good idea. He turned west on the 40.

It was nearly six, the sun low in the sky and blinding. He stopped at a diner in the middle of nowhere and ordered a burger at the counter. His cell rang. He noted it was Nicki and considered ignoring it, but answered with a weary "Yeah?"

Nicki sounded breathless again. "Listen, I've found something. It might be— I don't know *what* it might be, but it *could*, somehow—"

"What? What? What?"

"I'm casting a western, and we took a look at that HBO series—"

"Yeah, yeah—"

"There's this guy, this actor, an extra—he's a dead ringer for Martin."

Scott thought about this for a moment. "So?"

"I don't *know*! I'm just saying there's got to be a way to use it. I mean he looks *just like him*. It's like, totally unreal."

Scott sighed impatiently. "*I* look like Martin. Where the fuck did it get *me*?"

"This guy looks *more* like Martin than *you*."

"Great. We'll give him the fuckin' will, okay?"

"Scott—"

"Listen, I'm wrecked. I've been driving all day. I'm gonna stay over somewhere."

"You're not coming home?"

Scott tried for a split second to compute the word "home" but didn't dwell on it. "I'll be back in the morning."

"But this guy—"

He disconnected. He'd lost interest in the burger and Nicki and the whole fucking deal. Maybe he should just take the ready cash and get back to the relative safety of Mexico—leave Nicki to cope with the Martin shit. With the exception of the legal dumbos in Phoenix, no one but Nicki and Martin knew Scott was actually in the US. And Martin wasn't about to tell anyone. That left Nicki. And Scott didn't break his brother's skull, *she* did. It was her problem, her DNA, her fingerprints, her murder. All he had to do was make an anonymous call to the cops. He needed to sleep on it.

He beckoned the guy behind the counter. "Anywhere to stay around here? A motel, something?"

"There's one about a mile west."

*

6:56 P.M.

THE CRIMSON DESERT Motel was unprepossessing to say the least, but it boasted a pool and a barbecue and vacancies. Lots of vacancies. It stood alone on a single lane by a barren stretch of highway, ensuring it remained a well-kept secret.

As Scott entered the reception, the clerk was on the phone in a heated conversation with someone Scott guessed was his superior, if such a chain of command existed in a shithole like this.

"I want you to *fire* the guy!" The clerk was saying. "He's been using the business card to buy personal shit." His fist rested on a piece of paper. Of the figures scrawled on it, one was clearly a credit card number. By reflex, Scott committed the number to memory—it might come in handy some time. "Okay, so he's old Mendoza's son," the clerk went on. "That makes it okay? It's *stealing* for Chrissake."

Scott rapped on the counter to get the clerk's attention.

"Gimme a quiet room."

The clerk glanced at him for all of two seconds as if this were a redundant request and slid a key labeled "14" across the desk. "Forty-five bucks."

Scott put down cash and, as he was not asked for ID, signed the register "Fred Jones."

As Scott left the drab office, the clerk continued in his denunciation of the poor guy who'd been a little too free with the company's credit. With something like sympathy, Scott reflected that anyone who'd rob from this joint would steal used condoms from a whorehouse.

He pushed two dollars into a vending machine for a Coke. The machine swallowed his money and returned nothing. Scott yelled in the general direction of reception: "Hey, man, your vending machine's fucked!"

There was no reply.

Room 14 was at the farthest end of the run-down wooden structure. It contained two single beds, a token bathroom, and from the back window, a view of the pool. As pools went, it was far below Hollywood standards, but an effort had been made with underwater lighting. The barbecue was right outside his window, and a guy in overalls with the logo BBQ EXPRESS was bent over it priming a gas tank.

An overweight man in colorful shorts floated lazily on

the pool in a Baja chair. He held a beer bottle in one hand, and a cigarette dangled from the other.

"Hey, mister," the BBQ guy called. The man turned a somnolent gaze to him, and the BBQ guy pointed to a sign which read:

NO SMOKING

"Propane," he said pointing to the tank he held, adding, "gas" as if English might not be the guy's first language. The man blinked in slow motion, dowsed his cigarette in the pool, and tossed the butt onto the grass.

Scott hoped that exchange would be the last for the evening outside this particular window. He was tired and wanted no obstacles to a deep sleep.

He weighed options as he undressed and decided on a plan: An anonymous call to the cops, point them to the bloodied tire iron, then hightail it to Mexico—yeah, take what was left of the five grand and beat it. Leave Nicki to figure out what to do with the body all on her lonesome. The prospect of Nicki squirming under interrogation gave him the only genuine smile he'd managed all day.

*

3:14 A.M.

SCOTT WOKE WITH a start. He turned the nightstand lamp on to inspect his watch. What had woken him? It wasn't a dream—but something his mind had been turning over as he dozed off. He dialed Nicki's cell.

"It's three o'clock in the morning," she whined.

"This actor, this guy who looks like Martin, what do you know about him?"

"He's an actor. What's to know?"

"I mean is he famous?"

"He's an *extra*."

"Does he make money?"

"Sure, if he gets unemployment. He's a nobody. He just happens to look like Martin. I mean, the face, the build. So, the hair's not exactly—"

"Get everything you can on the guy. Photos, everything. I'll be back in a few hours."

*

TUESDAY, JULY 12
8:10 A.M.

JUST AFTER EIGHT, Scott was on the outskirts of Los Angeles and hit the worst of the morning traffic. He'd had five hours on the road to consider the intricacies of his plan. Complex, audaciously complex, but so devious, it would deflect all suspicion from him. Not foolproof, nothing was; he'd learned that at an early age. But there were emergency exits in the scheme, and he could bail out if things went wrong. And if things went right, he'd get away with twenty-four million bucks.

Nicki was sitting on the bare floor of the living room when he got back to the apartment. The plan was so elaborate, Scott boasted, that even the smartest of smartass cops would count his marbles before suspecting deceit. She listened, squirming occasionally, as Scott outlined the details, then got to her feet and walked to the window.

"It won't work. No way."

"It *could*."

She turned on him. "You want to risk life in the slammer for '*could*'? It's hit and miss. It leaves too much to chance."

"You got a better plan?" he shouted at her. "One that gets us off the hook? One that gets us the money? You got *any* fucking plan? You're the one who crushed his skull, baby, not me!"

Chapter Twenty-Four

TUESDAY, JULY 12
9:46 A.M.

SCOTT AND NICKI sat outside a shabby apartment build-ing in West Hollywood in Nicki's Mini Cooper. Scott munched on a hamburger, never taking his eyes from the entrance to the house. After five minutes, Nicki reached for the door handle.

"I need a cigarette."

"Stay where you are," Scott said with his mouth full. Nicki stayed.

Another twenty minutes passed.

At 10:20, Nicki sighed impatiently. "Maybe I should just go see if he's at home." Scott grabbed her arm and nodded to the front door of the house.

Jack McCauley emerged carrying a large manila envelope.

His resemblance to Martin was so startling that Scott wondered if there was a branch of the Dalstrom family he knew nothing about. The blond hair was longer and fuller than Martin's, but that was a detail. The eyes were a similar blue, the cheekbones a little more prominent, but overall, close—very, very close.

"Fucking amazing," Scott whispered. And repeated it several times as if to convince himself of what he was seeing. "I know my slut of a mother was spreading her legs, so who knows?"

Jack walked briskly to a parked beat-up Nissan. The engine, audibly reluctant to start, finally coughed into life. Scott and Nicki tailed him through busy traffic to a short concrete building on Santa Monica at Cahuenga. Like many Equity Waiver Theaters, the façade was painted black and bore hand-painted signs proclaiming a life-altering drama by a brilliant new playwright—coming soon.

Jack parked and joined a small group of young men on the sidewalk, some of whom he greeted a little too affably.

"It's an audition," Nicki observed.

"You'd better have something better to offer him," Scott said quietly.

Twenty minutes later, Jack emerged minus the envelope and minus the confident smile he'd worn on the way in.

Scott chuckled. "Loser."

They followed Jack back to West Hollywood. He parked and walked to the entrance of the building where a short, swarthy man waited. They couldn't hear the heated exchange, but it was all too obvious the guy wanted his rent, and Jack didn't have it. Jack yelled something at the landlord that couldn't be heard over the traffic, then walked away on the sidewalk, head down.

"Okay," Scott said, his mind in overdrive. "Who's gonna miss him? Agent?"

"Agent cut him loose. He's flying solo."

"Shit, this is perfect. Size him up. See if you think he'll fall for it."

"And if he won't?"

"In that case, we make him an offer he can't refuse."

"You can't just twist his arm—"

"*Listen*," Scott said vehemently enough to shut her up. "The guy's a bum. If he doesn't go for this on his own, I put a gun to his head."

"A *gun*?"

"Yeah, a gun and a few thousand bucks." Scott grinned. "Ten to one he'll go for it," he said as he got out of the car. "Call your office. Set up an audition."

"A test," Nicki said.

"A fuckin' test. Whatever. Just do it."

As he crossed the street, Scott jammed a baseball cap onto his head, tucked his hair well under it, and put on sunglasses to deflect any comment on his resemblance to the actor.

The chubby Armenian landlord was still fuming from his exchange with the actor when Scott asked if there were any vacancies. The landlord pointed to a sign that said otherwise. Scott peeled a hundred from the wad in his wallet, gaining the Armenian's undivided attention. The landlord wife joined him, resplendent in a stained velveteen bathrobe. She urged her husband to evict the lowlife actor and take this nice man. The landlord took the money but couldn't help complaining that the actor owed him two months. Scott tut-tutted and said if *he* were running a salubrious joint like this, he'd hold the tenant's possessions until he paid up. To back up this advice, he peeled another bill from the wallet. The landlord's wife took it with neither ceremony nor shame.

Back at the apartment, Scott used Martin's cell to call the Crimson Desert Motel. He recognized the voice of the clerk from the night before. He asked if there were vacancies. There were always vacancies. How about a room by the pool? There was no waiting list, the clerk said.

Scott drove the SUV to the Home Depot on Sunset, and as he started loading a cart with propane tanks, a thought struck him.

Mendooley? Mendola? What was the name of the guy the night clerk wanted to fire? "…*old Mendoza's son…*"

He abandoned the cart mid-aisle and ran back to the car. Information found the Nevada number for BBQ EXPRESS and connected him. A girl who sounded as if barely out of high school answered a little too brightly.

"Barbecue Express. How can we be of service to you?"

"Yeah, this is Mendoza, Crimson Desert Motel."

"Just a minute." Long fingernails clicked on a keyboard as the girl filed through client names. "What can I do for you, Mr. Mendoza?"

"I want to order some propane tanks."

"How many would you like?"

"Ten."

"Ten!"

"Ten."

"I believe we delivered one to you just last night."

"We're planning ahead."

"Okaaay. And when would you like these delivered?"

"Tomorrow. No later."

A pause as she clicked a few keys. "Could you confirm the last four digits of your credit card, Mr. Mendoza?"

Scott dredged up his memory of the paper on the reception clerk's desk. "Four two seven three." Kindergarten stuff.

A pause as she checked her records. "That's fine, Mr. Mendoza. Our man can't be there before 9:00 p.m. Is that okay?"

"He's gotta be there no later than twelve midnight, you got that?"

"No later than twelve? Oh, I'm sure our man won't want to work past—"

"Not a minute later! Or we can the deal and take our business elsewhere."

"We'll be there. Certainly."

"And listen, don't take any shit from the guy on the desk. It's kinda like a surprise party for him. Just tell your guy wheel 'em in, stack 'em by the pool, and charge it."

*

7:00 P.M.

SCOTT WAS AT the kitchen counter frowning over strips of dull metal when Nicki returned to the apartment.

She put a cigarette in her mouth and took out her lighter.

"Don't do that." Scott said quietly without looking up at her. "This stuff burns very easy, very quick, very hot."

Nicki removed the cigarette. "What is it?"

"Magnesium." Scott dropped a small piece of the foil into the sink. "It leaves next to no residue." He dropped a lit match into the sink, and the foil ignited in a searing white blaze that made Nicki jump. Scott turned on the faucet; the foil continued to burn. "And it's hard to put it out."

When the fire burned itself out, Scott bundled a handful of strips into an envelope. Then he proceeded to uncoil something that looked like black string from a card cylinder, measured several yards, clipped it, and wound the length around his fingers. This he also consigned to the envelope.

Nicki approached the sink cautiously and peered down at the dots of black, all that remained of the burnt magnesium. "Where'd you get this stuff?" she asked with a hint of awe.

Scott didn't reply. He heaved the sole propane tank he'd bought onto the counter and pulled a few pages of printout close to him. Referring to these pages frequently, he manipulated the valve of the tank with a wrench and a screwdriver.

"We leave the valves like this" he said as a faint hissing

sound emanated from the tank, "and it looks like a manu-facturing fault."

"A fault? In every tank?"

"It happens. That's why there are lawyers." He jammed a strip of magnesium into the breached valve.

"I hope this is gonna work," she said.

"Like I said, you got a better plan, you get rid of him." He closed the valve and glanced up at her with dramatic solemnity. "You'll have to take ole Marty out to the desert."

"What?"

"The SUV is bigger than the Mercedes."

Nicki backed away a few paces. "I can't!"

"Just don't get stopped for speeding."

"Scott, I can't."

"They pull you over, sure as hell, they'll take a look in back, and—"

"*I can't do it.*"

Scott regarded her deadpan for a few seconds, then laughed.

"You're kidding, right?" Nicki said.

"He'll be a tight fit in the trunk of the Merc," he said as he went into the hall. "I just hope to fuck he holds up in the heat."

Chapter Twenty-Five

WEDNESDAY, JULY 13
2:30 P.M.

AT 2:25 P.M., NICKI sat in a dilapidated soundstage behind a barren stretch of Sunset Boulevard. Her associate casting director, a failed actor, brought his world-weary cynicism to the session, seated in the dark next to her. Two less-than-illuminating auditions elicited audible yawns from him, while Nicki sat silent, rigid with nerves. Then, Jackson McCauley walked into the pool of light and took up position before the video camera.

Nicki had instructed makeup to clip his hair, rearrange

it, brush it back from his forehead. Now, his resemblance to Martin was striking. As she examined his face on the monitor, her pulse quickened, not so much for the plot to snare this guy, but for the startling resemblance to her dead husband.

He was desperate to get the job, that much evident from his manner, and the rest was bonus—he had no one in his life who'd miss him if he vanished from the face of the earth. She instructed him to be in Flagstaff by noon tomorrow, or no job.

As he settled his contract in the office, Nicki called Scott, who was engaged in shorting the ignition of Jack's car prior to driving it a few blocks away.

"Okay," she said, "the good news is he's all on his lonesome. No family, no relationships. No one's gonna give a shit about him."

"Great!"

"The *bad* news is he's *not gonna go for it*. I can tell you that right now! He's got this, I dunno, this holier-than-thou, humble kind of attitude."

"Which is why he's a deadbeat actor who can't get a job. No one, but *no one* is so fuckin' honest they'll turn up their nose at money, 'specially if they're dead broke. Just get moving."

*

SCOTT FOLLOWED JACK through the reporting of his stolen car to his frantic jog to the West Hollywood apartment building, from which, after a few minutes, he emerged at a run with just a backpack, his exit accompanied by screeching cries of "Police."

Scott wondered what crime he'd committed. Whatever, it meant the patsy would be in no hurry to return to this address. He watched as Jack sat, disconsolate in a bus shelter, then followed the Jeep in which some muscle-bound jock drove him away.

Is our Jacko a fruit? Scott wondered. *Is he gonna waste time fucking this guy before he gets on the road?* But Jack got out of the Jeep at the on-ramp of I-10 and stuck out his thumb.

As Scott approached to offer a ride, the heavy afternoon traffic allowed a tractor trailer to get ahead of him and take Jack with it. Scott cursed and followed, keeping the truck well in view. He passed it once, lingered in the slow lane until the truck passed him, and then he overtook it, again lingering in the slow lane with an eye on the rearview mirror. He let the truck pass him and watched until it lumbered off the freeway at the outskirts of Barstow.

It was just 7:00 p.m.

Here, Scott made a show of being lost and asked

directions of the truck driver, all the while keeping an eye on Jack, who slowed his walk to the freeway entrance ramp to inspect the Mercedes. It was no great feat to get him into the car.

Scott sized Jack up during the long drive and deduced confidently that the guy was at a dead end. He'd jump at the chance of assuming another identity. And if he didn't, Scott would simply put the proposition to him point-blank. Fifty grand for what amounted to an acting job: go to Phoenix, be Martin, sign a few papers, get the loot, then vanish.

He filled the dumbass in on as much of Martin's family background as he could during the drive, and to compound this, Nicki called and berated "Martin" for money she felt was her entitlement. The call signaled to Scott that she was at the motel, waiting. She'd brought all the necessary items that morning including a brand-new leather suitcase containing a wardrobe reflecting the measurements on Jack's résumé.

Scott stopped at a diner where a waitress conveniently pointed out the similarities in the men's appearance saving Scott the trouble. So far, so good. Everything appeared to be random. And big plus: Jack *was* gay! Scott played this to the hilt, proclaiming himself bisexual and up for some action.

Then, an event on which Scott hadn't counted.

They were just a few miles from the Crimson Desert

Motel on the deserted highway, a good spot to feign fatigue, the ploy to get them to the motel for the night. The actor talked about his career—*enough to put anyone to sleep*, Scott thought as he half closed his eyes and let the car veer off the road. He hadn't counted on the highway cop he almost downed as he straightened the car.

The cop wasn't too curious, no breathalyzer, no formal report. He checked the front lights and the rear, then played his flashlight over the trunk, and for one heart-stopping moment, it seemed he'd ask to take a look inside, where, in spite of the packs of dry ice, Martin was slowly and steadily thawing. Scott held his breath and wiped beads of sweat from his upper lip. The cop returned the license and suggested they pull over somewhere and get some rest, thus saving Scott the trouble. Jack was reluctant to digress from his planned journey, but sex was in the air, and clearly, Jack was starved for it.

The Crimson Desert Motel was just as lonely as the last time Scott had seen it and almost as deserted. A van with the logo BBQ EXPRESS was parked by reception, with the delivery guy wheeling gas tanks to the rear of the motel. Right on time.

Scott asked Jack to wait in the car while he checked in as Martin, showed Martin's license, and made quite sure the name "Martin Brenner" registered with the night clerk. He added "Jackson McCauley" very clearly to the register as the second guest. The clerk handed him the key to 14.

In passing, Scott wondered if the sheets had been changed since his last sojourn.

"I need to eat," he said.

The clerk, inspecting a delivery sheet, ignored him.

"Diner near here?" Scott tried again.

"Mile up the highway" the clerk said without looking up.

"Might drive on up there, get a sandwich." He planted this so the clerk would remember if questioned.

"Look, man, I got problems, you mind?"

But it had registered. Scott left as the clerk continued trying to decipher the delivery form for ten unwanted tanks of propane. He drove around the boxlike reception office to the far end of the L-shaped motel. A couple of motorcycles stood outside 12, where the flickering light of a TV seeped through the threadbare drapes. Jack backed the Mercedes right up to the door of 14, the last room in the row. Here, the car was not visible from reception, nor from the pool, and the motorcyclists were clearly riveted to whatever junk was on the ancient TV in their room two doors away.

He tossed Jack's backpack into the room, then pleaded blood sugar and urged Jack to return to reception to get a couple of snack bars from the vending machine, stressing the urgent need for sustenance.

As soon as Jack was out of sight, he popped the trunk and hauled out the tarpaulin and its contents, which fell heavily onto the doorstep with a dull thud.

"Come on, for fuck's sake! Help me here!"

Nicki rounded the corner of the building carrying a smart leather suitcase and a towel. Once the body was clear, she gave the trunk the once over with the towel, brushing the remaining shards of dry ice to the ground, where it would evaporate quickly.

"I've been waiting an hour," she whined as she dumped the suitcase into the trunk.

"Get inside."

Nicki darted into the dark and grabbed one end of the tarpaulin while Scott took the rear. They lifted, half dragged the body into the middle of the room.

"Anyone at the pool?"

"No. We're good."

"Gimme ten minutes." He slipped out of the room, closing the door behind him.

He'd just closed the Mercedes trunk as Jack reappeared with a bag of chips. Jack made to enter the room, but Scott deflected with a suggestion they cool off by the pool. They dipped their feet. Scott allowed the dork to indulge in a little philosophy, then pressed him on what he'd do with his nonevent life if he had money. Gaining a promising response, he put the frosting on the stopover by proposing sex. Jacko was drooling for it, and it took little convincing to get him into the car, get the food, and hurry back for a promised round of sweaty fucking.

Jack drove off with Martin's wallet in his jacket pocket.

Scott entered the dingy room where Nicki was inspecting herself in a grimy mirror. She wore a dull dark-blue jumpsuit with a paramedic insignia on the sleeves, courtesy of Fox wardrobe. She'd topped this off with Coke-bottle glasses.

"You sure he won't just bolt with the cash?" she asked.

"He'll be back," Scott said with a smug grin. "He thinks I'm gonna fuck his ass." He pulled at the tarp. "Where'd you park the SUV?"

"Other side of the pool. There's a service road and a row of trees—"

"Come *on*. We haven't got all night!"

Martin's naked body rolled out onto the floor, limp now and strangely misshapen. His face had turned a muddy color, and his lips pulled back over his teeth, giving the impression of a grim smile. Nicki's face contorted with disgust, and she bit her bottom lip.

"Don't you lose it!" Scott warned. He took Martin's shoulders, Nicki took the feet, and they carried the body to the bed nearest the back window and heaved it up onto the cover.

"Before I forget," Scott said as he took the gold necklet from around his own throat and held it out to Nicki. "Insurance."

She took it and turned it over in her hand. "This is 24 karat. It cost me."

"You know what to do with it. Just in case we need to point the finger at Jacko."

He pulled Jack's thin, worn wallet from his hip pocket, then darted into the bathroom and held it under cold water soaking it thoroughly. This, he lobbed outside the door, close to Jack's backpack, where it would be found more or less intact.

Meanwhile, Nicki pulled the curtains apart and raised the window in a series of grinding jerks. She scanned the darkness briefly, climbed over the sill, and took the folded tarp from Scott, who climbed out to join her. She dropped the tarp under the window, and together, they rolled the propane tanks onto it, as close to the window as possible. He hauled two of them into the room and set them by the body on the bed. He opened the valves and stuffed the apertures with magnesium foil.

Done with the tanks, Scott climbed out of the window to join Nicki once again. He flicked open his lighter, and a red glow sputtered up the fuse toward the windowsill. He smiled. "Bye-bye, Marty."

"Someone's coming!"

They ducked behind a row of shrubs as the bobbing pool of light from a pocket flashlight moved along the concrete path toward them.

Scott's eyes were riveted to the smoldering fuse as it inched closer to the window.

"The tanks are gonna blow," Nicki said in a panicked whisper.

"Shut up," Scott whispered back and pulled her into concealment as the motel clerk passed within a couple of feet of them, muttering under his breath. He rounded the corner at the end of the motel.

Scott grabbed Nicki's arm and dragged her across the patch of grass by the pool. They reached the row of trees at the far side of the pool as the clerk walked back into view. He surveyed the lighted pool briefly, and then he turned and started toward reception.

A shattering explosion laid the clerk out flat on his face. A ball of bright orange flame rose heavenward and lit up the night. Shrapnel thudded against the tree. Another tank went up, and then another, and another; the entire room was obliterated almost instantaneously. More tanks exploded. In moments, the adjacent room also blazed furiously.

Scott couldn't help smiling at the spectacle resulting from his ingenious plan. He ran over the bullet points for Nicki's next moves: Get to Jack before the real paramedics arrived, shoot him with Diazepam—enough to render him incoherent and out cold in a matter of minutes. He gloated. "By the time he comes to, the cops will have the wallet and identify him as Martin Brenner."

Anything Jack said to the contrary would be considered the ramblings of a man in shock.

*

THURSDAY, JULY 14

NICKI AND SCOTT arrived at the Lake Havasu General Hospital lot and parked close to the Mercedes, which a cop had thoughtfully transported there. They slept in alternating shifts until 5:00 a.m., and then Nicki went into reception and identified herself as a reporter for a local paper.

The duty receptionist was at the end of a long, dull night shift and only too happy to dish the details of the motel fire and its casualties: One fireman had been admitted for burns, two cops had minor scratches, and the young guy admitted for observation was still out cold. And the poor guy who'd been in the motel room when the tanks blew was plastered all over the countryside.

"So, the guy who's in for observation, when do you think he'll be released?" Nicki asked.

"We don't keep 'em any longer than we have to. Need the beds."

Jack would miss his call in Flagstaff; that much was guaranteed. Nicki settled herself by the big-screen TV in the lobby.

At seven, the morning news devoted all of two minutes to the motel fire—the third item in; the first dealt with the extreme temperatures for July.

Nicki waited. Her agenda was simple: If Jack protested he was anyone but Martin Brenner, she'd introduce herself as his wife, claim he was concussed, confused, get him out of there fast, and introduce him to Scott's more rugged persuasion. On the other hand, if he went for it and claimed to be Martin Brenner, they were a few moves ahead.

At eleven-fifty her cell rang. The assistant director on the Flagstaff western complained bitterly that her chosen actor, Jackson McCauley, had not turned up. Nicki's reply was succinct: "Get some local hick!"

At twelve-thirty, Jack emerged from the elevator and headed for the reception desk. He looked disoriented— there was no way for Nicki to tell which way he'd swing. She called Scott and talked him through Jack's every move—that he offered a brief argument to which the receptionist was oblivious, but then he signed papers, shoved Martin's overstuffed wallet into his pocket, and headed for the exit. Nicki followed at a discreet distance.

Outside, Scott and Nicki watched as Jack stood looking at the Mercedes for a few seconds before he opened the trunk and saw the suitcase.

Just then, a man in jeans and a sport jacket approached him.

"Fucking cops," Scott whispered.

The detective produced a plastic bag and very carefully took something that looked like photographs out of it. Eventually, he left. Jack turned back to the car, then walked slowly to the driver's side, opened the door, and got in.

"He's doing it!" Scott said slapping the steering wheel of the SUV joyously with the palm of his hand. "He's doing it!"

They followed Jack through the streets of Lake Havasu to the junction of I-95. There, he pulled over by a parked car and sat, idling. Scott stopped half a block behind.

"He's changed his mind," Nicki said.

"Wait."

"I *told* you."

"*Wait.*"

A minute later, a man in a gaudy shirt and baggy shorts approached the Mercedes and rapped on the window.

There was a brief exchange, and the Mercedes drove off, reached the highway intersection, paused, then turned left and headed south on I-95.

Chapter Twenty-Six

PHOENIX
MONDAY, NOVEMBER 7
6:32 P.M.

THUNDER RATTLED THE rotting boards of the derelict motel.

"Hey, Jacko, how's it hangin'?"

Jack sucked a breath audibly and held it. He fell against the wall and clamped his palms to it to steady himself. It was fully five seconds before he exhaled.

"Gained a little muscle! Lookin' good. You oughta be in the movies," the guy said with a wide grin. "Better sit down. Look like you seen a ghost."

Jack sat heavily on the edge of the bed. The guy was in a biker's leather jacket, tee, and jeans. His shock of thick blond hair had been shorn down to a buzz, but Jack recognized him unmistakably as Martin Brenner—the Martin Brenner who just as unmistakably had perished in the Crimson Desert Motel fire.

"So, how's life among the shitkickers? Been spending lotsa money, I hear—horses, parties. Gotta put a stop to that."

Jack was frozen, his throat dry, his heart pumping.

"Aww, I can see by the look on your handsome kisser you don't know what the fuck's going on, do you."

"No," Jack managed in a hoarse whisper.

"Let's put the kid in the picture." The guy turned to the laptop on the table before him and pressed a key. Jack's face filled the screen. A woman's voice accompanied the image, distant, echoed.

"Can you be in Flagstaff by noon tomorrow?"

"Flagstaff, Arizona?" Jack's image said.

A baritone sigh. "It's the only Flagstaff I know. It's not a big part. You'll have to get there on your own."

The man pressed Pause, and the image froze on Jack's jubilant smile. "Wanna see any more?"

Jack stared at the screen trying to understand, but

nothing made sense.

"Jesus, nobody ever said actors are the brightest bulbs in the billboard. But you, my man, are one dim fucker. You want it handed to you on a platter?" He pressed Play, and Jack's image came to life again, smiling in extreme close-up. A chair was heard scraping on the floor, followed by the *clack* of high heels—and then the casting director's voice as she left the sound stage.

"Be there twelve noon on the dot, or we'll have to cast a local." Nicki's voice.

"You set me up!"

"Give the guy a drink!" The man in the biker jacket poured a shot of vodka into the glass and pushed it across the desk. Jack grabbed the glass and drained it. Tears welled—part shock, part cheap vodka.

"How?" Jack asked.

"Long story!"

"*Why*?"

"Jack, my man, I can think of a million reasons. Around twenty-four million to be exact."

"But the money's yours!"

"Uh-uh. The money's Martin's."

Jack squinted at the face in the shadow. And, at last, he figured it out.

"You're the brother. You're Scott!"

"Bingo!"

"The fire—at the motel—that was…"

"Yep, that was ole Marty."

"You killed him."

"Nah, that was Nicki. Took a swing at him one night with a tire iron. Split his skull open."

The combination of stress and vodka churned Jack's stomach. "I think I'm going to be sick."

"Well, get it up, Jacko." Scott stood and tucked the Glock into the back of his jeans. "Gotta be at a wedding in fifteen minutes. Yours."

Jack got to his feet, stumbled, and nearly fell as he started for the door. "I'm going to the police."

"I don't think so. You've worked so damn hard to get all those hicks on that horse farm around to liking you. Think how they'll feel when they find out you killed Marty, stole his ID, and put yourself in line for twenty-four million bucks." He smiled confidently. "Nicki could be pretty convincing in a courtroom."

*

7:05 P.M.

SCOTT DROVE THEM west in the Mercedes to where the city met the low, barren hills. The acrid smell of an impending storm was evident, even inside the car. Lightning rent a uniformly ugly sky, followed almost instantly by a clap of thunder.

For most of the journey, Jack's mind was busy triggering defense mechanisms against shock, and twice, he blacked out only to jerk into consciousness a split second later to hear Scott chattering happily.

"…Trouble is, you were *too* good! You got to like playing the character. Three quarters of a million for a fuckin' horse? We figured we'd reached a point of no return, so we sent in the big guns." He let out an abrasive laugh. "And Christ knows, Nicki's got big guns!"

Bloated drops of rain splattered intermittently on the windshield, and Scott put the wipers on low.

"Ahhh, Nicki," Scott continued. "We sorta hoped you and her might hit it off without any help. We didn't count on you being a fag."

He turned the car into a neat suburban street and stopped at a bungalow with a manicured lawn and a solemn shingle which read:

JUSTICE of the PEACE
PUBLIC NOTARY
Marvin R. Jamieson

A shabby SUV was parked just ahead of them.

Scott turned to Jack and adopted a reasonable tone. "Look, Jacko, you'll make this a whole lot easier on yourself if you'll just be a good boy and get yourself hitched without a fuss. We'll cut you in. Think about it—you can go back to Hollywood, fire up your career again." He chuckled. "You'll have to do it under some other name since you used the old one up."

Jack was rigid and stared through the rain-blurred windshield, seeing nothing.

"Hey!" Scott went on. "You could even stay on in this shithole, seeing you like it so much. Go on playing Cowboys and Indians. Oops, Native Americans."

Jack's mouth was dry, his voice hoarse. "What if I just sign some of the money over to you?"

"Aw, that'd be nice Jack, but we don't want some of the money, we want all of it."

"I'll give you whatever you want if only you leave us alone."

"If only, Jack, if only," Scott said with a sympathetic smile. "Apart from the fact I don't trust you, how would it look if you suddenly gave a shitload of money to your ex-wife? People might talk." He glanced at the brightly lit shingle in front of the house. "Nah, there's something kinda binding about marriage, conjugal rights, that kinda thing."

He reached across Jack and opened the passenger door. "Showtime! Move your ass!"

"Listen," Jack said, "if I do this…"

"If? *If*!" Scott grabbed Jack's shirt and hauled him close. "Have you been listening to me? There's no fuckin' *if*."

"*If* I go through with this," Jack repeated firmly, "I want your assurance you'll leave Loretta and everyone at the ranch alone."

Scott pulled the gun from his jeans. "I'll give you *if*, faggot. I'm running this show. Now get your ass in there."

Jack remained still. Scott prodded him in the ribs with the gun.

"I don't want to have to do this before you're hitched."

"But you're going to kill me after," Jack said in a whisper.

Scott shrugged. "Not if you play your cards right."

Jack stumbled out of the car and walked unsteadily up the path to the front door. Scott sounded the horn, and in response, a woman with gray hair, dressed fussily and formally, opened the door. She smiled benevolently at Jack.

"Mr. Brenner? I'm Mrs. Jamieson. You'll get soaked! Come inside!" Jack moved into an over-decorated foyer where Nicki sat smoking. She'd dressed soberly for the occasion but still looked too glossy for the surroundings. She rose and searched for somewhere to put the cigarette out.

Mrs. Jamieson darted to a hall stand and snatched a glass vase from it. Nicki dropped the cigarette into it.

Visibly relieved at having saved her rug, Mrs. Jamieson turned to Jack. "Now, I have Nicole's details and the marriage license. I just need to see some ID from you, Mr. Brenner."

Nicki sidled up to him. "Show her your driver's license, babe."

When Jack didn't move, Nicki grabbed the lapel of his jacket, reached inside, and hauled his wallet out. She slid the license out and gave it to the woman.

"Is there a witness?" Mrs. Jamieson asked.

"Uh-uh," Nicki said. "I guess you'll have to be best man."

Mrs. Jamieson returned a coy giggle and ushered them into the living room where a bald man of sixty sat at a desk writing. He wore a gray suit plainly reserved for these occasions and rose to greet the party. Mrs. Jamieson did the honors.

"This is Mr. Brenner," she gurgled, "and the ex–Mrs. Brenner, who is the Mrs. Brenner to be!"

Mr. Jamieson beamed with good will. "It's not often I meet two people who want to remarry right after a divorce. Very romantic." He took a card from the desk while Mrs. Jamieson eased the couple into position. Mr. Jamieson cleared his throat and read from the card.

"We gather here to celebrate one of life's greatest moments and give recognition to the worth and beauty of love, as you are joined together, once again, in matrimony. You are the most laudable of lovers in that you seek a second chance for happiness, and—"

Nicki sighed. "Could we cut to the chase?"

Jamieson paused for a moment to digest the request, then obligingly turned his card over and read from the other side.

"Do you, Nicole, take Martin to be your husband? Do you promise to love, honor, and cherish him, forsaking all others, as long as you—"

"I do."

"Do you, Martin Brenner, take Nicole to be your wife? Do you promise to love, honor, and cherish her, forsaking all others, as long as you both shall live?" Jamieson looked up at Jack, whose whole body was rigid, his fists clenched.

As long as you both shall live.

"Are you all right, Mr. Brenner?"

"Stage fright," Nicki said.

"The response is 'I do,'" Jamieson prompted.

"I do," Jack said, barely audible.

"The ring?"

"Got the ring, babe?" Nicki asked sweetly.

Jack closed his eyes tight; a tear escaped and rolled down his cheek.

Mrs. Jamieson's gaze followed the tear's journey, and she uttered a heartfelt, "Aww."

"The ring," Nicki said firmly.

Jack opened his fist. The silver ring, the sole evidence he had of his mother, glinted in the overhead light of the living room; glancing down at it, the bittersweet longing of Jack's entire life actually to have known his mother overwhelmed him.

Nicki held out her left hand, and after a long moment, Jack slipped the ring from his finger and put it onto hers. Third finger, left hand. It was a loose fit, but Nicki closed her fist, determined to keep it there.

"Insomuch as you have agreed to be joined…" Jamieson droned on, but Jack barely heard. "…power vested in me…declare you to be…you may kiss the bride."

Jack didn't move. Nicki leaned forward and pecked him on the cheek, then wiped a smudge of crimson lipstick off him with her thumb.

"Congratulations!" Mrs. Jamieson said, joy in her voice. "Now we have a little paperwork."

"And there's the will. Don't forget the will," Jamieson said.

"Will?" Jack whispered.

Nicki shrugged. "Guy's a notary. Thought we could kill two birds, know what I mean?"

"Always good for young marrieds to establish a will. In the event of the unforeseen," Jamieson said.

Jack barely saw the paper they passed before him. It stated, of course, that in the event of Jack's demise, all property, possessions, and monies would be Nicki's.

Jack signed.

The Jamiesons escorted the newlyweds to the front door and onto the porch. Rain fell steadily now.

Mrs. Jamieson beamed at the couple. "We hope you'll be very, very happy!" A jagged spear of lightning was followed at once by a clap of thunder, and the Jamiesons darted inside, closing the door on the joyous events of the evening.

Nicki took Jack's hand and ran to where Scott waited in the car. Scott exited the Merc and threw the keys to Jack. Nicki let herself into the passenger seat and examined the rain spots on her dress as Jack got behind the driver's.

"Aren't you going with him?" Jack asked.

"I'm going home with my husband," Nicki said sweetly. "Gotta keep up appearances."

"Got the certificate?" Scott asked, and Nicki patted her pocketbook. "You'll need it when you go see Adams. Call me later."

Scott started the SUV and yelled out the window, "Don't use the house phone!"

Jack watched Scott drive off before he started the Merc. He drove back to the ranch without exchanging a word with Nicki. She dozed most of the way, snoring faintly.

*

8:49 P.M.

"YOU WIPE YOU goddamn feet you come in the house!" Consuela's voice shrilled in anger. She blocked the way forward for Nicki, who stood in the doorway dripping water.

"Fuck you, you fuckin' wetback. This is my house now. You take orders from me."

"Leave her alone," Jack begged.

Nicki pushed Consuela out of her way. "Bitch."

"*You* bitch, lady. Not Consuela."

Jack reached out to Consuela, either to comfort her, or to shut her up, even he wasn't sure. She shook her head angrily and took off at a heavy stride down the long hallway.

Nicki crossed the lobby and headed for the staircase. Jack stumbled after and took her by the shoulders, spinning her around to face him.

"You've got what you want," he said. "Give me some assurance you'll leave us alone."

"Get your hands off me! You're hurting me."

"It's not too late for me to go to the police."

Nicki laughed abrasively. "Oh boy, I'd love to know what you're gonna tell 'em. You're not in a movie now, you dumbass fairy."

"I'll kill you," Jack said steadily with menace.

Nicki's laugh mocked this.

"*I mean it.* You harm anyone in this house, *I'll kill you.*"

Nicki's laugh echoed around the high space above the lobby as she pulled free and started up the stairs. "Jesus, you're a pussy." At the top of the stairs, she half turned back to Jack. "I'll be talking to your lawyer in the morning. He'll need copies of the certificate and the will. Be there, don't be there, I could give a rat's." She went into Amy's room and slammed the door shut.

Jack stood motionless, his head devoid of rational thought, unable to compute the events of the night or a way forward. When a glimmer of reason returned, it was about Loretta. He hurried down the hallway and let himself quietly into the den.

The quilt had been pushed onto the floor by the sofa where she slept quietly. Jack picked it up and covered her gently, with care. Then he fell into the chair by the tall window and sat, exhausted, resting his head back against the soft leather. He closed his eyes, and fragments of the sights and sounds of the last few hours instantly invaded his mind.

...look like you've seen a ghost...

...cracked his skull open...

...now declare you to be Husband and Wife...

...as long as you both shall live...

...as long as you both shall live...

...as long as you both...

He opened his eyes. Loretta was watching him. He sat upright. "I didn't mean to wake you."

"So," Loretta said coolly, "how's married life?"

"Could you hear what we...?"

Loretta's cool segued into anger. "I told you to talk to *me* before you did anything dumb!"

"Don't. Don't ask me to explain."

"And did I hear mention of a *will* by any chance?"

"Please, Loretta."

"I don't know what she's got on you, and I..."

"I'll *tell* you what she's got on me!" Jack erupted, fully prepared to confess.

Loretta overrode his. "What's important is she's got you by the balls. She wants the ranch, the money, and given your idiotic compliance, she now has her clutches into all of us. All this"—she gestured widely—"the house, the property, the Wyatt name, the tradition, the money, the art, the fucking chair you're sitting on—it's hers! She has the power to destroy…" She searched for a word. "…everything!"

Pitifully depleted by Loretta's attack, Jack drew an audible breath to prevent dissolving into sobs.

Loretta relented. "Oh God. Come here!"

He went to the sofa. She grabbed his shirt and pulled him down into an awkward embrace.

"Fucking greenhorn," she whispered. She held on a moment longer, then let him go. "Go. Get some sleep. I've got a lot of thinking to do."

Jack started to speak.

"Go!"

Jack shuffled out of the room and closed the door quietly. He stood in the hallway for some time, incapable of clear thought. He turned toward the lobby, the staircase, and contemplated the cocoon of the yellow bedroom, but his feet refused to obey so simple a command as *walk*.

Diego.

He needed the solid assurance Diego emanated, the proximity of the man, a friend, an ally who would not question his motives.

He went through the morning room and opened the back door. The rain had slowed to a misty drizzle. Far across the field, a light burned in Diego's cabin. Jack crossed the field, trudged past the dark stable, and climbed the low rise until he reached the cabin door. He hesitated for a moment, trying to control his breathing, unaware that the drizzle had all but wet him through. He knocked. The door opened almost at once, and Diego stood facing him. He wore only baggy sweatpants and held a book, but when he saw the anxiety in Jack's eyes, he dropped the book, took Jack's arm and led him inside.

"I don't want to impose…" Jack began.

Diego put a finger to his lips and sat Jack on the sofa. He darted into the bathroom and brought back two towels. He pointed to Jack's shirt and waited patiently until Jack had removed it before gently stripping off his sodden jeans. As Jack dried himself, Diego reached for the bottle on the low wooden coffee table and poured a shot of bourbon into the accompanying glass. Jack took the drink and downed it in one. He coughed as the liquor burned. Diego poured a second shot and handed it to Jack. This one, Jack sipped. Diego took the folded blanket from the end of the sofa and spread it around Jack's shoulders.

Jack felt obliged to offer an explanation, though Diego gave no indication of wanting or needing one. "Everything—everything's a mess."

That seemed a monumental understatement. Diego's dark, steady gaze didn't waver from Jack's eyes. Jack suddenly realized tears were flowing freely down his cheeks.

He had no idea how they'd started. That Diego could not offer a verbal response spurred Jack into a confessional free-fall.

"That woman—she's not...she's nothing to me. She never was. I don't know her. I never knew her. They set me up. They used me. The ranch, Loretta—I've ruined it all. I have no idea what to do." He stopped and took a wheezing breath as he realized just how much information he'd given Diego.

Diego reached out and brushed tears from Jack's cheek with his fingers. Jack was startled, not by the gesture, but by the gentleness of Diego's touch.

"I'm sorry." Jack lowered his head. "I don't want to lay all my shit on you. Not like this." But Diego hadn't taken his hand from Jack's cheek. "Of all people, I never wanted to lie to you. You've given me nothing but support. You—your friendship." His voice became a broken whisper. "You mean so much to me."

Jack looked up as Diego's gaze remained fixed on him. The hand on Jack's cheek moved slowly to the back of his head and drew it close. Diego kissed Jack's lips. Gently. Very gently.

Jack welcomed the kiss, gave in to it completely, aware of how much he needed this man, how much he felt for him, how much he'd longed for this intimacy. But when they parted, the floodgates opened. Jack wept, painfully, unable to control the wracking sobs. Diego pulled him into a tight embrace and held him, rocked him gently as one would a child. Jack wrapped his arms about Diego's broad shoulders and felt—comforted, secure, safe. For the first time since this lunatic stunt began, someone with a strength he might never know in himself was there for him.

After some time, the tears subsided and utter exhaustion overwhelmed him. Diego lifted him easily from the sofa and carried him into the bedroom. He lay Jack on the bed and covered him with a comforter. Then, sure Jack was warm and comfortable, he stroked Jack's hair as Jack sank into a deep sleep.

Sometime during the night, he thought he heard a door open and close, but his mind dismissed it as a dream.

Chapter Twenty-Seven

IN AMY'S BEDROOM, Nicki pushed the neat array of sil-ver-backed brushes and combs to the edge of the dresser, paused, then thought, *what the fuck*, and continued the mo-tion. The items clattered to the floor. A hand mirror cracked. *Seven years bad luck*. She smiled. *Not!*

She found her makeup case stowed on the floor of the armoire, packed as if with a battering ram and cursed the Mexican bitch, thinking of the keen pleasure she'd take in firing her ass. As she undressed, Nicki reflected on the events of the evening. After the chore of tying the knot with the dumber-than-dumb faggot, she felt she was in the homestretch.

She slipped into her cream silk robe and admired herself in the dresser mirror. Money had never come easily to Nicki; what little had come her way had often been the direct result of the figure she was now giving the once-over.

Her parents, moderately well-off Philadelphians, had made their money in real estate. Her father was a rigid conservative, so it really shouldn't have come as a surprise that, on discovering she was sleeping with his business associate, he kicked her out of the house.

Business Associate left wife and family and trailed Nicki to New York, where she found work as a temp receptionist at a prominent talent agency. Business Associate didn't fare so well and, unable to bring himself to take employment unequal to his former status, languished in their cramped studio apartment on the lower East Side until his money ran out. Nicki quickly tired of paying the bills and just as quickly formed an alliance with a senior executive at the agency. Business Associate returned to Philadelphia, presumably to wife and kids—Nicki neither inquired nor cared.

Now, the agency senior executive's wife became antsy and gave her husband the old me-or-her alternative. He chose the "me," and the "her," Nicki, was put on a plane to Los Angeles with a reasonable payoff and a glowing letter of introduction to a casting agency. The work and the climate agreed with her. Casting actors in TV series and in minor movies was no tough call, and the feeling of power, particularly over men, gave her a warm and fuzzy feeling.

When she met Martin Brenner—twenty-four, tall, good-looking advertising exec on the way up—she was impressed; and when he asked her to marry him, she said yes without hesitation. After all, he was a good catch and would be at the top of his tree in no time.

They were a show couple, Martin with his blond hair and dark-blue eyes and Nicki with her almost natural red hair, perfect figure, and stylish couture. And for a while, the party crowd couldn't get enough of them.

But less than a year into the marriage, the nightly socializing began to tell on the daily routine, and vice versa, and life became simply dull. Perhaps the most irritating thing about their marriage was that there was never enough money to buy the things she wanted. She amused herself with a low-level guy at the agency and conducted the occasional casting couch liaisons with actors. If Martin cared, he didn't show it. Maybe he was screwing around too. She never asked.

Then Scott came along.

Tough and attractive, there was something excitingly dangerous about him. Scott was a go-ahead kind of guy, albeit with a wanted sign over his head. Nicki knew from experience *that* was the kind of guy who'd stop at nothing, *really* nothing, to get what he wanted. The kind of guy a girl like Nicki was invented for.

Looking back, after the trauma of the event had faded, she'd begun to think of Martin's death as no more than a glitch in the scheme of things. Considering the way Scott had turned the incident to their advantage, she'd done herself a favor by slugging her ex with that tire iron.

And now that she'd installed herself in the Wyatt house, antediluvian pile though it was, things were even better. The laws governing marriage would provide her with all the money she needed to give her life meaning. She was married to the actor sucker, and she had the will which left a shitload of money to her. Would she need Scott? Given a quiet afternoon, she could probably think of ways to pry Scott's share from him.

If necessary, over his dead body.

She reached deep into her makeup bag and took out the gold necklet—her wedding present to Martin way back when and which Scott had appropriated upon Marty's demise.

"Insurance," Scott had said.

She got it: Should their plan go awry, all she had to do was to plant the thing on Jack and let him take the fall for Marty's murder. But, oh, what a waste of something expensive, beautiful, gold, and glittery. She held it up to her neck, gazed at her reflection, and sighed.

Shit. He said to call him.

She dialed Scott's number on the phone by the bed but stopped short of connecting.

Don't use the house phone.

And somehow, a phone call wasn't the same without a cigarette. She shoved the cigarette pack and her lighter into one pocket of her robe and the necklet into the other.

The faint rustle of her silk robe was the only sound as she descended the grand oak staircase.

She found her way down the dark hallway, past the living room, and into the morning room. Here, she turned on a lamp at the bar and reached for her cigarettes—but the echo of her spat with Loretta made her hesitate. The logical place to have a smoke was outside. She went to the back door, relieved to find the rain had stopped, the sky clearing.

The stable would be nice and dry. And private. She could weather the stink of horse dung if it meant a hit of nicotine. And none of the hicks would overhear her conversation. The spill from the bar lamp was sufficient to light her way as she darted across the terrace onto the paved path to the stable door.

She slipped inside and found a light switch. A single bare bulb lit a stack of hay bales by a stall wall, located at the opposite end to where the horses were smelling up the place, so this was the obvious place to sit. She caught sight of rain spots on her pretty silk robe and cursed. But hey, soon she could buy a dozen silk robes. She sat on a bale and, at last, lit a cigarette and took a long, deep drag. The only sound she could hear over the rain was the rhythmic breathing of the horses in the stalls.

How the fuck do they sleep standing up? she wondered briefly as she took out her cell and entered Scott's number. It rang for some time, and then voicemail picked up.

"Where *are* you? You said *call*." She waited a moment and figured Scott must've turned his phone off.

"I'm out in the barn, and it stinks in here. I hate this fucking dump. It's like living in a museum. I'm going to sell it, soon as I can. Soon as it's mine." She paused. "And yours," she added to reassure Scott, though she didn't mean it. "I want to see that bitch Loretta out on her ass."

She took a long drag on the cigarette.

"And listen, I think the fag actor is gonna be a problem. I mean, a *big* problem. He keeps talking about going to the cops. Maybe—we should think about—shutting him up? She paused to give this suggestion weight. "For good." Another pause in case Scott missed the point and to let him think he called the shots. "Think about it, babe."

Another drag on the cigarette.

"I'll go along with whatever you come up with. I mean, you figured everything out great after I...after...I had the accident with Martin."

Another drag—enough time to let Scott's mental wheels grind into action.

"Okay, I'm wrecked. I'm going to bed. Call me in the morning." She considered adding, "Love you, babe," then thought better of it and disconnected.

She took a final drag and stood, looking for somewhere to put the cigarette out. She cleared strands of hay from the floor with her foot, dropped the butt onto a tile, and ground it under her slipper. As she rose and turned to the light switch, she put the phone into a pocket of her robe and, finding the gold necklet there, drew it out and admired it. She turned it over in her hand. Scott's directive made sense: "Insurance." But oh, so hard to let go of something as pretty, as expensive. Never again, she vowed, would she ever let wealth, no matter how paltry, slip through her fingers.

She neither heard nor sensed that anyone else was in the stable, so as she reached for the light switch, the solid impact of something sharp as it entered her back surprised her more than it hurt. The wind was knocked out of her, and when she tried to draw breath, found she couldn't.

The instrument that had attacked her was pulled free, and she jerked around. Her assailant stood just a couple of feet before her holding a pitchfork. Light glinted on the sharp tines as the fork was drawn back for another thrust. She held up a hand, the hand that clutched the gold necklet, to ward off the blow, but the fork plunged into her.

Her knees buckled, and she slid down the stable wall into a heap. She glanced down at her pretty silk gown as blood flowed freely from four holes just below her left breast. As life deserted her, one final, feeble thought crossed her mind:

The stain will never come out.

Chapter Twenty-Eight

TUESDAY, NOVEMBER 8
6:15 A.M.

JACK WAS DREAMING of his mother, the mother he'd never known. He sensed her smiling at him even though in this dream, as in others he'd had of her, she had no face.

In the dream, Jack was a child, and the faceless woman held his hand and led him through heavy traffic. Cars sped by, heedless of mother and child. A police siren pierced the air, and the woman began to run in an effort to get away from it. She let go of Jack's hand and ran on while he was frozen to the spot in the middle of a busy highway. He called out to her—and woke.

The siren continued. Somewhere in the waking world, a police car was approaching.

His watch read 6:20. He pushed the blanket away. He was naked. And in an alien bed—memory flooded back—Diego's bed. His clothing, soaked in the downpour of the night before, hung neatly over a rack by the freshly primed fire. His recollection was fogged by the heavy sleep of someone in shock. Then the memory of Diego's kiss returned and nearly overwhelmed him with emotion.

This man whom he so admired and respected cared for him. A man whose many strengths made Jack's tenuous hold on integrity seem even more feeble, a man for whom he desperately wanted to be himself. But what would Diego make of Jack McCauley? This was a man to whom honor meant everything, a man who would not have taken a leap of familiarity if it were not heartfelt. Jack knew there'd be no peace in a relationship with Diego, no future, if there was no honesty.

Nicki and Scott.

Maybe if he got to Miller first, confessed everything, accepted the consequences, he could preempt whatever accusations they might make. Jack hoped that among whatever of his scruples he might salvage, there'd be courage.

He called out for Diego. No response. He rose, used the

bathroom, and dressed, his mind churning, and went into the kitchen. Here, prominently placed on the kitchen table sat a blender filled with one of Diego's protein shakes—fruit, soy milk, protein powder, malt. A notepad page lay beside it, again with the instruction in marker ink: DRINK!

Jack smiled and drank, warmed by Diego's gesture of care.

He exited the cabin. The air was fresh and clean after the rain, the sky an unclouded blue. He started toward the house but faltered as he saw the two police cars that had cut across the lawn and parked on the muddy ground by the stable. A police officer was reeling out yellow tape at the stable doors.

A man emerged, slipped under the tape, and caught sight of Jack. In his late forties, dark, and heavyset, he wore an ill-fitting gray suit. Judging by his size and shape, he could've been a professional wrestler, but the badge he flashed defined him as a police detective.

"Mr. Brenner?"

Jack nodded.

"Detective Ian Cassell, Phoenix Police Department. I wonder if you'd make an identification for me?"

"Identification?"

The detective didn't reply but started back toward the stable. Jack followed. They squelched across the damp lawn, over the caked mud, and Cassell lifted the yellow tape to admit them to the stable. A man in what looked like hospital scrubs crouched over something in a corner near the door; a camera flashed as he took picture after picture.

Bewildered by the profusion of police, the determined activity, Jack asked, "What's going on? What's happened?"

Diego stood at the far end of the stable. Catching sight of Jack, he touched his lips briefly, a seemingly casual gesture Jack instantly interpreted as "say nothing."

At a word from Cassell, the crouched man lowered his camera and moved aside.

Nicki lay in a pool of blood, knees bent, one arm at her side, the other clutching the front of her silk robe in a parody of modesty. Rivulets of congealed blood traced patterns on her robe from their sources at her throat and breast. Her head fell unnaturally to one side; her eyes were open and stared, without surprise, at nothing.

Jack's knees buckled. Cassell took him by the shoulders and kept him upright.

"Is this Nicole Brenner?" Cassell asked.

There was no hint of the swagger, the brash confidence, the vulgarity that had defined Nicki in life. In death, she had a vulnerability Jack had never seen before.

Cassell asked again, evenly, "Is this Nicole Brenner?"

Jack uttered a feeble, "Yes."

He watched as a uniformed officer in rubber gloves carried off a pitchfork carefully, between forefingers and thumbs. Dried blood caked its tines.

"I'm sorry we had to spring it on you this way," Cassell said with the merest hint of sympathy. He beckoned to a sturdy female officer and instructed her to escort Jack to the house.

Jack trudged across the damp grass, numb and unsure if he could place one foot in front of the other. Several times, he faltered, and the officer reached to support him but never made contact.

In the morning room, a young female officer was taking Loretta's fingerprints. Loretta sat erect allowing her fingers to be manipulated with no more than tolerance. Consuela stood guard by her chair, her face stony in accord with the circumstances, but as Jack steadied himself against the bar, she inclined her head toward him.

"I get you something to eat, Mr. Martin?"

Given what he'd just seen, the thought turned his stomach. He shook his head.

"I bring coffee," Consuela said, then added to Jack, confidentially, "My niece, she have a boy. We gonna name him Martin, after you."

"Consuela, get out of here," Loretta said.

Unoffended, Consuela left the room.

The younger police officer turned her attention to Jack. He barely felt the pressure as she pressed finger after finger onto pad and paper. Meanwhile, Loretta took a mirror and a small cosmetics bag from the bar and began to apply makeup. When finished with Jack, the officer packed her fingerprint kit carefully into a vinyl case and left the room.

Jack shuffled to the bar and poured water from a pitcher into a glass and drained it in one.

He caught Loretta's brief and unreadable glance at him, no more than a flicker of her eyes, and then she returned her attention to her reflection. She wiped a minuscule smudge of lipstick from the corner of her mouth, then put the mirror and her makeup on the bar.

Now Loretta turned to Jack with a query in her expression.

"I spent the night— I passed out in Diego's cabin."

"I know." She darted a glance to the windows. Jack followed her gaze and saw Cassell and the sturdy female officer emerge from the stable and start across the lawn toward the house.

"This marriage," Loretta said. "I need proof."

"Proof?"

"A certificate. Anything."

"Yes, there's a certificate. And the will. Nicki kept them with her."

The hall door opened, and Consuela wheeled in a cart with coffee pot and cups and a plate brimming with incongruously festive-looking cookies. She anchored it by Loretta's chair.

Loretta kept her eyes on the approaching Cassell as she spoke quietly and firmly. "Consuela, go to Mr. Martin's room and move his things, all his personal things, into Amy's room."

"'Scuse?"

"His toiletries, his clothes, his shorts, socks, whatever you can find—put them on the bed, in the closet, on the dresser."

"With the bitch stuff?"

"*Do it. Now.* Before the police get up there."

Cassell tapped lightly on one of the glass doors. Jack stiffened. Loretta took his hand and held it tight enough to cut off circulation.

"You were here with me, all night," she said. "This morning, you went up to Diego's cabin to discuss extensions to the stable, but he'd already gone down there. Unknown to you, he and one of the hands discovered the body." Jack had no time to react as she continued in an intense whisper, "I'll do the talking." Jack tried to pull his hand free, but she held fast. "*I mean it.* And if you have to speak, follow my lead."

Cassell tapped again.

Consuela's eyes darted uncertainly from the terrace to Loretta and back again. "You want I open the door?"

Loretta let go of Jack's hand and nodded to Consuela.

The housekeeper slid open the glass door and greeted the detective with a curt, "Wipe you feet!" When he'd done so, she allowed him to come in. The female officer needed no prompting. Visibly daunted by Consuela's glare, she wiped her feet vigorously. Satisfied propriety had been served, Consuela turned to the hall door.

"Don't leave the house," Cassell called after her. "I'll need to talk to you again."

"I tell you everythin' I know!" Consuela said belligerently. "I dunno *nothin'!*" And she stormed out muttering, "*Cerdos!*" slamming the door behind her.

Cassell looked shaken.

"We're all a little rattled I'm afraid," Loretta said. "This has been a great shock. To all of us. Sit, please." She looked cool, her tone was gracious. Jack marveled at her poise. "Would you care for some coffee?"

"I wouldn't mind," Cassell said as he eased himself into an armchair.

She offered none to the policewoman stationed at the door.

"Are the horses all right?" Loretta asked as she poured.

"They're fine." Cassell accepted a cup from Loretta but declined a cookie. "Your man, Diego, is taking care of them. He's taking all this very calmly."

"Diego takes everything calmly."

Cassell nodded as if adding this to some database in his mind.

"He's an Afghanistan vet," Loretta added to qualify Diego's calm.

"We understand he'd never met the, uh" —a glance to Jack—"deceased."

Loretta took Jack's hand and squeezed it in a visible gesture of comfort. "Diego keeps to his part of the property. Nicki and Martin have been here in the house in the few days she—in the short time she was with us." Then, with an ingenuousness that surprised Jack, she asked, "Are you absolutely certain it wasn't an accident?"

"We're certain."

"Who could've done something so—" She searched for a word. "—monstrous?"

"That's what we want to find out, Ms. Dalstrom. There are no fingerprints on the weapon. None. There's no sign of a struggle and no attempt to make it look like an accident. It looks exactly like what it is—murder."

Loretta shook her head sorrowfully in grim acceptance of the vile deed that had been committed in her stable. "She was so sweet. She was one of the family." Her voice broke, and she wiped at an eye with a tissue, but not so it would smudge her mascara. "Everyone she met just adored her."

"That's not the impression I got from your maid."

"Consuela doesn't adore anyone," Loretta said flatly.

Cassell settled his cup on the table by his chair and took a notebook from his pocket. He glanced up at Jack, who made a great effort to stem tears and failed.

"I'm sorry, Mr. Brenner. I realize this is painful for you. I believe you and the deceased were about to be married for a second time."

Jack opened his mouth to reply, but Loretta squeezed his hand again in a gesture designed to look comforting, but her grip was a vise.

"We had a big celebration planned," she said as if the light had gone out of her life. "But my nephew always hated all that show, didn't you, darling?" Jack managed a feeble nod. "He crept off with Nicki last night, and they were married in secret."

Cassell's eyebrows lifted. "Last night?"

Loretta glanced up at Jack with sympathetic warmth. "You thought I'd be upset, being left out, but I know how you and Nicki felt about each other." A tear started at the corner of her eye, and she promptly wiped it away with a finger. She turned back to Cassell. "When he came in last night to tell me about the wedding, I was overjoyed, wasn't I, sweetheart."

Jack managed to nod again. Cassell made a note on his pad.

"Where was the ceremony?" he asked.

Loretta turned to Jack and took his hand as if to cue him.

"Justice of the Peace," Jack whispered.

"You have a certificate, I presume?"

"She—Nicki kept it," Jack said.

Loretta released Jack's hand, then patted his clenched fist gently. "I'm sure it's in their room." She inclined her head to the policewoman. "First door, top of the stairs."

Cassell nodded to the policewoman, who went out through the hall door almost on tiptoe. "You say you didn't leave the house last night, Ms. Dalstrom."

Loretta indicated her bandaged ankle. "I couldn't. I was in agony. The doctor forbade me to climb the stairs. I was comfortable in the den."

Cassell turned to Jack. Loretta anticipated his question.

"My nephew was with me," she said. "All night."

Cassell turned to Jack. "You stayed down here? On your wedding night?"

Loretta smiled as she might to a schoolboy ill-versed in matters of sex. "Not only were they married for some years, they've been sleeping in the same bed since Nicki arrived. I doubt that the mysteries of a wedding night were exactly sacrosanct."

Cassell looked mildly embarrassed. "When you went into the den to see your aunt, did your wife accompany you?"

Loretta looked up at Jack—this one was all his.

"No, she—was tired." His voice was little more than a whisper, and Cassell leaned forward to hear. Jack cleared his throat. "She was tired. She went straight upstairs. I—went to the den and, uh…" Loretta winced and massaged her leg. "My aunt was in pain. I decided to sit with her a while. I must've dozed off."

Cassell considered this. "But you weren't here when we arrived this morning."

"I needed to talk to Diego about—work we're doing on the stable. He wasn't in his cabin." He felt he was reading a script, making rote words seem spontaneous. "I—found the blueprints on his desk and went over them. I don't really know how long I worked there. Then I heard the police sirens and…" He lowered his head, knowing it would make him an object of sympathy. The bogus screentest popped into his mind. Expressing loss was his specialty. He'd done it then; he did it now.

A degree of sympathy was indeed in Cassell's tone

when he spoke again. "Any idea why Mrs. Brenner went to the stable in the middle of the night?"

"She must've been worried about the horses," Loretta said. "She loved them. Particularly the new stallion—she was so fond of that horse."

Cassell looked from one to the other. After a moment, he reached into the pocket of his bomber and took out a small, clear, ziplock bag. Inside was a gold necklet. "Have either of you seen this before?"

Jack swallowed hard. Of course he'd seen it before. On Scott when he was impersonating Martin. Loretta reached for the bag.

"Don't remove it," Cassell warned.

Loretta took the bag and turned it over to examine the necklet.

"It was found on the victim. She had it clutched in her hand." Cassell's eyes moved between them, waiting for a reaction. "How about you, Mr. Brenner? Have you seen this before?"

Loretta passed the bag to Jack, but his hands were icy fists, and he couldn't take it from her.

Yes, he'd seen it before. On Martin—only Martin was really…

"Scott!" Jack blurted. "Scott was wearing it."

"Scott?"

"Martin's brother," Loretta said as if she'd bitten on a lemon.

Cassell looked from Loretta to Jack patiently, waiting for one of them to expound. Jack looked down at Loretta and noted the steel behind the welling tears. He took the cue.

"Nicki and Scott had an affair. That's why—we divorced."

"Yet you decided to remarry?"

Loretta leapt in. "It was all over between Nicki and that bastard! But maybe Scott didn't think so."

"I take it you're not fond of your nephew Scott."

"He's wanted by the FBI for smuggling drugs. You probably know that."

"No," Cassell said with some surprise, "I didn't."

Loretta got a grip on her emotions with visible effort. "When Martin was named in my sister's will, Scott started making a nuisance of himself. He turned up in my attorney's office trying to extort money."

Jack supposed the temptation to relay the juicy story to Loretta must've been too hard for Maggie to resist, in spite of her insistence on confidentiality.

"I'll need to talk to your attorney."

"He'll tell you all about Scott Brenner," Loretta said bitterly as she wrote Adams's address and phone numbers. "I can only imagine he was insanely jealous when he heard Nicki and Martin were getting married again. You should be out there looking for him," Loretta said passionately. "I know I'd feel a lot safer if he was behind bars." She turned in the direction of the stable. "Especially after—this."

"We're not jumping to any conclusions, nor should you."

There was a tap at the hall door. Cassell stood as the policewoman entered and passed folded documents to Cassell. Jack recognized them as the marriage certificate and the will.

Cassell raised his eyebrows. "A will?"

Loretta glanced up at Jack—this one was all his.

"My attorney advised us to establish a prenup agreement. It seemed like—I don't know..." he said wistfully. "It seemed like a lack of trust between us. I thought it best to prove just what I felt for Nicki by making a will in her favor."

Cassell considered this, nodded, and slipped the documents into the back of his notepad. "I hope you don't mind if I hold on to these for a while." He gave Loretta and Jack a mildly reassuring smile. "We don't want you to leave the house until we've investigated thoroughly. I hope it's not too much of an inconvenience. I'll station an officer. Just in case your nephew Scott comes by."

"So you think he *will* come back here?" Loretta said, her voice breaking with anxiety. "Even after committing this horrendous…"

Cassell sighed patiently. "Ms. Dalstrom, don't assume anything until we have more information. Obviously, we need to move as quickly as possible without leaking anything. I've instructed my people to say nothing to the media, and I would ask the same of you and all your employees. Can your ranch hands be trusted?"

"My nephew hired them," Loretta said evenly as she took Jack's hand. "If he trusts them, I do."

"And your head man Diego?"

"He won't say a word."

Jack searched her face for a hint of irony but found none.

"Diego is more than a hired hand," Loretta added. "He's the most trustworthy person on the planet."

Cassell headed for the French doors, and Jack followed to open one for him.

"About my—about Nicki," Jack said. "I gave her a ring, last night, when we were—married. I didn't see it just now when I…"

"A ring?"

"A silver ring. We used it as a wedding ring."

"There was no ring. All we found on her was the

necklet, a pack of cigarettes, and a lighter." Cassell went out onto the terrace and started across the lawn.

Loretta watched him go. "I told that bitch not to smoke in the stable."

"Do you think Scott killed Nicki?"

Loretta didn't take her eyes from the departing detective. "Go take a shower."

"But why? Without Nicki, he has no way of getting money or the ranch." Jack took a determined breath. He was on the verge of confessing his identity. "If Scott talks…" Words petered out, and he swept a trembling hand across his forehead.

Loretta turned to him, watched him for a moment, then said quietly, "Take a shower. You're starting to smell up the place."

Chapter Twenty-Nine

AS INSTRUCTED, CONSUELA had strewn most of Jack's personal things around the main bedroom and intermingled them artfully with Nicki's, giving the impression of cohabitation. But Jack couldn't bring himself to shower in a bathroom where Nicki's perfume still hung in the air. He took refuge in the yellow bedroom and showered in the en suite. He stood in the stream of warm water for some time contemplating his situation.

Loretta's dissembling on his behalf was indication enough that if the truth of his relationship with Nicki were known, he'd be elevated from grieving husband to "person of interest." And once forced to reveal his actual identity, he'd come under the scrutiny of Detective Miller in the death of Martin Brenner. Either way, he'd painted himself into a corner. But Loretta was defending him, providing him with an alibi. Did she think *he* killed Nicki?

He dressed—not in Martin Brenner's expensive wardrobe, but in Jack McCauley's old jeans and denim shirt; it seemed the only honest thing he could do under the circumstances.

Jack stayed put while the police searched the house and then watched from the bedroom window as the squad cars and the coroner's van drove away from the house in slow tandem, belatedly respectful of Nicki Brenner. A lone police officer remained, trudging the gravel drive patiently, occasionally touching a hand to his holster as if to ensure it still held a weapon.

Jack found Loretta in the den, seated at a table with a set of solitaire laid out before her. A side table held a plate of cold cuts.

"I should've told the police everything."

Loretta didn't look up. "We'll figure this out for ourselves. Eat."

"I've got to do *something*."

"You can get me a drink."

Jack glanced at the grandfather clock. "It's only two-thirty."

"So call AA."

Jack poured two shots of scotch and handed one to Loretta, who took a hefty sip. She set her glass down on the desk and glared at Jack until he forced a couple slices of ham into his mouth. Still, Loretta glared. Jack added some cheese cubes to his meal.

Satisfied, Loretta turned her attention to a small candy-pink slab Jack recognized as Nicki's cell phone. "Diego took it before the cops got to the body," she explained matter-of-factly. "He thought it might come in handy." She held the phone out to Jack, "Call him."

"*Call* him?"

"Let him know just what kind of a hard place he's in. He'll lie, he'll bluff, he'll tell you the bogeyman killed her — he has a blue ribbon in lying. Just be cool and make him an offer in return for his getting out of the country."

"If he leaves, they'll assume he's guilty."

Loretta merely looked at him as if he was pointlessly stating the obvious. "I just want him out of the way so he can't cause any more damage."

"Maybe we should let the police…"

Loretta shot Jack a fierce glance that rooted him to the spot. "Listen! They arrest him, he'll squeal like a stuck pig. Pay him off, get him out of town."

Jack thought about the harm the truth would do to

Loretta and, an instant later, was surprised to realize it was his first thought. Not about *his* safety, *his* integrity, but about this woman he'd come to respect.

Jack took the pink cell phone. "It's unlocked," he noted with surprise.

"Diego's a man of many talents."

"Wait." Jack held up the phone. "If Scott killed her, why didn't he take this with him?"

"I neither know nor care! But soon as it hits him that he has no claim on the cash, he'll go after you."

Jack thought about it for about thirty seconds, then found a number with a California prefix at the top of the recent calls. He glanced up at Loretta, who simply held his eyes until he had no choice but to press Call. He put the phone on speaker. The number rang for some time during which Jack tried to formulate a ploy. Nothing came to mind by the time Scott answered.

"Yeah?"

"Hi, Scott."

"What are you doing with Nicki's phone?"

Jack glanced at Loretta, whose steady gaze urged him on. "Nicki's dead."

A short silence, then, "What is this, *Hamlet*? *Macbeth*? You're getting carried away with the character aren't you, Jacko?"

Was he shamming? Covering himself?

"She's dead, Scott. It looks a lot like you killed her," Jack said quietly.

Jack expected either an indignant denial at most, or cries of pained grief at least. What he got was silence, a very long silence. Then it occurred to him that, guilty or not, Scott's prime response would be neither to confess nor deny—it would be to consider options.

Eventually Scott spoke defiantly. "Don't forget. I got a load of shit on you. The feds take me, I spill the lot!"

Jack gained confidence in the game. "Just as long as you know that without Nicki, you have no claim on anything."

Now Scott's tone was even, his voice firm. "Then you better make it worth my while to get across the border."

"We can do that."

"We! *We*! Who's calling the shots, you or that ball-breaking bitch Loretta?"

"Name the place, the time. I'll be waiting with enough cash to make you happy."

"And how much do you think that is?"

Loretta scribbled a figure on a notepad and held it up.

"A hundred thousand."

Scott laughed abrasively. "*A hundred thousand*? Are you shitting me?"

Loretta beckoned for Jack to give her the phone. "Hello,

Scott," she said sweetly. "Nice to know you haven't changed in all the years since you were poisoning the neighborhood cats."

"Quit the bullshit!"

"Would I bullshit you? Martin is all for letting the cops know—"

"Martin! *Martin*? He's *not*…"

Loretta let this sit in the air for a moment before she said coolly, "He's not what?"

Scott was silent.

"Are you suggesting the person here with me in this room is not Martin Brenner? Because, if that's what you're saying, you must have a pretty good explanation as to who he is. And what he's doing here."

In Scott's silence, Jack knew he was pondering options again: how much could he reveal without implicating himself in the complexity of the deception in Martin Brenner's death?

"Let me tell you something, Scott," Loretta continued, "I'm willing to swear on a stack of bibles that the man here, by my side, in this room, is Martin Brenner. And if you have anything to say to the contrary, I'd like to hear it." She waited a moment. "I'll give you back to my nephew. He makes all the financial arrangements in this house."

She handed the phone to Jack. He hesitated, trying to

read her eyes, then took it.

"Scott?"

"You little asshole. You think you've got this all tied up." Scott's voice trembled with anger. "You think you've got me in a corner."

"You *are* in a corner."

"So are you buddy. You've got more to gain by getting rid of her than I do. They take me down, I can still finger you." Scott disconnected.

Loretta shuffled the cards. "He'll call back."

Jack watched her for a moment. "How long have you known? About me?"

Loretta didn't look up. "Since the night you arrived," she said as she dealt another round of solitaire.

"Why didn't you say anything?"

"Curiosity. I wanted to see how you'd play out. What you were up to."

"How? How did you know?"

"Oh, a hundred things only an old maid aunt could know. Martin had a scar on his right forearm. Just a little one, but I was the one who bandaged it and got him to the ER for stitches. Scars like that don't just disappear. The way he walked, like a cowboy, not a city slicker. All those years in the big city don't entirely erase bowlegs. And one other little thing. Martin might have been a kid of eleven last time

I saw him, but he was definitely straight."

"Straight?"

"Heterosexual." Now Loretta looked up at Jack. He suddenly felt as if he'd been stripped naked, and his breath caught.

Loretta turned back to her cards, laid a black six on a red seven, and shuffled three more cards off the deck. She paused, a card poised above the layout. "Diego means a great deal to me. He deserves to be happy." She laid down a card.

Jack sat opposite her and waited until she looked up from the cards. Sure that he had her eye and her undivided attention, he said simply, "My intentions, I swear, are honorable."

Loretta smiled, seemingly amused by the formality of the statement.

"I…" Was it too soon to use the word "love"? "I think more of Diego than any other human being I've ever known," Jack said earnestly. "I wouldn't do anything to hurt him in any way."

Loretta nodded, satisfied, then went back to the cards. After a long silence, she said, "You know, at first, I thought you might've killed Martin."

"I didn't. I swear," Jack protested passionately.

Loretta sighed with something like sympathy. "Yeah.

You'd think twice before swatting a fly."

"Nicki killed him. I found out last night."

"And they were blackmailing you."

Jack sighed deeply and rubbed his eyes. "I had no idea what they'd done to Martin, the real Martin. They set me up, both of them. They saw the resemblance and led me into a trap. I fell for it. No, I *jumped* in. I've lied, I've cheated. I can never forgive myself for what I've done. My whole life was at a dead end. This—" He gestured to the room in general. "—seemed like a new start. It wasn't the money. It was never about the money."

"I know that."

Of course. Maggie blabbed about the trust.

"I've loved my life here. For the first time, I'm not playing out some fantasy, I'm living real life. A rewarding life." He stood and went to the window. "I can't keep on like this. I have to tell everyone who I am, what happened."

"No, you don't."

"But I'm—"

"I want you here. And so does Diego."

Jack teared up. "He deserves to know who I am!"

"He knows all he needs to know, or he wouldn't have committed himself. He's not the kind of man who gambles. He told me how he feels about you."

"Don't you want to know my name?"

Loretta said, simply, "You are Martin Brenner."

The pink phone burbled the *Dance of the Sugar Plum Fairy*.

Jack connected.

"Five hundred grand," Scott said. "And I want it to-night."

"Five hundred thousand?"

"Don't tell me you can't get your hands on it. I know what kind of money that bitch keeps in the house."

Jack glanced at Loretta, who nodded.

"The place?"

"State fair, tonight, eight-thirty."

"State fair?"

"Lots of people around, in case you should get ideas. Go to the Ferris wheel and get on it. I'll wait till you come around to ground level. When you see me, leave the money, and stay put until I'm out of sight. If I see a cop, you're dead." He disconnected.

Loretta indicated a cupboard door by the clock. Jack opened the door to reveal a safe. He knelt and dialed the numbers Loretta dictated. The safe contained several metal boxes and cash, lots of cash. Jack loaded money into a leather bag. Loretta pointed her cane to the gun cabinet.

"Get the Winchester."

Jack turned a puzzled glance to the gun cabinet and

back to Loretta. She was on her phone.

"Diego? Get down here. We're going to the fair."

"No! You don't have to come. And I don't want Diego involved. This is all on me. It's my responsibility."

"Just give me the goddamn gun," Loretta said wearily.

*

7:15 P.M.

JACK AND LORETTA went down to the storm cellar and waited—Jack, rigid with nerves, Loretta calm in spite of the pain of her sprained ankle.

Jack wore his old western clothes; Loretta sported buckskin chaps and a fringed jacket, the outfit topped by a jaunty leather rodeo hat.

They heard the horse trailer pull up in the gravel driveway and then a single, quiet knock on the cellar door.

Jack helped Loretta out into the open while Diego watched for the duty cop.

As if in on the plot, the black stallion stood patiently in the trailer, while Jack and Loretta climbed into the truck cab and crouched low. Diego threw a horse blanket over them. Throughout this exercise, Loretta kept a tight hold on the Winchester, refusing to relinquish it even when it temporarily obstructed her entry to the truck.

Diego drove to the front of the house where the cop halted him, greeted him politely, and asked what he was doing.

As instructed, Diego produced a notepad and wrote:

State Fair — Show Horse

They heard the cop trudge round to the rear of the trailer and comment, "Nice horse."

Chapter Thirty

8:17 P.M.

THE ARIZONA STATE Fair sparkled with colored lights which lit the fairgrounds like day. Crowds thronged every ride, contest, concert, and display, glad of the clear, fine evening that followed the previous night's storm. Kids rode camels, bumper cars, carousels, and spaceships, while dads shot slugs at tin ducks and moms binged on cotton candy and ice cream.

The Ferris wheel towered above all, glittering with lights as it revolved, slowly, majestically.

Jack and Loretta now flanked Diego in the cab of the

trailer, free of the scrutiny of the watchdog back at the house.

At the entrance to the livestock pavilion, Jack showed a pass, and Diego parked the trailer in the designated area. Jack helped Loretta out. She winced as her injured foot hit the ground but waved Jack off when he tried to take her arm.

Jack and Diego made a show of backing the horse out of the trailer. Several of the stable hands paused to admire the sleek black stallion as Jack helped Loretta into the saddle; she pushed the Winchester securely into the saddle scabbard. Jack took the leather bag crammed with money and headed for the wheel, Loretta following slowly. Crowds parted as Diego led the stallion forward, Loretta smiling and waving.

Jack paused to buy a large bag of show souvenirs. He ditched the contents and wedged the leather bag into it. The wheel had a long line for tickets. He glanced at his watch and wondered if Scott was watching him. Eventually, he squeezed into a car with a party of five teens, two boys, and three squealing girls.

The wheel moved forward and up until Jack could see the Phoenix skyline, lit up against the night sky. He searched the crowd below for Scott but couldn't single out anyone.

By eight thirty-eight, Jack had been around twice, but no Scott. The ride operator asked him to get out of the car. Jack slipped him a couple of twenties, and he was allowed to stay put and ascend again. Then, he saw the buzzed blond head moving forward through the ticket line. Diego followed a few paces behind Scott, shadowing him.

Suddenly alerted by something, perhaps instinct, Scott swung around and froze. Jack followed his gaze, not to Diego, but to a half dozen uniformed cops converging on him.

Jack's car was almost at ground level again. Scott made a run for it and leapt in, pulling the Glock from his belt as he did so, pushing one of the teen occupants aside.

"Hey! Take it easy, dude!"

Scott slugged him with the gun, and the kid went down in a heap. His companions backed up, the girls screaming. The car had started upward again. Two of the teens, a boy and a girl, scrambled out of the car and fell to the platform six feet below.

"You double-crossing motherfucker," Scott yelled at Jack.

"I didn't do this! They must've followed us!"

A cop reached the operator and barked an order. The operator pulled a lever, slowing the wheel to a halt. Jack's car was now a hundred feet from the ground. Scott aimed the Glock at the operator below.

"GO! Start this fucking thing!"

The wheel stayed where it was.

Scott fired a shot that ricocheted off the platform where the operator stood.

Screams erupted, and the crowd at the base of the wheel stampeded. Scott aimed again. The operator pushed the lever, and the wheel jerked forward. Cops took up positions at the base.

Scott scanned the cars below, gun held aloft. Riders yelled and crouched as close to the floor of their cars as possible. Those who'd made it to ground level leapt from the cars and ran.

The wheel continued to revolve until Jack and Scott were at the zenith. The remaining teens cowered against the far door of the car; the two girls hunkered by the boy, sobbing. Then the wheel jerked to an abrupt stop. The car swung back and forth. Jack caught a glimpse of a cop at the controls who'd engineered the halt. The girls in their car were crying hysterically now.

"Shut up!" Scott yelled at them, sweeping the gun in their direction.

The shrill, metallic sound of a bullhorn sliced through the night air. "This is the Phoenix Police Department. Throw your weapon down and put your hands behind your head!"

Scott replied by firing a shot into the cluster of police

officers. One of them clutched at his shoulder and fell to his knees.

Scott crouched in the car as all of the officers retreated. He turned the gun on Jack.

"I swear I didn't call the cops," Jack insisted. "Maybe I can hold then off while you—"

"What? Shoot it out?" He looked over the side of the car.

Jack followed his gaze. Devoid of police and fairgoers, the brightly lit expanse of bare earth surrounding the wheel stirred occasionally as wisps of breeze lifted the dust. Only a distant, wheezing calliope playing the "Destiny Waltz" broke the otherwise eerie quiet.

Jack caught sight of Loretta as she emerged from the shadows, urging the stallion forward. He grasped at straws. "Listen. Loretta's down there with a horse. Maybe—maybe she could cover while you…"

But Scott was no longer listening. He slumped against the side of the car, eyes closed. A sob escaped him. "Fuck Loretta," he said quietly and took a gasping breath. "Fuck all you rich assholes. You always treated me like shit."

Jack suddenly felt an overwhelming pity for Scott.

"Gotta think. I gotta think," Scott muttered.

A commotion broke out below. Jack looked down and saw Diego shrug off a cop who'd tried to restrain him. He climbed onto the lowest car, and from there, onto the cross-bars that held the car, leaping up to the next higher, then the next higher yet.

Scott leaned over and aimed the Glock at Diego. Jack pulled him back, and as Scott tried to break free, the wheel started up again. Both were thrown off-balance and tumbled to the floor of the car. Scott struck a stinging blow to the side of Jack's head with the gun. Stunned, Jack nevertheless struggled to take the gun from Scott.

As the car reached the halfway point, Jack caught sight of Diego clinging to a car in which an elderly couple held each other in a terrified embrace. The change in pitch allowed Diego to scramble along the now horizontal spoke to the hub of the wheel. Scott fired off a shot at Diego, but the swinging of the car defied his aim, and the shot went wide.

The car crested and began to descend, and as it passed halfway, Diego slid down the taut steel cable and landed in the car between the two.

Scott shifted his focus to Diego and aimed the gun at him. Before he could fire, Diego delivered a right to Scott's jaw, stunning him. Scott reacted by pulling the trigger. The shot went wide and ricocheted off the adjacent car. The occupants screamed.

The bullhorn again: "Drop the weapon!"

The wheel continued to turn, and the car began to

ascend again.

Diego and Scott struggled, battling for possession of the gun, teetering as the car rocked erratically.

Jack clutched at the side of the car to hold his balance and saw Loretta, a solitary figure in the deserted lot, firmly astride the stallion, put the rifle to her shoulder.

Diego delivered another right to Scott, who went down flailing. Scott took advantage of the rocking car to push Diego off-balance. He tumbled over the edge.

Jack yelled in alarm and grabbed for Diego's wrist. Diego slid, almost losing Jack's grip, but got hold of the door of the car with his free hand. He hung, swinging, a hundred feet above the ground. Scott brought the side of the gun down on Diego's knuckles, trying to dislodge him. Jack tackled him and pulled him back, away from Diego.

Scott shifted focus and thrust the gun into Jack's face. "You're dead."

A single shot echoed around the fairgrounds.

The neat hole in Scott's forehead somehow compounded his look of surprise as he slumped forward onto the floor of the car.

Jack held tight to Diego's wrists as the wheel turned and their car descended. At ground level, Diego landed securely on the platform. He hauled Jack out of the car and held him in a tight, protective embrace as the police swarmed the scene. One of their number knelt to examine Scott's lifeless body.

Jack searched the growing crowd of rubberneckers until he saw Loretta.

She sat astride the stallion but at an angle. She'd dropped the Winchester to the ground, and her left arm hung limp—indeed, her entire left side seemed to have collapsed under some unseen weight, and she stared ahead of her.

A cop examined her briefly and yelled for assistance.

"Medics!"

Chapter Thirty-One

WEDNESDAY, NOVEMBER 9
12:14 A.M.

JACK SAT IN the stark fluorescent glare of the ER waiting room, Diego at his side, a still sentinel.

They'd spent an impatient hour at the fair giving guarded statements about Scott, his suspected involvement in Nicki's murder, and his demand for money with the intention of fleeing the country. Shortly after 10:30, they were released and hurried to the hospital.

A medic emerged from surgery and asked for Ms. Dalstrom's nephew. Jack leapt to his feet.

"Your aunt," he began, "there are complications."

"What kind of complications?"

"Her blood pressure is abnormally high. That, coupled with the stress of the situation—"

"What complications?"

"She's suffered a stroke. We're not sure yet of the extent of the damage, but it seems considerable."

Jack sat heavily onto the bench. Diego put an arm about his shoulder.

"Mobility might be improved with therapy," the surgeon said in an effort to tender a little hope. But the images that flooded Jack's mind were of a proud, handsome woman striding the vast acreage of the ranch, controlling a galloping horse with lithe authority, or standing with her feet firmly on the ground as she shattered clay pigeons.

"There's no point in waiting here, Mr. Brenner. She's in good hands, and we'll keep you posted."

*

JACK AND DIEGO returned to the ranch and relayed the news to Consuela, who instantly abandoned her celebrated stoicism and dissolved into uncontrollable tears. The men soothed her and sat with her for a while, but eventually, the exhaustion of a half hour of wracking sobs weighed, and Consuela trudged slowly, silently up the tower stairs to her bedroom.

Jack contemplated the prospect of the yellow room and told Diego he couldn't bear to be in the house that night. Diego led him across the fields to his cabin.

Diego turned on a lamp, and by the low light, poured hefty shots of bourbon. He sat by Jack on the sofa, and they drank in silence. Jack realized his opportunity to come clean to Diego.

"I want to tell you who I am."

This statement hovered in the still air for a moment, and then Diego turned toward Jack and without looking at him directly, shook his head slowly, *no*.

"I need to. I want to be someone you can trust, someone you never have to doubt. I want to be…" His eyes fell on the framed photograph of Diego's dead lover.

Diego followed his gaze and turned back to look deep into Jack's welling eyes. He pressed two forefingers gently against Jack's mouth. Then, he reached for his notepad and wrote swiftly.

I want YOU. No more, no less.

"Diego…"

Diego dropped the pad and took Jack's shoulders firmly in his massive hands, then leaned in and kissed him—less with the gentleness of his first kiss, more with a passion that indicated his intentions clearly. Without breaking the kiss, he stood, bringing Jack to his feet too. When he stepped back, they stood quite still, facing each other for a time, each searching the other's face for — permission? Approval?

It seemed to Jack they agreed on both. He pulled Diego to him, and his kiss matched the heat of Diego's. How long had it been since he'd had any sensual contact with another human being? When had it ever felt so secure? So just plain right? When had the touch of a man's hands, his lips, made Jack tremble with anticipation?

Diego removed Jack's shirt and dropped it to the floor; he then tore at his own and let it fall.

They stood a moment more, each scanning the other's bare torso as if seeing it for the first time. Then Diego took Jack's hand and led him slowly to the bedroom.

*

DURING THE FOLLOWING three weeks, Jack and Diego alternated visiting Loretta at the hospital and managing the ranch.

They'd endured several visits by Detective Cassell, answered question after question until, it seemed, the Phoenix Police Department accepted the theory that Scott had murdered Nicki in a fit of jealousy, then tried to extort money to escape. Cassell even seemed forgiving of Martin Brenner's sympathy in wanting to pay off his own brother and let the matter slide. After all, as Loretta had said, as long as Scott was at large, she feared for her and her nephew's lives.

Though unspoken, the doubt about Scott's guilt lingered in Jack's mind. Why would he kill his accomplice when they verged on the big payoff? Jealousy wasn't a factor, though he never said as much during the questioning. Had Nicki perhaps decided to cut Scott out of the deal? As he ran over his phone call with Scott, he had the impression that something of the sort had happened. Otherwise, Scott would've shouted the place down when accused of killing her.

Four weeks after the night of the fair, Loretta was moved to a therapy ward, where she was stretched and pummeled. Eventually, she assumed a little mobility, though her left arm remained inert. She was taught to speak again. By some perversity, the stroke had robbed her of English, her first language, and left her in command only of her adequate but limited Spanish. After seven weeks, they brought her home.

Her once handsome face sagged to one side, and they moved her from one part of the house to another in a wheelchair. It seemed unlikely she'd climb the grand oak staircase again, so they set up the den, which adjoined the living room, as a bedroom for her.

Jack employed a reed-thin, overly fussy therapist. She spoke to Loretta as one might a backward child, and Consuela took delight in translating Loretta's Spanish profanities into colorful English. The woman resigned after nine days.

A plumper, jollier, but no less officious woman replaced her. She addressed Loretta as "Honeybun," but Loretta let it be known, in Spanish, that "Honeybun" wouldn't last long either.

Jack and Diego always reported the day's activities to Loretta. They sat side by side and found it hard to keep their hands off each other—a pat of one hand on the other's, the hand of one on the other's knee, frequent glances between them. Loretta watched this with a tilted smile of amused approval.

Consuela guarded her mistress like some ogre at a mythical gate, scrutinizing every therapeutic move employed by Nurse Honeybun. When the time came to move Loretta from wheelchair to bed, Consuela brushed off any offer of help by the therapist and relocated Loretta herself.

Early every day, Jack took her to the morning room. Evenings, they convened for dinner in the grand dining room, just Loretta, Diego, and Jack at one end of the long table. Consuela bustled in and out with food, lovingly cooked by her but carefully scanned by Honeybun to conform to Loretta's diet. But Consuela would allow no one else to spoon feed Loretta, coaxing the food into Loretta's slack mouth with gentle encouragement.

Activity at the ranch became ordered again. The younger mare was pregnant, which was good news, but of course, the outcome would not be apparent for at least ten months. Jack bought a second stallion and then another female foal.

Diego and Jack worked side by side, their common purpose to sustain the ranch and to better it. They planted vegetable gardens and four groves of fruit trees and refurbished the barns. But when Jack told Loretta their intention to demolish the distant, rotting shack, she rallied in broken Spanish.

"No toques la maldita choza!"

The shack was left intact.

Jack and Diego's relationship became apparent to all at the ranch. Even Consuela became a little soft and fuzzy in their presence and doted on them. They took their meals in the big house, lovingly prepared by Consuela, but chose to sleep in Diego's cabin, which had become more like a home to Jack than any he'd known.

*

THE COURTS DELIBERATED over the fairground shooting, and Jack wheeled Loretta in to give evidence. Consuela translated for her, and given the state of Loretta's Spanish and Consuela's English, there was much to be deciphered.

The verdict was justifiable homicide, and Loretta was actually congratulated for potentially saving lives by her action. But the ordeal had a grave effect on her, and she relinquished some of the little feistiness she had left. She spent less and less time in the morning room looking out over the fields and more time in her bed in the den.

Cassell visited the ranch three times more, questioning all and taking formal statements. He reexamined the stable and the main bedroom, poring over Nicki's every possession. Later, at the hearing into the murder of Nicole Brenner, Jack was grilled again and again. He stuck to the story he and Loretta had devised. Maggie and Adams confirmed that when Scott had made his outrageous claim on the family's wealth, he'd been wearing the gold necklet, the necklet Nicki clutched when her body was found. This became the damning evidence, albeit circumstantial, implying Scott had been motivated by jealousy. Despite Cassell's plea to regard the case as cold, a posthumous verdict came against Scott Brenner for murder, and the case was closed—as it was for Jack, who put aside his doubts to just get on with his life.

Chapter Thirty-Two

SUNDAY, DECEMBER 25

CHRISTMAS WAS CELEBRATED with the ranch hands and their wives, and Loretta reigned over the gathering from her wheelchair, wearied by the event, but nodding approval as each of her gifts to the workers was meted out. Adams and Maggie brought modest gifts for all and were given lavish gifts in return.

Jack gave Diego a new electronic reader; Diego gave Jack a buckskin jacket.

To Consuela, Loretta gave jewelry from her own collection. Her gift to Jack and Diego was entirely practical and not entirely selfless—she'd ordered a complete refurbishing of the kitchen and bathroom in Diego's cabin. Hitherto, the rooms had been practical, but in need of updating and the gesture was welcomed by the two, though they realized what was in back of Loretta's benevolence—while the re-building went on, they'd have to relocate to the big house, and they'd be closer to Loretta.

January segued into February and on Valentine's Day, a visit from Adams and Maggie. Maggie corralled Jack, Diego, Consuela, and Loretta into the morning room.

Adams cleared his throat several times before words actually formed. "Maggie and, um, Maggie and I... We...we've, uh, well, after long and careful consideration, we've decided, both of us..."

"Oh for the love of God," Maggie interrupted, "we're getting married."

Hearty congratulations were offered by all.

"No big surprise," Maggie added. "We've lived in each other's pockets for years."

"Can't wait to get her hands in my pockets," Adams said with a wry smile.

The wedding was in early April and held at the ranch in the field by the morning room, so Loretta could attend without the inconvenience of being trundled to some public venue. About a hundred people came, and Jack and Diego ruled over the event as the heads of the Wyatt Ranch—which now they were.

Adams and Maggie bickered throughout the ceremony and the alfresco reception, at one point breaking up Jack to the degree that he excused himself and went into the house for a hearty laugh.

After the guests had gone, Diego led Jack back to their cabin, closed the door, and stood close, peering into Jack's eyes with undiluted adoration. He lifted Jack's left hand and pointed to the third finger. Jack glanced down and then back up to Diego, whose eyes held a question.

"Yes." Jack swiped at tears as they wet both his cheeks. "Yes!"

*

AS APRIL ADVANCED to May, Jack and Diego began to reap the profits of their labors. Though for now, this meant watching things grow, it seemed certain this would evolve into self-perpetuating and escalating financial gain.

Every evening, by ritual now, they sat by Loretta's bed and related the events of the day. On one such twilight meeting, Loretta looked longingly at the array of liquor on the drinks tray. Jack got the message and poured a small shot of bourbon. Honeybun wagged a reproving finger, but Loretta told her in broken Spanish where to put her finger.

Jack held the glass to Loretta's lips as she sipped.

Late in May, Consuela took a call from Detective Miller who announced that the investigation into the death of Jack McCauley was closed. Would she kindly pass on the news that accidental death had been ruled. Consuela found Loretta and Jack in the den and relayed the news.

"I dunno who is this McCauley guy, but is accident, so forget him," Consuela reported.

Jack shot a glance to Loretta who didn't react by so much as an eyelid flicker. But both knew the truth of the matter. When Consuela left the room, Jack took Loretta's hand and said quietly, "You know how grateful I am for—"

Loretta pulled her hand from his and said, just as quietly, "*Estas lleno de mierda.*"

Jack laughed. "So are you!" Then he became serious. "I need to talk to you about something. To ask you…" He took a breath. "Diego and I—we want to get married."

Loretta turned to him, trying hard to command her fallen features into an expression Jack couldn't read.

He stuttered. "I know! I know! Legally, it'll be a problem. I'll have to come clean, but—"

Loretta brought her hand down on the folding table by her side with such force, it toppled a glass of water. "Consuela!" she said with as much force as she could muster. "*Consuela!*"

Consuela came running. Loretta inclined her head, and Consuela went to her and bent close. Loretta whispered. When Consuela came out of the huddle, she darted a look at Jack and then back to Loretta as if she was loco. "Why you tell me this? I don't need no—"

"*Mi dormitorio. Armario. Consíguelo.*"

Consuela shrugged and left the room.

Jack mopped the spilled water. "If you think this isn't a good idea—"

"*Callate!*"

Jack tried to open a debate a couple times, but Loretta merely closed her eyes, deflecting discourse.

Consuela bustled back into the room bearing a manila folder. Loretta nodded to the folding table, and Consuela placed the folder before Loretta and opened it. Loretta stared pointedly at Jack, who went to the table and peered down at the folder's contents.

Martin Brenner's birth certificate.

Loretta turned to Consuela and whispered, "Mr. Martin—*se va a casar.*" She struggled painfully for the English. "Mr. Martin, Diego, they—marry."

Consuela considered this for a second or two, then fell upon Jack with a hug that nearly knocked him off-balance.

Loretta banged the table with her hand and gestured to Consuela tersely to get her ready for bed. As Jack left the room, she glanced at him briefly with the small, tilted smile her stroke allowed. He was incapable of words and simply returned the smile.

*

THE NEXT DAY, Jack went to Adams's office and gave him the news.

Maggie fluttered about, expressing joy in similes, hugs, and congratulations. Adams absorbed the news with a puzzled frown, and then he followed Maggie's example and offered congratulations with a handshake.

Tea was brewed, cookies were found, and conversation lapsed into ranch business. That done, Jack left the office. A second after he closed the outer door, he heard Adams clearly.

"I don't get it."

Jack did something he'd never done in his life: he eavesdropped. He stood close to the door and listened.

"What don't you get?" Maggie asked with minimal patience.

"I've known young Martin since he was a child."

"And?"

"He's been married. Twice. To a woman."

Maggie's patience wore even thinner. "So maybe he's bi."

"Bi?"

"Bisexual, Harry, bisexual."

There was a silence, and Jack considered it was time to leave. He started for the stairs with a broad smile he couldn't contain only to hear Adams's renewed puzzlement. He paused to listen.

"Can it happen? Just like that? Can a man turn?"

"Maybe it's something in the water."

"I don't get it."

Now Maggie lost it. "Oh for God's sake Harry! What does it matter? He's happy. Be happy for him. And don't look so worried. No guy's gonna put the moves on you."

Jack ran down the stairs stifling a laugh which erupted as soon as he hit the street.

*

MAY ENDED, JUNE began.

Honeybun had been replaced by a large woman who never smiled but was efficient and most importantly, patient. She was tough and took no crap. Consuela dubbed her "Godzilla."

Harry and Maggie, now Mr. and Mrs. Adams, came by weekly and spent an hour in the den, now Loretta's bedroom, talking in the brightest tones they could muster. But one afternoon, as they left, Harry collared Jack in the hall and spoke in a whisper.

"I'm worried, lad, worried."

"She's lost so much weight," Maggie observed.

Adams wore a deep frown. "She's got that look, that same hopeless look I saw on Amy's face when she took to her bed."

"I don't know what else I can do," Jack was unable to keep his voice from breaking. "I've taken her to everyone who might be able to help."

Consuela passed them on the way to the den, carrying a small tray with a teapot and cup.

"What've you got there, honey?" Maggie asked.

"Tea from herb," Consuela said. "Camouflage."

"No dear, chamo*mile*."

"Whatever."

Maggie was effusive. "It'll do her good! I make it for Harry. He loves it."

"I *hate* it!" Adams said.

"See how it calms him down?"

Jack saw Adams and Maggie off, then returned to the den. Godzilla was not inappropriate nomenclature for the woman who hovered over the bed, holding the teacup to Loretta's lips. Consuela watched with beady eyes as Loretta sipped, dribbling tea onto her chin. Godzilla dabbed at her patiently with a tissue.

*

SATURDAY, JUNE 10

THEY HELD THE simple, casual ceremony in the living room.

Adams acted as best man and clicked his tongue frequently at Maggie, a blubbering mess throughout, stifling sobs, mopping tears.

Godzilla guarded the door, gruff and unmoved by the proceedings, which it was clear she thought peculiar.

Consuela stood by Loretta's wheelchair and held her good hand throughout. Now painfully thin, Loretta watched the ceremony impassively, seeming to release a held breath only when simple gold rings were exchanged and the Celebrant said, "I pronounce you husband and husband."

*

THROUGH THE REST of June, business at the ranch proceeded as usual, though Loretta grew weaker. She summoned Jack and Diego and announced that she'd ordered a complete overhaul of Amy's grand bedroom. The shrine to the eldest Dalstrom sister would be dismantled in favor of refurnishing to Jack's taste should he and Diego ever choose to move into the house. She offered no debate, just a statement of intention, take it or leave it.

July brought unseasonal storms. Winds lashed the newly planted trees, and torrential rain left the vegetable gardens awash, but the ranch hands remained on top of the situation and maintained order and growth.

One evening, against the roll of thunder outside, Loretta summoned Jack to the den. Godzilla had the night off, and there seemed to be no purpose to the meeting except that Loretta wanted Jack's company. Consuela came in with broth and the food she thought could be tolerated, but Loretta declined to be fed and dismissed her — but only after nodding thanks while she gripped Consuela's hand, holding it for some time, and giving her a small smile of pure gratitude.

As always, Jack related the status of the ranch: One of the new horses had developed equine herpesvirus and had to be quarantined for fear of infecting the pregnant mare. The mango trees were doing well, and the profusion of buds in the orange groves promised eventual fruit. And stock in Wyatt Enterprises was rising and would soon be at an all-time high.

Loretta nodded, satisfied.

At her bidding, Jack found an LP and put it on the antiquated turntable hidden in a cupboard. They listened to a selection of Debussy nocturnes, her favorites. She held her stroke-tilted smile throughout. At the conclusion, they sat in silence for a minute. Eventually, Loretta inclined her head to Jack and, straining to recall her English, asked haltingly, "You and Diego—are you happy?"

Jack chuckled as if surprised at his own response. "I'm happier than I've been in my entire life." He wanted to give weight to this declaration, and he dredged up fragments of the philosophies of Plato and the Aristophanes both he and Diego had read. "Diego makes me whole. Every minute I spend with him, I hope I'm... What's the word? Worthy. I hope I complete him in the same way he does me."

Loretta smiled her half-smile and nodded once. "*Lo sabras.*"

She seemed to be pondering something for a moment, and then she waved her right hand in the direction of the wall safe. Jack got her drift and opened it. He turned to her for further instruction. She rolled her eyes and sighed as if dealing with an idiot. Jack reached in and took a manila envelope out. Loretta nodded. "*Mañana.* Read tomorrow. Not tonight."

Jack shrugged. "Okay. Want me to put you to bed?"

She shook her head. "Here. *Yo duermo aqui. En la silla.*"

Jack settled the quilt over her, tucking it in at the sides of the wheelchair. He bent and kissed her forehead. "Thank you for giving me a life," he whispered.

She grabbed his hand and held it tight, gazing for some time into his eyes. Then she nodded and let him go.

"Sleep tight." He turned out the light and left the room.

The storm raged through the night.

Next morning, one of the ranch hands ran to the cabin and pounded on the door to rouse Jack and Diego, urging them to get down to the house.

They found an ambulance parked outside the back door and stood in the rain as Medics eased Loretta's lifeless, wasted body into it. Her wheelchair was overturned in the mud nearby.

During the night, she'd wheeled herself out of the house and into the storm.

Chapter Thirty-Three

TUESDAY, AUGUST 1

THEY BURIED LORETTA, according to her request, by the ancient, tumbledown shack on the far hill of the ranch. The ranch hands, Consuela, Jack, Diego, Adams, and Maggie all attended the funeral.

Reverend Carnley, in fine form, spoke of God as if he'd dined with Him the night before. The dear departed, he assured the gathering, was happy and glorious in the hereafter, as though that was enough to assuage their grief.

When the time came to throw earth onto the casket, Jack held back, the finality of the gesture something he couldn't bear to commit himself to.

Harry Adams put a hand on his shoulder. "It's all right, lad. We're here. We're all here for you."

When it was all done, Maggie took one of Jack's arms and Diego the other as they walked back to the house.

*

SATURDAY, AUGUST 12

UPWARD OF A hundred people attended the memorial at the Mountain Preserve Center. As well as those Loretta had allowed to be close to her in life, many who feared, envied, or frowned upon her turned out in earnest respect.

Unlike the last hollow address Jack had given in this same room, his tribute to Loretta was honest and heartfelt and emotional. He could barely speak as he concluded: "More than anything in my life, I'm proud to have known her. Proud that she thought of me as family. I never knew anyone like her, and I'll never know anyone like her again. And I'll never forget her."

A luncheon followed for all the guests. After, as they left, every one of them had something appropriately sympathetic to say to Jack, even those who hadn't spoken to Loretta for many years.

Consuela was the last to approach. Jack hugged her,

and without hesitation, she reached up and put her arms around him and held him tight.

After some time, she stepped back and smiled. "Today, I am sixty-eight years. Is my birthday."

"I didn't know," Jack said. "Many happy returns!"

"I am at the ranch forty-nine of these years," she added, her head high.

"I wish it could've been a happier birthday."

Jack led her to a bench and they sat.

"I have something to say," she opened haltingly, and then, in a rush as if carefully rehearsed, "My sister, the old one, she very, very sick. I must be with her. You understand if I leave the ranch?" Suddenly her resolve weakened and tears ran down her plump cheeks. "I must do this. I must go to her. Now."

Jack nodded. "I understand. I don't want you to leave, but I understand."

She pecked him on the cheek, then hurried away to join Diego.

Chapter Thirty-Four

TWO YEARS LATER
SATURDAY, MAY 17

MARTIN TURNED TWENTY-EIGHT—at least, according
to the driver's license in his wallet. Jack had actually turned
twenty-six in February, but several days had passed before
he realized it. It felt like a date connected to someone with
whom he'd fallen out of touch long ago, someone he hadn't
known very well.

Life had been good to Jack in three years of
concentrated work, and the security he found in loving
Diego. Routine, far from dull, became a pleasure, and the

ranch flourished. He and Diego had remained in the cabin, so the vast Wyatt mansion, while maintained meticulously in Consuela's absence, became a rarely visited museum.

He visited Consuela regularly and took gifts for her and her family. Each time, he noted that she'd deteriorated a little—a little weight lost, a gauntness in her now seventy-year-old frame. He begged her to see Dr. Verne, the Dalstrom family doctor, but she stubbornly refused, maintaining confidence in her own medical advice.

The ranch was running well enough for Jack and Diego to take a little time off now and then—a dinner downtown, a classic rock concert at the Coliseum, art galleries. On their first anniversary, Diego took Jack to a concert at Symphony Hall, where they played Rachmaninoff's *Symphony No. 3*. Though unstated, this meant something special to Diego, an emotion he wanted to impart to Jack. He'd held Jack's hand throughout, and Jack felt, that night, that his life never could be better.

*

WEDNESDAY, SEPTEMBER 10

SEPTEMBER WAS DOWNRIGHT cold, heralding a winter in which caution would have to be applied to the ranch's resources.

Consuela sent one, sometimes two of her nieces to the vacant house every week to clean. Her grandniece, Dolores, a high school student, worked Saturdays to supplement her expenses. She cleaned and dusted Diego's cabin, a chore hitherto the exclusive province of Consuela. Always, Jack asked after Consuela, always Dolores had a happy anecdote of some kind.

The refurbishment of the master bedroom in the big house had been completed more than a year before, and after long debate with Diego, they decided to take up residence in the house and give the cabin over to a family they'd employed to supervise the workers.

Diego transported the things he deemed precious, principally his art and books, while Jack collected smaller items—several pots of Santa Fe origin, two San Ildefonso vases, a box containing several pieces of Hopi silver jewelry. There was no sign of the framed photograph of Diego's former lover. He assumed Diego had consigned it to a drawer in the small bureau after their marriage. Jack turned the drawers out in search of the picture. All of them had been emptied, yet wedged in the back of the lowest, he found a manila envelope. It took a moment for recognition to kick in.

This was the envelope Loretta had given him the night she died—*knowing* she was going to die. In the wake of the many details Jack had been obliged to attend to as a result of her death, the envelope had been forgotten. He had a vague memory of leaving it there, on the desk. Diego, *eternal neat freak*, Jack thought affectionately, must've put it into this drawer two long years ago.

He inserted his forefinger under the seal and was about to tear the envelope open when something inside the drawer caught his eye. A glint of reflected light. He pulled the drawer all the way out and rested it on the surface of the desk. Wedged in the rear corner was the silver ring—his mother's wedding ring, the ring he'd worn since he was twelve years old, the ring he'd been forced to use when he married Nicki—and which had been missing since the night she was murdered.

The implication struck him and turned his knees to jelly.

A movement at the cabin door startled him, and he turned. Diego stood in the doorway, watching him. Jack was frozen, holding ring before him. Diego regarded it without expression and took a step toward him. Reflexively, Jack took a step back.

Now Diego's face reflected pain, anguished disbelief. Jack read his expression, as he'd learned to in their years together, and it asked clearly:

Do you really believe I could harm you?

They stood this way, immobile for several seconds. Jack's mind raced. This was the man he loved—was he a cold-blooded killer? He had a history of violent revenge.

"When he'd done, there were more than two hundred bodies."

Had he committed murder to free Jack from the trap he was in? Had it been an act of temper? Rage? Jealousy?

Ask for an explanation. Beg for one. Tell him whatever he's done, it would change nothing between them.

Or would it?

Now Diego read Jack's face—and Jack was unable to veil the doubt there.

Diego turned and stumbled out of the cabin. Jack ran to the door as Diego ran, stumbling down into the small valley that led to the farthest perimeter of the ranch and the deserted shack.

He yelled, "Diego!"

Diego didn't turn.

Jack was about to take off after him when Dolores ran up from the house. She called to Jack, and when he turned to her, saw she was in tears.

"Consuela!" she said. "Come, please Mr. Martin! She doesn't have very long!"

Jack shoved the ring absently onto his finger, folded the envelope in two, and pushed it into the hip pocket of his jeans as he ran to get his car.

Chapter Thirty-Five

SOUTH MOUNTAIN WAS an area largely populated by Latino families, some moderately affluent, many poor. The house to which Consuela had retired was that of a large middle-income family. One of her many nieces, her nephew in law, and their four children occupied the house.

Jack drove an inconsolable Dolores, who wept silently throughout the entire journey. "Why didn't I know sooner?" he demanded angrily.

"She didn't want to make you unhappy."

"I'm unhappy now! I'm unhappy that it's taken everyone so long to tell me she was so ill!"

This prompted audible sobs.

"I'm sorry, Dolores. Sorry. I'm upset."

Dolores calmed a little. "Mr. Diego should be here too."

Jack's eyes welled now. *Yes, he should. He should be by my side.* "Call him!"

Dolores started punching numbers on her cell. A click as Diego picked up. Dolores barely got through explaining the situation before he disconnected.

Jack parked haphazardly by the front door and ran inside. He was startled when a priest rose abruptly from a chair in the entrance hall.

"This is Father Sebastian," Dolores said.

Jack realized fully just how little time he had. "Where is she?"

Dolores led him up the narrow staircase to a bedroom at the end of a long hall. The shades were drawn, and it took a moment for his eyes to adjust to the gloom.

"Mr. Martin?" There was no evidence of the sturdy conviction of Consuela's broken English he'd known in the past. Her voice was weak, brittle, like the emaciated figure in the bed.

"I'm here," Jack said gently as he went to her.

"You come. You come," she said with a measure of relief.

Jack sat by the bed and took her hand, bony now, veins visible beneath the taut, thin skin. "Consuela, why didn't you let me know!"

"What you do, huh?" A little of the old feistiness sup-ported the query. "I tell you, what you do? You worry!" He stroked her hand. "The girls, they tell me ranch is good," she said in a croaked whisper.

"It's very good," Jack said. "But we miss you so much."

Consuela nodded. "Me too." Her eyes turned a hopeful glance to the doorway. "Is Diego…"

"He'll be here soon." Guilt settled heavily in Jack now that he hadn't gone after Diego, brought him here himself. His eyes moved to Consuela's hair, once a luxuriant, silver-streaked black, now gray and sparse, exposing scalp.

She mustered a smile when she saw Jack frown. "Chemo," she said simply. "Is why I leave the ranch. I don't want you are embarrass by Consuela."

"Oh, Consuela, why didn't you tell me? We could've—"

She squeezed his hand and shook her head. "No! I have good doctor! He tell the truth to Consuela!" She turned his hand over so that the silver ring was evident. Her eyes fixed on it. She cleared her throat and visibly mustered determi-nation, though her bottom lip trembled. "Now I tell you truth."

She shot a glance to the closed door as if to make sure they had privacy, then turned back to Jack and held him with a steely glare. "I tell you now. Then I tell Father

Sebastian." She closed her eyes briefly, then opened them again. "I kill her."

Jack froze, his hand still in Consuela's.

"I kill the bitch. The Nicki slut."

"No," Jack whispered. He tried to withdraw his hand, but even in her weakened state, Consuela found the strength to hold on.

"She gonna ruin the ranch, *destruir todo*! That's why I do it!"

Jack considered this and a glimmer of suspicion entered his mind. "Just—how did you do it, Consuela?"

"I stab her! I stab and stab! With fork. Just like you find her!"

After a moment, Jack said quietly, "I don't believe you, Consuela."

"Is true! I gonna confess to Father Sebastian."

He took his hand from hers, but she grabbed for it and held it so that the light on the nightstand reflected from the ring, giving it a classy gleam it really didn't deserve.

"I take it offa her after I kill," Consuela insisted with as much energy as she could muster.

Jack shook his head. "You're protecting Diego, aren't you?"

Now, tears welled in Consuela's eyes. "No, it was me! It was me!"

Jack took a tissue and dabbed gently at her sunken cheeks. "No," he said gently.

Consuela's insistent tone weakened. "You love Diego. He love you. He is good man."

"Where did you find the ring?"

A pitiful sob escaped Consuela before she answered timidly, "I see it in the drawer of his desk when I clean. I put it back, then I think…" She trailed off for a moment and then, with surprising strength, clutched at Jack's shirt with both hands. "He do it for you! Because he love you so much!"

She fell back against the pillow, and the sobs multiplied. Then, her breathing became deep and labored. "Father Sebastian," she said in a feeble whisper.

Jack darted to the door and threw it open. "Dolores! Father Sebastian!"

They came, followed by her niece's entire family, seven of them, the women in tears. All waited patiently outside the room as the priest administered last rites. He rose and beckoned the family inside.

As they gathered around the bed, Diego burst into the room. The family, aware of how much he meant to Consuela, parted respectfully to let him through. He fell to his knees by the bed. Gently, very gently, he put an arm behind Consuela's head, lifted it, and cradled it against his chest.

Consuela recognized him and smiled. He kissed her forehead, and then she was still.

Jack backed up to the door. The family had priority here. He took a long look at Diego, who wept unashamedly, something Jack had never seen before. Then he went downstairs, got into his car, and drove back to the ranch.

Chapter Thirty-Six

JACK PARKED IN the driveway by the front door and sat contemplating the vast, empty house that towered above him. Now tears came. He'd lost two of the kindest, most supportive people he'd known in his life.

And now, perhaps, he would lose Diego too.

He took deep breaths to control the wrenching sobs. He'd talk to Diego. He'd tell him how much he loved him. That his secret would remain just that, a secret. But could they continue their idyllic life together with this horrific act a forethought?

He slumped back onto the car's headrest and guilt swamped him—the sleek Mercedes he called his was actually Martin's. Jack had secrets of his own which he'd never confided in Diego.

He was phony, a hypocrite.

Jack opened the door, and as he stepped out of the car, something fell to the ground—the envelope he'd shoved hastily into his hip pocket. He picked it up and resumed his seat in the car as he tore it open. He took out four pages, recognizing Loretta's hand on the uppermost, weakened by the stroke but undeniably her bold, impatient scrawl.

"Dear Jack," the first page began.

> *I can call you that now, for all the reasons you'll find herein. And I can tell you why I embraced your deceit, right at the outset. I wanted Martin to be here at the ranch. I wanted him desperately. I wanted him so badly I let you be Martin.*

> *Martin was not Geena's child. He was mine.*

Jack read this statement twice more before it really registered.

> *You asked me once why I never married. Simple. I was in love with Ed Wyatt, Amy's husband, Martin's father. From the time I was eighteen, we*

conducted an affair in that shack you were so eager to tear down. Amy never suspected until long after Ed's death. Until I told her. That's when she took to her bed and changed her will in Martin's favor.

As for Geena, she did just one decent thing in her shabby life—she became a party to the deceit to give my child a name. I add that Ed's money was a persuasive factor in keeping her mouth shut. When I began to show, we traveled abroad—a sisters' vacation, we told everyone. Geena called around, claimed to be pregnant by her soon to be ex-husband, Errol Brenner.

I gave birth to Martin in a hospital in Los Angeles. A perfect, beautiful baby, who, I realized within minutes of his existence, I could never call my son.

But Martin Brenner grew up with a name, a pedigree.

Jack's mind pulled up an image of the yellow bedroom. Martin's childhood bedroom. No wonder it had been preserved in such pristine condition. Every toy, every souvenir, every report card for Martin Brenner up to age eleven had been stored lovingly, obsessively by a woman who accepted that her son would know her only as a doting, overly-affectionate aunt.

> *But wait, kid, there's more. This is one crazy, mixed up family!*

Jack turned to the second page, skimmed it, then stunned by what he saw, straightened the paper and read it over, slowly, carefully. Then he cried out—a loud, involuntary, primitive single syllable of sheer shock.

He scrambled from the car and ran into the house, down the deserted hallway to the living room. The heavy drapes were drawn and the room pitch dark. He turned on the small ceiling lamp, lighting the portrait of the three sisters—Loretta, Amy, and Geena. He moved as close as he could to the painting and examined the third Dalstrom girl closely. Then he turned his back to the fireplace and leaned against the mantel, trying hard to stop trembling.

He stumbled into a chair and turned on the lamp next to it. He read the page again, carefully, word for staggering word. The letter was dated two and a half years before, two months after he'd come to the ranch. The neatly typed information was crystal clear.

Maurice J. Freeman
Private Investigation Services
confidentiality guaranteed

Dear Ms. Dalstrom,

Regarding your inquiry of this last August 18, I'm pleased to report the following:

<u>Subject</u>—Jackson Edward McCauley

born 2.18.1999

<u>Father</u>—Edward Maxwell McCauley

born 5.22.1972—died 7.3.2010

<u>Mother</u>—Geena McCauley — formerly Brenner, nee Dalstrom

born 3.7.1974—died 8.8.2001

The rest became a blur. He glanced over to the portrait of the Dalstrom sisters for a moment before he found the strength to get to his feet and examine it closely. He clutched the mantel for support and peered at the painting. The girl on the right—blonde like all the Dalstroms, eyes a deep icy blue, the full lips parted sensuously, Geena Dalstrom.

His mother.

He stepped away from the picture and stumbled back into the armchair. He read the final page of Loretta's letter.

> *English comes so easily as I write this. Why does my hand defy my mouth?*
>
> *Know one thing—in the years you've been here, I've come to think of you as my son, my Martin. Knowing you are actually the flesh and blood of this family only supports my care and the lengths I've taken to protect you.*
>
> *You'll read this when I've gone. Use it as you will. After all, knowledge is power.*
>
> *Be well, my dearest boy.*

There was another page that read more like a formal statement than a personal missive.

Chapter Thirty-Seven

MONDAY, NOVEMBER 7

A LOW RUMBLE of thunder roused her from a fitful sleep. The pain killers barely made any impression, even when kicked along with a couple of shots of scotch.

Now she heard the raised voices. Initially, she made little sense of the few words she deciphered. Consuela, Martin, and Nicki were yelling at one another in the lobby; that much was obvious.

She winced in pain and massaged her bandaged ankle briefly before easing off the sofa and limping to the door. Opening the door a crack, fragments of the angry exchanges became clearer.

Fuck you, you fuckin' wetback!

…Bitch!

…You bitch—not Consuela

…go to the police

… not in a movie now, you dumbass fairy

…harm anyone in this house, I'll kill you

…marriage is binding

…a will.

Loretta settled back against the door. She heard Consuela stomp down the hallway toward the kitchen, the slam of the door to Amy's bedroom upstairs, and then Jack approaching down the hall. She eased back onto the sofa and stretched out, eyes closed, but alert, her mind in overdrive in an attempt to defeat the effect of the drugs.

The door to the den opened and closed quietly. She remained still as Jack placed the quilt over her gently, with care. Once he'd slumped into an armchair, she opened her eyes and examined him. She saw exhaustion, grief, defeat.

He caught her gaze, and there followed his anguished admission of marrying the manipulative, common little slut Martin had foolishly married, wisely divorced, and who'd barged into Jack's life to blackmail him.

About what? His identity?

Jack hadn't killed Martin; she was certain of that. As

certain as she was that Martin was dead. That left Nicki and Scott, but clearly, they had the ammunition to point the finger at Jack.

Her heart went out to Jack as he revealed the ignominy to which these two assholes had subjected him. He was eager to admit his deception, reveal his identity to her, and assume guilt for all that was happening, but that was another discussion for another time. There were more pressing issues.

When he'd gone, Loretta sat quite still for some time, turning options over in her mind. She'd never suffered fools, never remained a passive bystander in a scrap in which she had a moral investment, and never relinquished her dignity to anyone. Now she was being railroaded into subservience, irrelevance, exile.

Offer them money?

There'd never be enough. And knowing Scott, he wouldn't be satisfied until he'd destroyed her and everything the ranch stood for. To him, Jack was merely collateral damage.

A will?

No doubt with Nicki as prime beneficiary.

She heard the *slap, slap* of Nicki's slippers as she walked down the hallway. Was the bitch going to contaminate the house with cigarette smoke? She pulled on her robe angrily as she went to the door, ignoring the pain in her ankle. She opened the door and peered out into the darkened hall.

A light snapped on at the far end, in the morning room.

I won't have her smoking in this house!

She started toward the morning room, then heard Nicki leave the house by the back door.

The stables? Smoke and horses?

The dim shaft of light from the morning room lit the path to the stables, and she saw Nicki ease through the door and go inside.

Loretta started across the lawn, slowly, haltingly, hampered by the ankle's insecurity—not by pain. Pain had been conquered by determination and was no longer an issue. When she reached the door, she heard Nicki's whine as she babbled on—to Scott? No, to his voicemail.

"I hate this fucking dump. It's like living in a museum. I'm going to sell it, soon as I can. Soon as it's mine." She paused. "And yours. I want to see that bitch Loretta out on her ass!" She took a long drag on the cigarette. "And listen, I think the fag actor is gonna be a problem. I mean, a *big* problem. He keeps talking about going to the cops. Maybe—we should think about—shutting him up? For good. Think about it babe." Loretta peered out from the shadows by the door and saw Nicki take another drag on her vile cigarette. "I'll go along with whatever you come up with. I mean, you figured everything out so great after I—after—I had the accident with Martin."

Nicki had killed her son, her Martin.

And now Jack was in her sights.

"Okay, I'm wrecked. I'm going to bed. Call me in the morning." Nicki disconnected, stood, and ground the cigarette out on the floor. She turned to the wall switch.

Loretta pulled back into the shadows and brushed against a pitchfork. She grabbed it to prevent it from falling.

Nicki paused by the switch to take a gold necklet from her pocket. She turned it over and over in the dim light, smiling, running her thumb over the glinting links.

Loretta had the solution to everything in her hands.

She stepped out of the shadow and drove the fork into Nicki's back with all the force she had in her being.

She pulled the fork out. Nicki turned, a surprised look on her painted face.

Loretta thrust again, just below Nicki's left breast. And withdrew the fork.

Nicki slumped against the wall and slid slowly to the floor.

When she was laid out, Loretta pushed the fork into her throat, through flesh, and into the earth under Nicki's perfectly proportioned, once invitingly sensuous, now dead body.

The fork remained vertical, solid, unyielding, a monument to revenge.

*

LORETTA KNOCKED GENTLY at the cabin door.

Diego opened it almost at once. His eyes traveled from her head to her feet, taking in the blood-spattered bathrobe. His face revealed nothing, but she knew his instincts well—she knew he understood what had happened. And to whom.

He stood aside to let her into the living room. After he'd scanned the landscape, he came in, closed the door, locked it, and removed her bathrobe. Diego checked briefly, but thoroughly, to ensure that the sweatpants and shirt Loretta wore under it were unstained. He rolled the robe into a ball and went to the bathroom and consigned it to the washing machine, along with a quantity of bleach.

From where she stood, Loretta had a clear view of the bedroom and Jack, sleeping soundly in the vast bed. Somehow, the sight comforted her: Jack loved, he was loved, he would live.

Diego took his own bathrobe from a chair as he walked back through the bedroom, glancing briefly at Jack. In the living room, he put his robe around Loretta's shoulders and sat her in an armchair.

A slight tremble in her hands betrayed a reaction to the bloody murder she'd committed. Diego poured a hefty shot of brandy and watched as she drank it.

She'd not uttered a word, not a sound, yet she knew Diego understood what had to be done. He indicated the bedroom, Jack, then put a finger to his lips. Loretta nodded once. She watched as he pulled cleaning fluids and cloths from a kitchen cupboard and left the cabin.

About fifteen minutes later, he returned. Loretta hadn't moved, but her eyes followed him as he replaced the containers of fluids and put the cloths into the wood stove which he lit.

He reached into the pocket of his sweats and took out the silver ring—Jack's silver ring that had been on Nicki's finger. He considered it for a moment, then put it into a drawer of his bureau, far in, at the back.

Now he turned to Loretta and indicated he'd take her back to the house. She shook her head and rose. "I'm fine," she said quietly, calmly. She went to the cabin door, turned back, and nodded toward the bedroom. "Take care of him." And she left.

Chapter Thirty-Eight

JACK LOOKED UP from the pages scattered on his lap and took in the grandeur of the living room, as if seeing it for the first time.

His eyes rested briefly on the portrait of the sisters, on the woman he now knew to be his mother, but even this revelation meant little in comparison to the confession he held in his hand, by the lengths this remarkable woman had gone to protect him, to allow him to live, to encourage him to love…

Diego!

Sometime during his reading of Loretta's letter, he'd heard Diego's car pull in at the side of the house, but his attention had been on the page.

He leapt to his feet letting the pages flutter to the floor as he ran to the door, into the hall, through the morning room, and out into the open field.

He was out of breath when he reached the cabin, and he stood for a moment to pull himself together.

He knocked heavily on the door.

No response.

He pounded on the door.

"Diego!"

The door opened to reveal Diego, a puffiness around the eyes marring his handsome face, evidence of his grief over the loss of Consuela—and perhaps at the prospect of losing Jack.

Jack could find no words to express how he felt, his shame in thinking for an instant that Diego would ever harm him, could ever harm him. Suddenly, he was as mute as the man who stood before him searching his face for meaning, Jack held up his hand to show Diego the silver ring. And Jack found his voice.

"I know," he whispered. "I know everything." He took a deep breath before he could continue. "I'm ashamed. I'm…"

Diego grabbed Jack's shoulders and pulled him into an embrace that forced the breath from him. He held him with one arm, his hand firmly on Jack's shoulder, while his other hand stroked Jack's hair, his face. Jack wound his arms about Diego and held him tight.

They stood this way for some time, and then Diego drew breath, and huskily, with painful effort, he spoke for the first time in eleven years.

"*Te quiero*, Jack."

Acknowledgements

The author thanks:

Editor, Elizabetta McKay for her tenacity in keeping story, characters, and points of view in line, and whose punctuation is beyond reproach.

First reader Ted Merwood for his always valuable, sometimes wry observations.

Shawn Thompson for his enviable knowledge of contemporary vernacular.

Vaughan Edwards for his patience in reading every draft, providing wise insight, finding those pesky typos, and for just putting up with the author on a day-to-day basis.

About the Author

Barry Creyton has worked extensively in British theatre and television, and in his native Australia where he's known nationally as a star of stage and television. His plays are produced in more than twenty languages. His young adult novels are published by Random House, and his awards include the LA Weekly Annual Theatre award, the LA Ovation Award, the Kessell Award for his contributions to Australian theatre as actor, director, and playwright, and the Noel Coward International Writing Award. He lives in Los Angeles, California.

Facebook

www.facebook.com/barry.creyton

Website

www.creyton.net

Other NineStar books by this author

The View from Olympus Mons

Connect with NineStar Press

WWW.NINESTARPRESS.COM

WWW.FACEBOOK.COM/NINESTARPRESS

WWW.FACEBOOK.COM/GROUPS/NineStarNiche

WWW.TWITTER.COM/NINESTARPRESS

WWW.INSTAGRAM.COM/NINESTARPRESS